Maureen Pacifici Smith and Fran Thomas, co-authors and neighbors, live and work in the historic district of Savannah, Georgia. They were inspired to write the Full of Grace series to preserve a snapshot of growing up in the South in the sixties. While vacationing together a few years ago, a nostalgic conversation sparked the idea. They realized that even though they had grown up in different towns, their experiences and circumstances were very similar and begged to be recorded in a fast-changing world.

Maureen has been a commercial interior designer and space planner for over thirty-five years. She continues to work almost full-time in her own design business and with a local commercial furniture dealership. She balances her work with traveling with her husband David and writing with Fran.

Fran received her BFA from Auburn University. While working as a graphic artist, she continued to paint, studying summers with Henry Henche at the Cape School, and traveling many times to Italy to paint *en plein air*. In 2003 when her husband Hue retired, they returned to their native Savannah and opened Gallery 440. In 2020, she closed the gallery to write and paint full-time. Taking writing classes and workshops spurred her on to realize a twin passion, writing.

Working together to write this novel, the first in a trilogy, has added a new dimension to their friendship and lives.

To David and Hue.

Maureen Pacifici Smith and
Fran Thomas

Full of Grace and Mischief

AUSTIN MACAULEY PUBLISHERS
LONDON * CAMBRIDGE * NEW YORK * SHARJAH

Copyright © Maureen Pacifici Smith and Fran Thomas 2025

All rights reserved. No part of this publication may be reproduced, distributed, or transmitted in any form or by any means, including photocopying, recording, or other electronic or mechanical methods, without the prior written permission of the publisher, except in the case of brief quotations embodied in critical reviews and certain other non-commercial uses permitted by copyright law. For permission requests, write to the publisher.

Any person who commits any unauthorized act in relation to this publication may be liable to criminal prosecution and civil claims for damages.

This is a work of fiction. Names, characters, businesses, places, events, locales, and incidents are either the products of the author's imagination or used in a fictitious manner. Any resemblance to actual persons, living or dead, or actual events is purely coincidental.

Ordering Information
Quantity sales: Special discounts are available on quantity purchases by corporations, associations, and others. For details, contact the publisher at the address below.

Publisher's Cataloging-in-Publication data
Smith, Maureen Pacifici and Thomas, Fran
Full of Grace and Mischief

ISBN 9798891559912 (Paperback)
ISBN 9798891559929 (Hardback)
ISBN 9798891559943 (ePub e-book)
ISBN 9798891559936 (Audiobook)

Library of Congress Control Number: 2024923350

www.austinmacauley.com/us

First Published 2025
Austin Macauley Publishers LLC®
40 Wall Street, 33rd Floor, Suite 3302
New York, NY 10005
USA

mail-usa@austinmacauley.com
+1 (646) 5125767

We would like to express our gratitude for the experiences of growing up in the South in a less complicated time when beauty and adventure proliferated. We were cared for, surrounded by love and help, even though it was not always obvious to us. To the characters who were the inspiration for this book, you know who you are.

Along the way we have been validated by early readers and helped by those who took time to edit and offer suggestions: the Writing Circle at the Learning Center in Savannah, Charles Boniface, Diane Brannen, Patrick LoBrutto and most importantly, Eben Lee Thomas, who has been with us since the beginning and deserves a gold star for all the faith and effort he took bringing this work into fruition.

Prologue

Savannah, Georgia, 1981

A bolt of lightning illuminated the tiny apartment. Startled by the explosion of thunder that followed, Mary Margaret slumped down onto the stripped bed and began to scream hysterically. The truth spread over her stiff body. She jumped up, grabbed the wine bottle from the counter, and flung it toward the wall. It shattered. A bloody burgundy color spread over Theresa's painting as shards of green glass tinkled to the floor. Now she had nothing but disdain for the artist, her confidant, trusted friend, and soulmate.

Mary Margaret slammed the door, started down the steps, slipped, and tumbled to the bottom. She brushed off the dust, ignoring her pain. Determined, she ran like a whippet around the corner to Theresa's gallery.

Theresa saw Mary Margaret coming and ducked into the gallery office. She couldn't face her best friend. Mary Margaret stormed in, pushed Tommy aside, and demanded to see Theresa. He looked at Mary Margaret's contorted face, torn blouse, and smeared mascara.

"Theresa, you'd better come out here," said Tommy, leaning into the office and motioning with his finger.

Theresa took a deep breath, said a Hail Mary then stepped out of the office.

Dangling the necklace in front of her face, Mary Margaret yelled, "Are you missing something?"

Theresa brought her hand to her bare neck. Her mouth dropped open. She gasped.

"You're so stupid. You should have been more careful. The clues are everywhere," Mary Margaret ranted. Her arms flailed.

Theresa reached out to get control of her, only to get a slap in her face.

"I'm sorry, Pucci. I never in a million years would have done it if I had known."

"I hate you. I thought you were my best friend. You were supposed to be the good one," Mary Margaret yelled, throwing the key and the necklace at Theresa's face. "You're nothing but trash."

The sky opened and dumped buckets of fat raindrops. Mary Margaret pushed past a woman who was coming in the gallery door, almost knocking her down. Theresa ran after Mary Margaret.

"Pucci, please, let's talk this out. I can't lose you now. I need you more than ever. I'm so alone now. You're all I have."

Outside, Theresa grabbed Mary Margaret's wet arm. She slipped away. Gullies of rainwater rushed past them.

"I don't ever want to see you or talk to you again," Mary Margaret screamed, wiping the spot where Theresa had touched her. "Stay away from me and my family."

Theresa slid down the brick wall of a building into a squat and allowed the rain to wash away her tears. Her mind flashed back to the summer of 1959. *If only we could start over.*

One

1959 Savannah, Georgia

"Jesus, Mary, and Joseph. That car has wings," said Sister Fatima. She grabbed Sister Mary Joseph's arm. "It's taken to the air." Sister made the sign of the cross and put her hand on her heart. The other nuns followed suit.

Under a canopy of live oak trees, dripping with Spanish moss, three nuns stood in front of a rustic wooden cabin, waiting to greet this summer's campers. Green metallic fins followed the sleek body of the car as it bumped along the rutted road in a cloud of dust.

"Holy shit, you'd think those nuns would at least pave the goddamn driveway," George McDermott yelled, as he slammed on the brakes.

The 1958 Chrysler Imperial came to a stop. Theresa rolled onto the floor. "Daddy!"

She had been asleep, stretched out in the front seat with her feet in her father's lap and her head in her mother's.

"George, hush, the sisters will hear you. You okay, honey?" Elizabeth McDermott said. She pulled Theresa up from the floorboard and straightened her hair with her fingers. "Look, we're here. The nuns are waiting."

Theresa crawled onto the seat and looked through the windshield at the three nuns in their black habits, long veils, and stiff white collars. They were stair-stepped in height from short and stocky to tall and husky.

George frowned, "They look like a row of penguins." He discreetly wiped his balding forehead with his handkerchief, then removed and dried his glasses with it. He put on his seersucker jacket to cover the sweat stains under the arms of his crisp white shirt and walked around to open the door for his wife. Elizabeth stepped out of the car. Her blue shirtwaist dress was unruffled, and her dark brunette pageboy fell neatly at her squared shoulders. Even in her high-heeled pumps, she barely came up to George's shoulder. A tiny mustache of sweat glistened above her full pink lips.

A cloud of gnats swirled around Theresa's head, sticking to her tear-stained cheeks. All her arguments for not coming to camp raced through her head. She was convinced that nobody would like her. Elizabeth reached into the car and grabbed her daughter's arm, trying to pull her out. Theresa saw something that caught her attention, so she quit resisting and flew toward her mother. The leather seat pulled at the damp skin below her shorts as she lurched forward.

"Ouch!"

"Hush, Theresa. Smile at the nuns, and look them in the eye," her mother whispered. She straightened Theresa's shirt, then ran her fingers through her dark curls again, and gently pushed her forward.

Sister Consuela rubbed the cross on the end of the Rosary beads around her waist. Her pale wrinkled face looked tired. The hazel eyes of Sister Fatima, the nun in the middle, followed a group of children by the marsh. A gazelle-like girl with long sunburned legs raced a few paces in front of a group of boys holding something out toward her. Her strawberry blond pigtails bounced behind her as she ran across the lawn. Theresa couldn't take her eyes off the approaching girl.

"Dr. McDermott, thank you for your generous support of the Sisters of Mercy. We are so thrilled to have Theresa with us at Camp Villa Veronica," said Sister Joseph, looking into his eyes, level with her own. Her stern face relaxed almost into a smile.

"We appreciate her being here while we're traveling. I see she'll be in good hands," said George, shifting from foot to foot. Elizabeth swatted at a mosquito with her left hand as she reached out with her right to shake the nun's hand.

Sister Fatima turned toward the approaching girl and cupped her palms, "Mary Margaret Puccini, get over here at once. Your bunkmate has just arrived."

"Sister, they were chasing me with crabs," said the girl, pushing back a strand of hair that had come loose and hung in one of her eyes. A spattering of freckles across her nose decorated her pale glistening skin.

"Hold on, Mary Margaret," said Sister Joseph, introducing everyone. "Now show Theresa where she'll be sleeping."

Mary Margaret took Theresa by the hand. Blue eyes locked blue eyes. The girls jumped up and down. With her other hand, she pointed to a row of weather-beaten cabins, connected by a dirt path. Mary Margaret, a full head taller, bent down to whisper into Theresa's ear. "We're in Cabin Three. It's the one at the end. Perfect for sneaking out."

"Oh dear," Sister Joseph said to Sister Fatima behind her hand. "I hope Theresa will be a good influence on Mary Margaret."

"It could go the other way," said Sister Fatima, covering her laughter.

The two girls ran ahead. Inside the dimly lit cabin, rows of bunk beds lined the pine-scented walls. A footlocker was placed at each end of the neatly made-up bunks with stuffed animals adorning the pillows. One stood apart. The lower one had no stuffed animals, and the upper one was unmade with sheets stacked on top.

"That's our bunk," said Mary Margaret.

"But the sheets aren't on it," said Theresa, narrowing her eyes and holding up her palms.

"You have to make it up yourself. Don't worry, I'll help you. Over here is the bathroom. That trough is for washing your hands and your feet. You won't believe how dirty our feet get. That black sandy soil sticks to your shoes and creeps onto your feet and if you don't wash it off its gritty gross on the sheets." She slipped off her sandal and showed Theresa her blackened sole. "It's really gross if the sand gets in your sheets."

"There's only one shower?" Theresa said, pointing down the row of open toilets to a stall at the end.

"Oh, that's not a shower. It's a toilet in case you have to, you know, poop. The showers are in the bathhouse. You must be scheduled for that, but I know where there's an outside shower that we can use. I love outdoor showers."

Mary Margaret was telling Theresa about her seven siblings when Dr. and Mrs. McDermott came in carrying Theresa's footlocker.

"Tell us goodbye now, Theresa," said her mother. Theresa gave them each a hasty hug and a kiss before turning back to her new friend. She couldn't imagine having four sisters and three brothers. She wanted to hear more.

Theresa's parents entered the cabin.

"Miss Puccini, I've just discovered you are Joe Puccini's daughter. We were in medical school together. We were quite close at one time but have lost touch over the years. Please give him my best regards. Perhaps we can arrange a reunion sometime."

"You knew my daddy?"

"Great guy. Studied all the time. Glad to see he has a family. He never had time for girls or parties. Finished school before the rest of the class."

"He works a lot. Me and my seven brothers and sisters tease about him loving his patients more than us."

"Eight children," said George and smiled. "You be sure and tell him George McDermott says hello."

"Come give me one more hug," her mother said, wiping her eyes.

"It's okay, Mama. I'll be fine."

"But I thought you'd be the one crying."

"I'm fine," Theresa said, giving her mother another hug, then hurried back to her new friend.

Dr. McDermott was inching toward the door. "Come on, Elizabeth, we need to get on the road."

The girls plopped down on the lower bunk.

"Your mama's so pretty. My daddy's a doctor too," said Mary Margaret.

"Where are all the others?" Theresa said, pointing to the empty bunks.

"Betsy and Katie are in religion class. They live in the country, where there aren't any Catholic schools. So, they have to learn religion here."

"Why aren't you there?"

"Oh, I get enough of that at Sacred Heart where I go to school. I live here in Savannah and my daddy treats all the nuns for free, plus he gives donations. So, they pretty much let me do whatever I want."

"Don't you get into trouble?"

"Sometimes, but my parents don't want to hear about it. They send me here to keep me out of trouble and out of their hair. I have these scathingly brilliant ideas, which they don't like. They think I do them for attention, but they're really fun. You'll see."

Outside, a bell rang. Mary Margaret jumped up, and the sounds of children running and shouting filled the air.

"Come on, let's hurry to lunch. If we don't get there early, there won't be any potato chips left."

Mary Margaret grabbed Theresa's hand, pulling her toward the door. "I'm eleven, you're ten and you're from Macon, you go to St. Joseph's school, and you don't have any brothers or sisters."

She never stopped talking as she ran across the lawn, dragging Theresa toward the dining room. "Your parents travel all the time, and you're going to stay here a month while they go to Europe."

"How do you know all this?" Theresa asked.

"I overheard the nuns talking about the new campers. Sister Consuela is from Macon, and she knows your family. They didn't say you were so pretty. I wish my hair was dark and curly like yours. Your daddy gives them money like mine does. You make good grades, and you are quiet and shy. Let's sneak in the back door. Come on, I'll show you."

The cacophony inside the mess hall echoed against the rafters of the open ceiling. The intensely hot air smelled of sweaty children and stale fried foods. Mary Margaret managed to get them to the head of the line where they heaped their plates with potato chips, a clump of grape jelly, brown goo, and slices of white bread. On the table were pitchers of green Kool-Aid.

The swishing sound of Sister Joseph passing across the front of the room quieted the children, and the pushing and shoving stopped. She was large in girth and commanded more authority than the other nuns. Her wrinkled skin set her mouth into a permanent scowl.

"Dear children, we are gathered here to thank God for yet another glorious day, and revel in His blessings; the clothes on our backs and the nutritious food we are about to eat. Join me in saying our grace. Bless us oh Lord and these…"

A group of girls were motioning to Mary Margaret from one of the picnic tables. She and Theresa made their way over there and squeezed onto one of the benches. Most of the campers had consumed their lunch before Sister stopped praying. As soon as she did, the noise level began to rise again.

"She says the same thing every day. Every day's a glorious day even when it rains." Mary Margaret took a bite of her sandwich. "She calls peanut butter nutritious. It's awful. Meet Katie and Betsy. They're in our cabin. Betsy lives in Claxton. They don't have a Catholic school, so she's not used to nuns," said Mary Margaret. "Her daddy makes those famous fruitcakes. My mama gives them to friends at Christmas time."

Betsy stopped chewing and looked up from her plate and gave Theresa one of the sweetest smiles she had ever seen. She reminded Theresa of one of the cherubs in her mother's art books.

Theresa smiled back but looked down.

"Mary Margaret told us all about you," said Katie.

"Now we have to go back to our cabin and rest for an hour. On the way out, you can get a dried apricot. See that bin over by the door? That's our dessert. You're only allowed one," said Mary Margaret.

"If you don't want yours, I'll be glad to have it," said Betsy, licking her fingers.

As they walked toward the cabin, Katie and some other girls jostled each other for the chance to walk next to Mary Margaret.

After rest, Sister Fatima came into the cabin to take Theresa for orientation. Mary Margaret turned over on top of the *American Girl* magazine she was reading and pretended to be asleep. When Theresa walked into the arts and crafts room, she was mesmerized by the smell of the tempera paint, the colorful paintings, and the bowls crafted from clay. The room was bright. Long tables stained with dabs of paint ran down the center. Stacks of construction paper in a rainbow of colors sat on the shelf next to reams of white, and rolls of brown craft paper.

"I love art," Theresa said.

"Art sessions are at ten o'clock every day," said Sister Fatima. "Your counselor, Carol, is the instructor."

At five o'clock, the dinner bell rang. Theresa looked all around for Mary Margaret. She walked up to the buffet with hesitation. After filling her plate with green beans, meatloaf, and mashed potatoes, she scanned the room and heard a familiar laugh behind her. Mary Margaret was in an animated conversation with a group of girls. They were all laughing hysterically. Katie nudged Mary Margaret with her elbow, then pointed to Theresa. She had drawn within herself and was just about to run out of the door, thinking that they were all laughing at her. But then, Mary Margaret patted the bench beside her making room for Theresa.

"Betsy was just telling us about her uncle who went to work as a traveling salesman for the fruitcake company. When he ran out of money, he ate all the fruitcakes and sold the company car," said Mary Margaret.

The girls broke out in another fit of laughter.

When they got to the cabin for the evening, Mary Margaret took Theresa aside. "Now let me tell you about our counselor, Carol. She is a Crabby

Appleton and a real pain. She's also a rat-fink, so you have to be smart and not get caught."

"What's a Crabby Appleton?" Theresa asked.

"You know, he's that character from the TV show *Tom Terrific and Mighty Manfred the Wonder Dog*. He was short, fat, and bald. Had a scrunched-up face…"

Theresa stood with a blank stare having no idea what Mary Margaret was talking about.

"Geez, never mind."

Theresa was not quite sure what Mary Margaret meant by any of that. Exhausted, Theresa climbed into her bunk and was out like a light, listening to Mary Margaret prattle on.

She awoke from a sound sleep when Mary Margaret shook her gently and said, "Come on, we've got to hurry."

Carol was snoring softly. The sleeping figures in the other beds were still. Theresa climbed down from the top bunk, taking her Keds from Mary Margaret.

"Put these on outside. The nuns will be finishing their prayers soon and I have a scathingly brilliant idea."

"But, Mary Margaret," whispered Theresa, as she stumbled into her shoes.

It was too late. Mary Margaret was already a yard ahead of her, sprinting noiselessly across the grass. Theresa ran to catch up. Just before they got to the gate, which separated the nuns' living quarters, Mary Margaret reached into a sand bucket and pulled out a crab.

"Where'd you get that?"

"I stole it from the boys," Mary Margaret said with a grin. "This is for Sister Mary Joseph's bed. This will teach her not to be so mean. You have to hold them from the back like this, or they'll pinch you with their claws."

"Is that thing alive?"

Mary Margaret shook the crab. Its claws flailed as the pincers opened and closed. She aimed it at Theresa's face menacingly, then with her other hand, she reached through and unlatched the gate.

"Sister told me we weren't allowed inside there," said Theresa.

"Ha, ha, ha."

Theresa's heart stopped, then started up again at an accelerated rate. Her stomach lurched. She thought she was going to throw up. Mary Margaret was inside the gate, creeping slowly toward the bedroom. She gestured for Theresa to follow. They entered the nuns' private space. Inside were three narrow cots, a crucifix above each bed, and three chests of drawers. A fan whirred on a small table near the cots. The windowsills were lined with African violets. A dim nightlight revealed a person asleep in one of the beds.

Mary Margaret quickly threw the crab under the pillow of the closest cot. The sleeping figure stirred, muttered something, then turned back over. With a gurgle, she resumed snoring. The girls rushed outside and ran a safe distance before Mary Margaret stopped Theresa.

"That was close," Mary Margaret said. "I guess Sister Consuela doesn't go to Friday evening prayers anymore. She's old, you know. I think she taught my mother. My mother's from Macon like you. But she left there a long time ago."

From the direction of the chapel, the nuns were returning to their quarters. They walked single file, two dark ominous shapes, their pale candle-lit faces, glowing angel-like. Their low singing rose and fell. Theresa held on to Mary Margaret's arm trying to steady her own trembling body. They waited, pressed against the wall, until Sister Joseph screamed. Mary Margaret gave a satisfied nod. The two raced across the lawn, sneaking safely into their cabin where the others still slept soundly.

Adrenaline pulsed through Theresa's body, giving her a charged feeling that she liked. Sleep eluded her. In the bunk below, Mary Margaret slept peacefully while guilt began to spread through Theresa's body like the sap in a maple tree. When she finally dozed off, her dreams were filled with red devils sporting crab claws, trying to push her into the fire.

"May the sacrifice we offer You, O Lord..."

I must be in heaven thought Theresa, now half awake, shielding her eyes from the sunlight creeping in through the window. "Give us life always and defend us through our Lord. Amen," the loudspeaker continued.

She leaned over the side of her bunk. Below, Mary Margaret had the covers pulled over her head. Theresa checked her Mickey Mouse watch. It was seven-thirty.

Theresa jumped down and shook Mary Margaret.

"Holy Toledo, let's get dressed," she said. She hopped up and pulled on her shorts and shirt, buttoning it as they raced across the grass. "Wasn't that fun last night?"

At breakfast, the buzz going around the room was that a boy was being punished for putting a crab in Sister Joseph's bed. They were sure Fred Mosley did it. His crabbing bucket was found outside the gate. Mary Margaret elbowed Theresa. They put their heads together and giggled.

Mary Margaret, smelling like the marsh, came into the art room. Theresa was engrossed in weaving a keychain out of strips of colored plastic. She pretended to admire Theresa's creation but quietly said, "Come on, McDermott. The boys snuck the boat out and got some chicken necks from the cook to go crabbing. She'll give us extra banana pudding if we bring her some crabs."

"I don't know, Mary Margaret. I need to finish this."

"Don't be silly, Mac. What do you need a keychain for? You don't even have any keys."

"All right," Theresa said. shrugging her shoulders.

Fred and Matt were holding the rocking boat against the dock when the girls jumped in. Theresa almost lost her balance. Matt pushed off. Theresa plopped down on the seat next to Mary Margaret. She ducked just in time to miss Fred passing the oar over her head. The boys rowed across the river up into one of the channels in the marsh grass and dropped anchor.

They pulled out some sticks with a dirty string tied around them and a package of chicken necks. Theresa gagged as she tied the slimy, stinky chicken onto the weighted string the way the boys showed her.

"Do crabs really like to eat this putrid stuff?"

"Yeah, the stinkier, the better," said Matt.

"Okay, now lean over the edge and lower it into the water. When you feel a nibbling sensation, slowly pull up the line and use the net to grab the crab."

"Like this?" Theresa said, dropping it in. She looked doubtfully at her reflection in the river. "Now what?"

"Just sit here quietly and wait," said Mary Margaret.

Just then a speedboat went by and rocked the boat. Rivulets of water washed up onto the black mud bank of the marsh. Tiny holes appeared to breathe. They made a sucking sound as fiddler crabs darted in and out of the holes.

Mary Margaret noticed the disgusted look on Theresa's face. "We call it pluff mud. I can't stand it to get on me."

"Ooh, I think I feel something," said Theresa. She pulled gently on the string and could see the blue claws of the crab. She leaned over. Fred rushed to her side with the net, almost tipping the boat over. The crab darted off the line, back to safety.

"It's okay, you'll get the hang of it," he said.

Soon the bucket was full. The crabs clicked and gurgled under the croaker sack the boys wet to keep them shaded. Frank and Matt were patient with Theresa when she let a few of them go.

"Fred likes to name them after the nuns and priests," Mary Margaret said.

"Look at this one," he said, untying the line. "It's got barnacles all over it. She must be old. I'll call her Sister Consuela."

"How do you know it's a she?" Theresa said.

"Look underneath," he said, carefully holding it from behind and turning it over.

"See how she has on an apron, just like a woman, and the boy crab has a well, it looks like uh. Here look at this one."

Theresa's face turned red.

"Go ahead and say it, Fred. It looks like a boy's pee-pee. I have brothers, remember?" Mary Margaret said, laughing.

The tide was dead low when they got back. They had to get out and push and pull the boat through the shiny black sludge of pluff mud. It sucked Theresa's white Keds off.

The sharp oyster shells embedded in the mud cut her feet. Father James stood on the dock, his hands on his hips, and a frown on his face. He shook his head. Matt threw the front line to the priest, who hauled the boat to the dock and tied it up.

The four campers smelling like the bottom of a fishpond were covered in mud. They hung their heads as Father James pulled them up, one by one onto the dock. The caked mud had begun to dry on their skin. They slapped at giant horseflies whose stings felt like tweezer pinches.

"The sisters will deal with you girls. Boys, come with me and bring those crabs. I'll give them to cook, and she'll give me extra banana pudding," he winked at them.

The girls ran off to the outdoor shower. They got in, clothes and all, and rinsed off the mud. After they stripped and used the bar of soap with dirt in the cracks, they realized they had no towels and would have to put their wet clothes back on.

"I don't think I ever want to go crabbing again," said Theresa, looking down at her sunburned arms dotted with whelps from the horseflies and itchy mosquito bites. "What do you think they'll do to us?"

"Oh, I don't know. The boys will be in more trouble for taking the boat without permission and not getting back before the tide was out," said Mary Margaret, with a smirk on her face.

As punishment, the girls were confined to their cabin for a day and assigned to write essays on *What Catholicism Means to Me*. It was sweltering inside the cabin. Outside they could hear the gleeful, birdlike cries of the other campers.

"Jesus, I wish I had some of Essie's sweet tea," said Mary Margaret, making slurping sounds.

"Is Essie your maid?" Theresa asked.

"She is and I love her. She never tattles on me, even when I'm guilty. I like it when she combs my hair and plats it. She's got the biggest boobies in the world," she said, sitting up on the side of the bed and holding her hands out in front of her chest indicating Essie's size. "And she wears a wig."

"How do you know that?" Theresa asked.

"Because I snuck into her room and there it was lying on the dresser. Essie has her own room off the kitchen. It has an entry door to the outside where she is supposed to come in and out, but Anne won't let her. She says she can come in the front door like the rest of the family."

"Who's Anne?" Theresa asked.

"Oh, that's my mama. It's her name. That's what I call her, but not to her face. She would kill me. So anyway, when Essie is eating lunch in her room, she lets me come in and put on her wig. I don't understand why she won't eat in the kitchen. She says it's because she wants peace and quiet. The only thing is, sometimes nobody is even home. She told me we were her other family. I was her favorite. One day I got to go with her on the bus to my father's office. We got to sit in the way back. That was so much fun. That's where the maids get to sit. I love her better than Anne."

"Our maid's Pearly. I love her too, but not like I love my mother. When I was little, Pearlie would take me to the park to play. All the other neighborhood maids brought the children they took care of. She would tell me I was the prettiest of all. I got to drink cold water out of her Mason jar. I know white people aren't supposed to drink after black people, but Pearlie let me anyway."

"Anne told me that too. I wonder why? Hey, I've got a scathingly brilliant idea. I know how we can get it cooler in here."

Mary Margaret began hatching her plan to steal the oscillating fan they had seen in the nuns' bedroom. She sketched a map of the camp. The nun's quarters were close to the dining hall. She jumped up and showed the map to Theresa.

"Look, I can get from there to the room in two minutes flat. Here's what we'll do. At breakfast, I'll sneak in a jar that I have for collecting lightning bugs. I'll dump our milk and some eggs and grits and stuff in it, then at lunch I'll bring the jar. You pretend to be sick. Make a big commotion about gagging then pour out the fake vomit. Everyone will gather around. Someone will get the sisters from their dining room and meanwhile, I'll run over and get the fan."

"No, Mary Margaret, that's just dumb. We can't use it, they would see. Instead of thinking about how to steal the fan, why don't you write your essay?"

"Okay, Mac, be quiet so I can concentrate."

Ten minutes later, Mary Margaret announced, "I'm finished."

"How could you be?"

"Here, Mac, read it," she said, pulling out her *American Girl* magazine and handing Theresa the paper.

Being Catholic is a crock, especially confession. I will never go to confession again. I was told that eating meat on Friday was a mortal sin and if I died, I would go straight to hell. When I was ten, I ate meat one Friday. I spent the night with a friend and they had hamburgers, so I ate one. I knew I shouldn't have, but I did anyway. Then on Sunday, I went to Communion before realizing, you can't go to Communion with a mortal sin on your soul or you would be committing another mortal sin. So, I knew that meant I had to go to confession. But it would be five days before our class would go. I was a wreck. What if I got hit by a car and died? I would go straight to hell. My parents would be pretty upset if I was the only one of us not in heaven. When I finally confessed my two mortal sins, Father Brennen said, "Say ten Hail

Mary's, five Our Fathers, and one Act of Contrition." The same penance as always, no matter what I confessed. I had worried for a whole week; scared I would die and go to hell. I thought I would have to say one hundred Hail Mary's, fifty Our Fathers, and ten Act of Contrition's. Everybody else would be finished with their prayers and I would still be praying and praying and praying. I was so mad. So, that's why I think confession is a big crock and so is being Catholic.

"Mary Margaret, you can't hand that to Sister," Theresa said, leaning over the side of her bunk. "You'll be sent to Catholic prison and must do that penance thing for the rest of your life. Besides, that wasn't even a mortal sin. Didn't they explain in religion class that mortal sins are when you disobey a commandment? You know, like stealing or if you murder someone or if you're an adult and you commit adultery, whatever that is. We don't have to worry about that right now. Here, let me write something for you."

Mary Margaret was reading articles from *American Girl* out loud while Theresa composed both of their essays, trying to imitate Mary Margaret's back-slanted handwriting. She jumped off the bunk and handed Mary Margaret the essay.

"I like the way you call me Mac. I'll call you Pucci."

Mary Margaret smiled, "I love it. I won't let anyone else call me that, ever. Just you, Mac."

After two days of rain, which coincided with the girls' house arrest, it was announced that river swimming would be at high tide. The swimming hole was floored with ground-up shells and sand which was kinder to the feet. A rope divided the shallow end from the deep. Sometime after lunch, the whistle blew indicating the tide was high enough. Mary Margaret jumped up from her bunk to get there first.

"Pucci!" Theresa said. "It hasn't been an hour yet. You have to wait. You might get cramps and drown."

"You can wait, I'm not," Mary Margaret yelled as she bolted out of the cabin.

Theresa swam out to the rope and watched Mary Margaret rough-housing with the boys. She thought about the cramps but was not worried. They tumbled through the water, dunking and squirting each other with a plastic water gun. Not wanting to get involved in their activity, Theresa ducked under the rope and swam out. Mary Margaret noticed but figured she would be okay. Theresa was a strong swimmer, but when she hit the river's current, the undertow pulled her down. Swimming as hard as she could fatigued her arms and legs. She gulped to catch her breath, bringing in a mouth full of briny water. Her scream came out as a gurgle. Her struggle to stay afloat was failing. She let go completely and felt herself sinking to the bottom. Losing consciousness, she wondered if she was descending to hell.

"Where is she, where's Theresa?" Mary Margaret turned her head around skimming the water, looking for her. She became frantic. "I heard something over past the ropes where she was."

"She was right there a second ago!" Matt yelled.

The two swam out to where they last saw her. Mary Margaret dove down where they saw bubbles on the water's surface. Matt swam in to get help. The saltwater burned her eyes. It was dark and murky and she could feel seaweed pulling against her legs. She swam as hard as she could unsure in which direction she should go. Then she felt something. It was Theresa. She was lifeless.

Two

Someone was pushing on Theresa's chest, causing her to regurgitate a huge spray of salt water followed by pink foamy bile. The crowd around her came into focus. She tried to sit up to speak. Sister Fatima was kneeling beside her, her black habit soiled with the spume. She made the sign of the cross, then blessed the air over Theresa's head.

"She's breathing," said Sister Fatima.

The campers crowded around her, each making the sign of the cross. Father James and one of the older boys put Theresa on a stretcher and took her to the infirmary. Someone had slipped off her swimsuit and covered her with blankets. She could not stop shivering. A tall man in a beige suit with kind, brown eyes examined her. She looked away, embarrassed by her nakedness under the covers, but his hands were gentle as he pressed her stomach and listened to her heart.

"Sister Fatima, she's going to be fine, but she'll need to rest here for a couple of days. Monitor her temperature and make sure she eats only bland food, mostly liquids. Her muscles will be weak and sore for a while."

Sister listened intently as she took notes. The doctor turned and smiled, then walked over to Theresa and kissed her forehead before leaving.

"Doctor, I'll see you out."

Outside they blinked against the intense sunlight; she explained to him that Theresa's parents were abroad. Her grandparents lived in Connecticut.

"Should I contact them?" She looked directly into his unforgettable brown eyes and wondered if he recognized her.

"I don't think we need to worry them. If she's not fine tomorrow, call me, and I'll reexamine her. If necessary, we can contact the grandparents then. She should sleep through the night. I gave her a very mild sedative." He slapped a mosquito on his face. Sister took her handkerchief and wiped the small smear of blood off of his cheek.

He smiled and thanked her, but showed no sign of remembering her. It had been a long time ago. She couldn't help but think to back that time. She took a deep breath and sighed. She made the sign of the cross before returning to the infirmary.

"Sister Fatima, I thought I was dying and going to hell," said Theresa.

"Why would you think that?"

"I've broken some rules since I've been here. They said in religion if you're bad you go to hell."

"It is against the rules to swim past the rope, but you didn't know. It wasn't a sin. No, dear, you haven't broken any commandants or committed a sin."

Theresa loved hearing the nun's soft Irish brogue with its sweet lilt and quietly listened as she told of Mary Margaret's daring rescue. Everyone loved Sister Fatima. Young and beautiful with pale skin and bright hazel eyes, she was never stern.

Theresa began to doze. She opened her eyes and saw Sister Fatima still sitting by her bed, watching her. She tried to sit up, but Sister pushed her gently back down and caressed her head. Theresa saw tears on her cheek.

"You looked so peaceful I couldn't quit looking at you."

"I dreamed you were my mother. I miss her so much."

Fatima gave her a hug. "Try to go back to sleep, I'll be right here if you need me."

The next day, the sun came up hot again. Theresa blinked at the light reflected off of the glaring white wall. In the corner, a fan whirred. She tried to sit up but was overcome by weakness.

"I thought you'd never wake up," said Mary Margaret, from the other infirmary bed. Theresa rolled over toward her. "Oh, my goodness, how'd you get here?"

"I've been here all night. You didn't think I would leave you, did you?"

"Sister Fatima said you saved me. How?"

"I saw you swim beyond the rope, but I wasn't worried. Then Matt and I didn't see you so we swam to where you were so I dove in to find you. You gave me such a scare. I thought you were dead. You've become my best friend."

"But you have so many friends and so many sisters and brothers."

"Yeah, Mac, but you're my best friend now, and I don't want to lose you. I love the way you go along with my ideas. Katie and Betsy are too afraid of the nuns. But that's because they aren't used to them. They don't realize nuns are just people and can be fooled."

Mary Margaret reached into the pocket of her shorts and pulled out a needle.

"Let's be blood sisters." She pierced her finger, and then Theresa's, pressing the wounds together. "Now, I'm going to get us some breakfast." She stood up and pressed out her shirt with her hands and straightened up the covers on the cot.

"By the way, my daddy said you would be fine and when you are stronger, you can come back to the cabin."

"Your daddy?"

"Yes, that was my daddy who took care of you. He's a very good doctor. He works all the time. When I was little, he would take me with him to St. Joseph's Hospital. I thought it was named for him. Daddy's my whole world and the only man I'll ever love. He calls me his 'Piccola Stella' which means little star in Italian."

Many of the campers came by the infirmary and brought gifts and cards, made in art class. Sister Consuela brought one of her prized African violets and Sister Joseph, a daily missal. Katie came by and took a picture of her. The day Theresa went back to her cabin, Mary Margaret borrowed a wheelbarrow and loaded all the gifts and the fan into it.

Carol noticed the fan in the window. "Where did that fan come from?"

"The doctor insisted that Theresa have it. She can't get overheated," said Mary Margaret. Carol crossed her arms and glared at her.

After breakfast the next day, Theresa was back to her old self.

"Let's stop by the cabin. I'm about to wet my pants," said Mary Margaret.

"You're gonna make me late for art class."

Mary Margaret shot her a bird.

Theresa stood outside the bathroom door. "Listen, someone's crying. I think it's Betsy. I wonder what's wrong," Theresa said.

"I'll bet someone was mean and teased her about being fat again," said Mary Margaret. "She's so sweet and funny. I wish they would just leave her alone. Let's go see what's wrong." She quickly dried her hands. They were by Betsy's bunk trying to turn her over when Sister Fatima came in and pried the bag of M&Ms away from Betsy's clenched fist.

"Betsy took these from the canteen without paying," said Sister.

"She got them for me," said Mary Margaret, reaching into her shorts pocket. "I was having a low blood sugar attack and about to faint. Here's the nickel. I forgot to give it to her."

"If you're lying, Mary Margaret and she was stealing, you'll both have to go to confession," said Sister Fatima, trying to look stern. She handed the candy to Mary Margaret before leaving.

Theresa was standing with her mouth open, Betsy turned toward them, wiping her nose with the corner of the sheet. "I'm sorry, y'all. I can't believe you took up for me. Everybody's always mean to me because I'm fat. You two have been so nice. Mary Margaret, you could have gotten into trouble."

"We like you a lot. But Betsy, why'd you do it? You know how they watch over that canteen."

"I don't know. I was just so hungry. I've been trying to diet so I skipped breakfast. I can't get into my good shorts for Parent's Day."

"Have some M&M's before we faint from low blood sugar," said Mary Margaret, laughing and tearing into the bag. "Hey, I've got a scathingly brilliant idea."

On Saturday afternoon, after rest, the girls stole a pair of shorts from Carol's footlocker for Betsy. They cut up a pair of Betsy's flowered shorts; removed the name tag, then appliqued the flowers onto the purloined pair, and sewed in the name tag. They rolled up the bottom to form a cuff. Carol would never recognize them.

The next week the camp began gearing up for Parents' Day. It marked the end of one month's session and the beginning of another. They practiced for a pageant and displayed the best artwork around the studio.

Theresa removed the candy box from her footlocker and retreated to her bunk to study the postcards her parents sent from England and Ireland. She picked up the one with the London Bridge and gave it a sniff. It smelled of chocolate and very faintly of the fragrance her mother always wore. Her grandparents who lived in Connecticut had written to her several times and had even sent the Whitman's Sampler, which made her briefly popular. She felt sorry for herself that no one was coming for Parent's Day. The other campers were so excited with anticipation of their family's visit.

Theresa looked up when Katie and Betsy ran into the cabin. Katie was ripping off her shirt and clawing at her shoulders and back in a fit. Betsy was scratching her legs so hard they were bleeding.

Mary Margaret followed. "Geez, why in the world would y'all do something so stupid?"

"We thought it would be fun. It was Katie's idea," Betsy said.

Theresa jumped down off her bunk. "What happened?"

"These two decided to make a bed out of the Spanish moss and took a nap on it. Now they are covered in chigger bites."

"What's a chigger?" Theresa leaned over and looked closely at Betsy's legs. "Tiny red bugs that live in moss. They bite you and it itches like mad." Mary Margaret opened her trunk and took out a first aid kit. "Here, use this cream Daddy gave me for mosquito bites. It'll help."

"So much with your new shorts for the pageant. You might want to wear long pants," Theresa said, rubbing the cream on the back of Betsy's legs.

Sunday morning, after Mass, the camp was abuzz with excitement. Cars arrived amid clouds of red dust. Shrieks of joy could be heard throughout the camp. When Dr. and Mrs. Puccini arrived, a stair-step string of tow-haired children followed. Dr. Puccini was wearing the beige seersucker suit that Theresa remembered from his visit to her in the infirmary. He held his wife's arm as Mary Margaret sprinted toward them. Her mother was tall. Her peach-colored dress was cinched at the waist with a wide matching belt. A small straw hat, with a cluster of feathers in its fold, was cocked to the side of her platinum blond hair. Theresa, alone, hung back in the door of the cabin watching families reunite. Rivulets of tears wet her cheeks. She brushed them aside when she saw Sister Fatima coming toward her. An older couple followed closely behind.

Theresa looked again, and blinked her teary eyes, to clear them, "Oh, Nana, oh, Papa. I didn't know you were coming."

"We wanted to surprise you," said Sara Willingham.

"You've come all the way from Connecticut?"

The handsome, well-groomed couple looked out of place in their heavy, city tweeds. They bent to hug their granddaughter. Theresa grabbed her grandmother around the neck, displacing a strand of gray hair from her perfect French twist. She could smell the powder on her smooth bright face.

"Yes," said Sara, straightening her jacket and adjusting her pearls.

"We have another surprise, darling. We're going to buy a house in Savannah. It's on Isle of Hope," said Oliver, wiping the sweat from the top of his bald head. "Later, we'll take you to see it. It's not far from here."

"Now dear, we want to meet this Pucci you've written so much about."

She led them to the huge live oak by the tennis court where everyone was gathered to watch the pageant. It would be followed by a procession to the statue of the Virgin Mary beside the river. One of the children was handing out round fans with wooden handles printed with the name and logo of Fox and Weeks Funeral Home.

"Look, Pucci, it's my grandparents. They surprised me," said Theresa, her cheeks rosy with excitement.

Mary Margaret introduced them to her parents, then her siblings, the twins, Joel and Frank, and her sisters Jeanne, and Nan.

"The older girls and my other brother Charlie didn't come," she said.

"Hey, young lady, you look better than the last time I saw you," said Dr. Puccini.

Theresa looked up into his tanned face with its strong Roman nose and kind brown eyes, "I feel fine now. Thanks for helping me."

The adults ducked behind the tree for a smoke.

"I knew they were coming," Mary Margaret whispered to Theresa. "I didn't tell you because I wanted you to be surprised."

"No, Pucci. Really?" Theresa made a fist and playfully boxed her on the arm.

"That's why I've been sort of avoiding you. I didn't trust myself to slip up and ruin the surprise. I've been accused of having ears in my fingers and toes." She reached down and scooped up two-year-old Nan.

"What's so funny, May May?" Nan asked, squeezing Mary Margaret's lips with her pudgy fingers. "Did you know about the house too?"

She shook her head. "What house?"

"I'll tell you later," Theresa said, looking at Mary Margaret with her little sister and feeling a pang of jealousy.

On the other side of the tree, Mrs. Willingham was conversing with the Puccinis.

"Oliver just retired from Metric Corporation. He was the CEO. We just went ahead and put our Greenwich home on the market. It was rather large, and we overpriced it, not being in a hurry or anything. But it sold in a week. We couldn't believe it. Could we, Oliver?"

"Uh, no, do you think it would be all right if I take off my jacket?" He said, wiping his forehead with his handkerchief. "We wear wool year-round in Connecticut."

"You won't need those down here," said Dr. Puccini, lighting another cigarette.

"Anyway, as I was saying, we were hoping to move south, closer to Elizabeth and George. When they brought Theresa to camp, they found this charming house right on the bluff for us. We're moving next month. She waved the fan in front of her face." "Is it always this hot?"

Anne laughed and looked at Joe. "It's just a heat spell. Why don't you take off your jacket too, dear? You'll love Isle of Hope. It's an enchanting place. Joe takes the children out there for ice cream. And those gorgeous houses look like something from an antebellum film. It's like time has stopped."

A voice over the intercom announced the pageant was about to begin. Sister Consuela gave each camper a fresh flower to place on the statue. The girls rushed to take their place in the procession. The parents followed as the children walked to the statue and placed their flowers next to the statue of the Virgin Mary by the river. Afterward, the children broke the line and rushed to the dining hall, pushing and shoving to be first in line. A feast of fried chicken, butter beans, corn, tomatoes, and biscuits was served in the mess hall. Theresa sat with the Puccini children while the four adults continued their conversation at the other end of the table.

"Eight kids?" Oliver said. "We only had one, Elizabeth, and she was off at boarding school. That's where she met George."

"Yeah, it's been a ride, and the children are each as different as night and day," said Joe. "Anne takes the brunt of it. I'm at the hospital or on house calls, often after office hours."

"I was an only child, so I love the chaos. Our help, Essie, she's a lifesaver," Anne said, choosing to ignore the piece of chicken she saw fly by at the other end of the table. "The older children pitch in, but Mary Margaret? She's a handful. She actually tried to convince our neighbors that she was an orphan so they'd feel sorry for her and let her live with them. That was mild compared to some of her other schemes. She needs more attention. The nuns keep her somewhat in check. I think Theresa has been a good influence on her. They've become really close."

"That girl of mine is special, but too smart for her own good," said Joe.

For the last two weeks of camp, the heat wave continued bringing hot rain and more mosquitoes. Everyone was getting testy. Carol was still looking for her missing shorts. She figured Mary Margaret had something to do with it but couldn't prove it. They all cried when it was time to go, but were secretly glad to be leaving.

After camp, Theresa and Mary Margaret stayed with the Willinghams in their new house on Isle of Hope. Mary Margaret loved it when she would go to the Isle with her father when he took the family to Barbee's Pavilion to eat ice cream and look at the turtles. She loved looking at the large homes on Bluff Drive. They reminded her of pictures of Tara from *Gone with the Wind*. She was awestruck when she saw the Willingham home with its wraparound porches and huge oak trees. The foyer was grand with a beautiful staircase leading to a second-floor galley. She stood and stared.

"Come on, Pucci, let me show you my bedroom." Theresa pulled her by the arm and led her up the stairs.

At night with the windows open, a warm breeze ruffled the white lace curtains. A large attic fan pulled the air in from the river and by morning the girls would huddle together and pull up the blanket.

Every morning they smeared fresh cream butter on thick raisin toast while Delia, the Willingham's new housekeeper, fried bacon in the old-fashioned kitchen on a green enameled electric stove which stood on legs and had a raised oven on the side. On the other wall was an old wood-burning stove which Delia still used to fry chicken. She insisted it made the chicken taste better.

On their own to buy candy at the little store on the bluff, before sneaking down to the dock and smoking Theresa's mother's French cigarettes, or wandering down to Barbee's Pavilion for a homemade peach ice cream cone, they filled every moment. At low tide, Mr. Willingham took them crabbing across the river in the marsh. He taught them how to row his beat-up bateau. Once they even stole a watermelon from Smith's, one of Mary Margaret's scathingly brilliant ideas. Of course, Oliver made them return it.

On Friday night, they walked down to Barbee's in their pajamas where they laid on blankets and watched old Charlie Chaplin movies with the other local children. Sometimes they would sit on the porch and watch the barges and yachts come down the Skidaway River, part of the Intercoastal Waterway. They stayed up late every night telling each other their innermost secrets, then sleeping late in the lumpy brass bed left by the previous owners. Two bathrooms were at the end of the hall. They soaked in the claw-footed tub in the one that was painted pink for girls, not daring to go in the blue one next to it. It had been for boys and had a tank above the toilet with a pull-down chain.

The night before Theresa's last day Mary Margaret hung up the phone from talking to her mother.

"Anne wants us to have lunch with her tomorrow in town at the Southern Kitchen. I love their pot roast and mashed potatoes. I told her we'd come."

"That sounds great. I'll ask Nana."

"No need to. I already checked with her. She said it's okay, she was invited too, but she can't come."

"But you just hung up talking to your mother."

"I know, well…" A look came over Mary Margaret's face, the one she got when she was up to something.

"Did you do something, Pucci?"

"It's just this has been the best week of my life, and Anne wanted me to come home and bring you. I told her your grandmother was sick and we needed to stay here. So tomorrow just don't say anything."

"Oh, Pucci, I hope I don't slip up."

The girls rode the bus downtown and caught up with Mrs. Puccini just as she was leaving The Lady Jane shop. She handed the girls her packages and gave Theresa and Mary Margaret each a hug. She looked at her daughter's unkempt hair and made a tsking sound while tucking a stray piece back in.

"Sorry, Mrs. Puccini, I just couldn't get that French braid thing right. You'll have to show me sometime. I thought this was a beauty parlor. It looks like a shop."

"There's a salon in the back. Every week when I have my standing appointment, I can also get my shopping done. Girls, what do you think of my new bouffant?" Anne took her hand and cupped the bottom of her hair.

Both girls snickered. "It's awfully big, Mama. How are you going to sleep without messing it up?"

"Oh, I have a hair net for that. With all this hairspray, it should stay in place. Look, there's Myrtle. Go ahead and I'll catch up in a minute. I want to show her my new hairdo."

"Gosh, your mama walks like a model, Pucci. She looks pretty in her navy suit and high heels. My mama gets all dressed up too when she goes to the beauty parlor."

When they entered the restaurant, the delicious aroma of fried chicken and biscuits permeated the entire space. Mary Margaret's mouth watered.

They were greeted by Mama Saseen, who along with her sister, the chef, owned the place. Mary Margaret cringed when she leaned down and gave her a big wet kiss on the cheek. She did the same to Theresa, assuming she was just another Puccini.

"How's the wonderful doctor today?" She looked around and toward the door as if he would be with them. "Will he be joining you?"

"No, he visits the nursing homes on Wednesdays."

"Of course, it's Wednesday, the doctor's afternoon off. That's too bad. My brother caught a mess of shrimp, so our special today is fried shrimp and hush puppies."

"The doctors in Macon take Thursday afternoons off. That's when they play golf," said Theresa, looking around. She spied a photograph of Doctor Puccini and an older man.

Mama Saseen noticed Theresa's stare. "Yeah, that's our daddy with Dr. P. He takes such good care of our family."

They took their seats at a booth with Anne across from the girls. Mary Margaret noticed nothing ever changed. She had been coming here since she was a toddler. Wooden tables and metal chairs with red vinyl seats were scattered around. A mirror behind a long counter had glass shelves on it that held the same family pictures and whatnot for as long as she could remember.

When she went to sit in her booth, she noticed the vinyl was split. She moved way over to avoid landing on a crack.

Theresa nudged Mary Margaret. She tilted her head toward Anne a couple of times and made a sour look. Mary Margaret looked over and widened her eyes.

"Mama, what's wrong with your eyebrows? They look different."

Anne took her ring finger and gently wiped one of them.

"Oh, Tillie dyed them darker than normal. They'll fade." She picked up her menu and scanned it. "So, let's see what looks good to eat. I think I'll get the special."

Theresa leaned over to Mary Margaret and whispered in her ear. "She looks like Joan Crawford."

After pot roast, mashed potatoes, butterbeans, and peach cobbler, the girls walked down to Broughton Street. When they passed Weiser Jewelers, Mary Margaret said. "I have a scathingly brilliant idea."

Theresa cut her eyes. "What now, Pucci?"

"Let's go in here."

They entered and were greeted by a man in a black suit with a yellow tie.

"Hi, Mr. Wiser."

"Good afternoon. Miss Puccini, can I help you?"

Theresa looked back toward the door, but Mary Margaret stepped up to one of the long brass-fitted glass cases. "We'd like to see some friendship rings."

He stepped behind the counter and pulled out a tray of silver rings. Theresa's mouth dropped open as Mary Margaret selected one. "Mac, try this on."

"It's beautiful. I love the three perfect hearts on top. They look like diamonds. I love it."

"How much is it?" Mary Margaret asked.

"It's five dollars."

Theresa took the ring off of her finger and put it back in the box.

"You girls are in luck. We're having a special today. Buy one and get the second one free."

"Oh," said Mary Margaret, drawing in a breath. She picked up the ring from the box and tried to slip it on her own finger. "It's too small. Do you have a larger one? Just one size up."

He pulled out a drawer and handed Mary Margaret the same ring in her size.

"Ok, we'll take them both. Just charge it."

"Do your parents get mad when you just charge things, Pucci?"

"No, they send the bills to Daddy's office. I always let him know when I do. He doesn't mind."

They walked down the street to the bus stop. Every few minutes, one of them would hold out her hand to admire her ring.

Three

Christmas, Savannah, 1960

As soon as school was out for the Christmas holidays, the McDermott's left Macon and headed for Isle of Hope. They turned onto Bluff Drive. Theresa rolled down the window and took in the musty smell of the marsh.

"I love it here," she yelled.

When they approached the house, she felt confused. The rambling old frame house with the wraparound porch and overgrown shrubs and vines was now restored with a new coat of paint and manicured lawn.

Inside the house was pristine with modern bathrooms off of the bedrooms and a stark white kitchen with long laminate countertops. They covered the heart pine floors with carpet except in the kitchen and entry hall. The only thing recognizable was the wraparound porch with gingerbread trim and the wood stove they kept for Delia's fried chicken. Theresa saw very little of Mary Margaret over the holidays, busy with her family. They talked on the phone since it wasn't a long-distance call and caught up with everything they had failed to report in their weekly letters over the spring. They both looked forward to going back to camp.

In June, they arrived at Camp Villa Veronica at the same time, Theresa with her mother in their wood-sided station wagon, and Mary Margaret with her father who was making a house call to Sister Consuela. The statue of the Virgin by the river could have heard their shrieks when they saw each other. Carol was standing by the cabins with a clipboard. When she told Mary Margaret that she and Theresa weren't in the same cabin, Theresa started wailing.

"Are you sure?" Mary Margaret said. "There must be some mistake."

"Absolutely not," said Carol, looking down at the paper. "Theresa's bunking with Katie."

"No, I don't think so. Where's Sister Joseph? I'll ask her myself," said Mary Margaret, looking around.

"She's with Sister Consuela and the doctor."

Mary Margaret trudged off toward the nun's residence meeting her father on his way out. She told him what was going on.

"Please, Daddy, talk to Sister Joseph."

"Okay, Mary Margaret, I'll see what I can do."

He turned and walked back in. Mary Margaret sprinted back across the lawn where Theresa and her mother were struggling with the footlocker.

"It's okay," Mary Margaret said, winking at Theresa.

Carol was standing by the door when Mary Margaret pushed past her and plopped down on her old bunk.

"No way," Carol said, balling up her fist and planting her right foot firmly on the ground. "You are not in my cabin. Sister Joseph promised."

Dr. Puccini walked in carrying Mary Margaret's trunk.

"Over here, Daddy. Look, they've got fans this year," Mary Margaret said. She gave Theresa a little hug.

Carol insisted on switching cabins with the new counselor, Nancy.

The girls skipped across the lawn to the mess hall. The noise, the peanut butter, the green Kool-Aid, the long lecture, the prayer, and the blessing. Life was good. They both felt they had come home.

In the afternoon, they made their beds, organized their clothes, and slipped away to the swimming hole. Mary Margaret dove into the water and raced to the rope. She turned around and motioned for Theresa to join her. Theresa dangled her feet into the water then slipped cautiously over the edge of the dock holding on until she was sure she could touch bottom. She walked out a little way and then retreated to the safety of the ladder.

"Sorry, Pucci, I can't just yet. Give me a moment."

Mary Margaret swam in. "Oh, Mac. I'm so sorry, how could I forget? You must have been so scared. Please forgive me." She started up the ladder and held a hand out to Theresa. "Come on, let's go."

Mary Margaret led her to the outdoor shower. The water was frightfully cold. They giggled at the goosebumps on their arms and legs.

"Look, it's the same bar of soap from last year," said Theresa. "Here, wash my back." Mary Margaret moved the bar in small circles then ran all ten digits down her back.

"Okay, now it's my turn," said Mary Margaret. Theresa turned around to get the soap. "Holy Toledo, Mac, you've got boobs." Theresa's hand went to her breasts as she stared at Mary Margaret, who was still flat above her pronounced ribs. She covered herself too, as they retrieved their suits from the floor.

"Lucky, we remembered to bring towels," said Theresa. They averted their eyes as they dressed.

A new camp feature this year was a Friday night bonfire. The boys collected the twigs from the nearby woods while the girls found old newspapers, magazines, and cardboard to add to it. Sister Fatima told them of a tradition in her family in Ireland to write down prayers and wishes and throw them into the fire. They would rise up with the smoke and go directly to heaven.

The campers were mesmerized as they sat around in a circle and sang songs, watching the rising embers and warm glow reflected in each other's faces. Theresa loved singing rounds of *One hundred bottles of beer on the wall*, but Mary Margaret told her it was totally ridiculous.

"Hey, have any of you heard the story about the monster Plaid Eye?" Matt said.

He leaned in toward the fire and narrowed his eyes looking mysteriously back and forth at the campers.

"Who's that, somebody you made up?" Mary Margaret said. She could see everyone's eyes were glued to Matt and decided to follow along.

"No, it's true," he said.

The bonfire was in an area down by the river. It was tented with many oak trees dangling with Spanish moss. Because of the position of the trees, a whistling sound was heard when the wind blew a certain way. They all listened intently as he told the story.

"Years ago, there was a monster who lived in the swamps over in South Carolina, not very far from here. It had one eye that looked strange," Matt spoke in a low voice. He looked around toward the river as if Plaid Eye were somewhere nearby. All the campers followed his eyes and began to huddle closer to each other. The wind was blowing and began to make that high-pitched airy sound. Betsy grabbed Katie's hand.

"Late in the day, when it was becoming dusk, it would leave its nest and look for children taking them back to the swamp. Never to be seen again. If anyone interfered, it would cut their throats with the long nails on its fingers. One early evening the monster came through the woods toward a house where several children were playing."

Matt sped up his words and became more dramatic.

"It approached them. The oldest child spotted the frightening monster and screamed. 'It's Plaid Eye, everybody run'. The children ran as fast as they could. The youngest sister fell as the beast came very close to her. 'Hey, over here', the oldest yelled and waved his arms to distract it. The boy bolted toward the stairs of the house."

Mary Margaret was completely transfixed hanging on to every word. Theresa saw something and nudged her. She jumped and brought her hand to her heart.

"Jesus, Mac, you scared the fire out of me." She followed Theresa's eyes and saw a large shadow moving behind one of the oak trees. They both screamed. That caused all the others to scream too.

Matt chuckled. "It's just the moss. It's nothing." He continued. "One of the brothers grabbed his sister who had fallen as Plaid Eye headed away toward the boy. That gave them a chance to make it to safety. As the monster approached the steps of the house, it stopped short. It screeched loudly and cowered as if afraid of something. The children watched from the window as Plaid Eye took off into the woods."

"What happened? Why did it stop"? One of the campers said. "I thought it would go inside and take them to the swamp or worse, kill them right then a there."

"You want to know why? It's because the family painted their windows and doors blue. Plaid Eye is afraid of the color blue. It causes excruciating head pain that becomes crippling and causes its death. That's why all those old houses you see in South Carolina, especially the ones near the swamps, have blue doors and windows."

"Really?" Betsy said. "Oh, dear, our front door is red and our house is near the water."

"No need to fear. It was killed by a group of hunters years ago. However, old legends have it that somewhere its ancestor lurks."

That night Betsy climbed into Mary Margaret's bunk at three am. Theresa woke up and leaned over.

"What's wrong, Betsy?"

"I just saw the ghost."

Mary Margaret rolled over, "What ghost, Betsy? You mean Plaid Eye?"

"No, you know, the one Sister told us about. The Holy Ghost."

"Geez, it's not that kind of ghost. Tell her, Theresa."

"The Father, Son, and Holy Ghost make up the one God. He's a spirit and they're all part of Him. You mustn't be afraid they're all good. I think what you saw was the night watchman shining his light on the cabin to make sure we're all safe."

"I don't understand," said Betsy. "And I don't like scary stuff." She pulled the sheet up over her head.

"Neither do I. Why don't you come and sleep with me?" Mary Margaret said.

Theresa was holding her breath waiting for Mary Margaret to have one of her ideas. They had been there a week and reconnected with Katie and Betsy, who had lost weight and had become much more confident and outgoing. She was the prettiest girl at camp that summer and none of the other campers teased her.

It had been raining for two days and the campers were beginning to get antsy. Sister Joseph had to go into town, so she left Nancy in charge. Carol had a boyfriend who was a counselor on the boy's side. When Nancy wasn't looking, Carol and the boy snuck out to be together.

"You know, I don't think it's that far to your grandmother's house."

Theresa leaned over the bunk. "Why are you asking, Pucci?"

"I have a…"

"Don't tell me, please. We've been so good."

"But this would really be a gas. No one is around. We could light a small fire down by the dock. That'll get Nancy's attention then we'll sneak out and walk down to Smith's and get some…No, we'll go to Barbee's and get an ice cream cone." She walked over to where Betsy and Katie were playing Go Fish and whispered her plan to them.

They jumped up and started giggling.

"Come on, Theresa, we'll have to hurry so we can be back in time for lunch." They set a small fire of twigs and moved along the river and through the lawns of private homes. They came to a fence which Mary Margaret quickly scaled. Betsy sat down in the grass and cried.

"Give her a boost," said Mary Margaret. After a few tries, Betsy and Katie decided to turn back.

Theresa was torn but knew she would never live it down, so she climbed the fence and she and Mary Margaret ran up to the road.

"I think we're going the wrong way. There's the sign for Villa Veronica," said Theresa, pointing. "Let's get back so we're not late for lunch."

"Yeah, we better. I know a shortcut, let's cut through the woods," said Mary Margaret. "I explored this whole area last year. This is the way we should have come. Next time we will."

"Shh, Pucci, I heard something in the woods."

It was a rustling sound followed by a moan. They stood by a tree and listened to voices coming from under the low-growing palmetto bushes which encircled a cleared-out area.

"That's where I shot marbles with the boys last year and behind there is where they used to hide. I think I see someone moving. Let's go around that way. Stay behind the trees."

"No, Pucci, let's go back."

But Mary Margaret moved stealthily through the woods. Under a bush, they saw a couple; the boy was lying next to a girl with his arm across her body under her tee-shirt.

Theresa stepped on a pinecone and twisted her ankle.

"Ow," she cried out.

At that, the girl sat up and looked their way. Mary Margaret whispered, "It's Carol and some guy. I wonder if she saw us."

The girls ducked down behind a huge azalea bush. They quietly waited to see what Carol was up to. Several minutes later, they could hear Carol moaning.

"Come on, let's crawl over there and see."

"No, you go, I'm scared."

Mary Margaret inched her way over toward the bush they were behind to get a better look. She watched. The boy was on top of Carol, her bare legs wrapped around him. His naked bottom going up and down.

She jumped up and ran over to Theresa, pulled her up, and started running toward camp. Theresa hobbled behind her.

"Wait up. Mary Margaret, what were they doing?"

"They were doing it."

"It? What?"

"You know the stuff in that book *Growing Up and Liking It*. It's about periods, sex, stuff like that. Didn't your mama give you that to read?"

"Oh, yeah." Theresa lowered her head and blushed. It embarrassed her that she had no clue as to what Mary Margaret was talking about.

Four

The next day, Mary Margaret came into the art room laughing out loud. Theresa was in the corner painting a still life while the others were weaving strips of colored construction paper. Mary Margaret sat down next to Theresa. The others went back to their projects.

"What?" Theresa said. "I'm busy."

"I have to tell you what just happened."

"Tell me then," said Theresa, swishing her brush around in the jar of mud-colored water.

"I can't tell you here. Put up your stuff and meet me at the cabin."

Carol saw Mary Margaret leaving and came over to where Theresa was cleaning off her palette. "What's going on?"

"Oh nothing, I just don't think the painting needs anything more."

"No, I mean about Mary Margaret, what did she want?"

"Oh nothing, she just stopped by to tell me she was going to the chapel."

Carol slightly turned her head and narrowed her eyes at Theresa. "You two better not be up to anything."

Carol leaned down to scratch her leg. Theresa noticed an angry rash just below the cuff of her shorts.

"We'd better go somewhere else, I think Carol's on to us," said Theresa, once inside their cabin.

"I know a place. Get the pack of cigarettes you stole from your mother."

A narrow clearing in the wooded area near the river led to a shed full of tools, discarded oars, and junk. Behind the shed was a lean-to with a broken door covered in vines, almost invisible.

Mary Margaret pulled the door open. The rusty hinges creaked. Inside a moldy mattress atop a wooden frame and a broken bentwood chair were the only furnishings.

"Carol will never find us here. She's way too prissy."

"Me too. Who lived here?" Theresa said screwing her face up like she smelled something bad.

"It was an old hermit. That little shed down by the river was his outhouse. When the tide came, in it washed away the poop."

"Ugh, let's get out of here."

"I'm kidding, it was for the gardener. Here, I brought a towel for us to sit on." She spread it out over the cot and lit a cigarette. Theresa coughed as the pungent smoke began to cover the musty smell.

"Here's what happened. I was waiting to shoot marbles with Matt and Fred in a little place we cleared last year. I heard them laughing in the woods nearby. They had a magazine they were all passing around, looking and pointing to something in it."

"Who was there?"

"It was Matt, Fred, and that good-looking new guy we saw at dinner last night. They threw the magazine down and covered it with leaves. Matt said 'Come meet Ted', so I walked a little closer. He smiled at me with the biggest grin, and I looked into his eyes. They were bluer even than yours, that pale blue. He looked like Troy Donahue. Then Matt came up to me and said, 'We were just talking about how cool you are. We want to show you something'."

Mary Margaret paused, took a drag off of the cigarette, and passed it to Theresa, who stood and walked to the window. "It's okay, I just heard something, but it was only a squirrel. Go on."

"I moved a little closer and Matt touched his zipper. He said, 'We'll show you ours if you'll show us yours'. I said, 'Okay' and they dropped their shorts, underpants, and all, right there, right in front of me. I bent over like I was to pull down my pants and grabbed Matt's shorts. I ran as fast as I could and threw his pants in the clearing."

"Pucci, you did not. You did not do that?" Theresa's heart was pounding as if it had happened to her. "What did their pee-pees look like? My friend at school said you've seen one, you've seen them all. Then she showed me a picture of Michelangelo's David."

"It's not true. I didn't have time to look closely, but Ted's was big and stood straight up."

"What do you mean?"

"You know, when they get excited. I was peeking through the keyhole in our bathroom and saw Charlie like that. I hid in the closet when I heard Anne coming. She knocked on the bathroom door, real loud, and told him to come out of there. She knew what he was doing."

"So, what was your brother doing?"

"You know, making it get big."

"No, I don't know," Theresa said.

"You don't know how babies are made, do you? So, you really haven't read that book. Remember what we saw, or at least I saw, Carol and that guy doing the other day? Well, that can make a baby."

Theresa walked back across the room and knelt on the bed next to Mary Margaret.

"Tell me, I don't understand."

"That's what I meant when I said they were doing, it. First, the man has to make it big, then he puts it in his wife's, you know." Mary Margaret pointed between her legs. "Sounds pretty gross, don't you think?"

"You've gone too far this time, you're teasing me again, Pucci. My parents wouldn't do that," said Theresa. She jumped down and ran all the way to the cabin.

Theresa, curled up on her bunk reading Jo's Boys had her back to the door. Mary Margaret climbed up on the ladder. "Come on, Mac, your parents only did that once. I promise it's like that. Let's ask Betsy, she knows everything about this kind of stuff from living on a farm."

Theresa put her hands over her head with her elbows to her ears.

Later, that same night Mary Margaret climbed the ladder again and shook Theresa gently to wake her up.

"What?" Theresa asked, "Leave me alone, I want to go back to sleep."

"I have a surprise for you."

Theresa sat up, rubbed her eyes, then climbed down the ladder and put on her shorts. "Where have you been all day, Pucci? You didn't even come to supper."

"I've been busy. You'll see. Come on. We don't have to sneak. Nancy's asleep and Carol's in the infirmary. She has a bad case of poison ivy on her bottom."

Theresa followed Mary Margaret out of the cabin. When they got to the hideout, Theresa stopped short. "I'm not going into that spooky place at night."

"Come on, just wait until you see. Katie and Betsy are here."

Mary Margaret shone her flashlight on the path. The Kudzu vines had been cut back to reveal windows. Light flickered from within. The cabin was swept clean. Candles burned in a votive stand, which stood slightly askew. A broken chair and the cot were covered in khaki green wool blankets, like the ones folded at the end of each bunk. A lopsided table, its half-missing leg propped up by a brick, held some candles, a flask, and a pack of cigarettes.

"Holy Toledo, Pucci, we have a clubhouse. Where'd you get all this stuff?"

"You wouldn't believe what's in that shed. Of course, I had to get the actual candles from the chapel. The flask is yours."

It was true; she had stolen it from her father, that and the French cigarettes her mother bought at the duty-free in Paris. She brought them to camp, hoping to prove to Mary Margaret that she was not a prude.

The girls settled in, passed the flask, then lit a cigarette. They confirmed to Theresa that Mary Margaret wasn't lying about what men and women do. They told the others that they had seen Carol in the woods with a boy.

"Even animals do it," said Mary Margaret stubbing out the cigarette they had been passing.

"Yeah, I've seen those bulls go after the cows on the farm, and heard the horses too," Betsy said. "The bulls jump right up on top of those cows. My sister told me that's what men and women do, too."

Katie then talked about hearing her parents in the next room. "It must hurt," she said, "my mama cried out. I'm never going to let a boy stick his thing in me, even if he is my husband."

"You'll never get a baby if you don't," said Mary Margaret.

She laughed and passed the flask to Theresa who took a swig and spit it out. Katie just pretended to drink it, but Betsy took a huge swallow and then another. They giggled and smoked as the flask went around.

"I think we should get back," said Betsy, knocking over the chair when she stood up.

They snuffed out the candles, hid the flask and cigarettes under the mattress, filed back to the cabin. Nancy was sleeping soundly, with a little help from some Phenobarbital Mary Margaret had taken from the medicine cabinet at home and slipped into Nancy's milk.

The next morning was cloudy, holding in the heat which added to the humidity. At eleven o'clock, Sister Joseph announced over the loudspeaker that it was time to line up for pageant practice. The sun came out making it hotter than Hades. It was low tide and not an iota of a breeze. The girls from Cabin Three, bleary-eyed and tired from the late hour of the previous evening, nudged each other in their conspiracy. Sister Joseph went on and on with her remarks and prayers. The girls shifted from foot to foot, slapping at mosquitoes.

"Betsy's face is awfully red," Theresa whispered to Mary Margaret.

"So is yours," she answered, waving the fake flower Sister Fatima had passed out for practice in front of her face. "I'd kill for a sip of water."

"Silence, girls, we'll begin the procession now," said Sister Joseph.

The girls and boys fell in line two by two and walked the three hundred yards to the statue by the river. Two boys and two girls genuflected in front of the statue, the girls leaving their flower offering.

"Matt calls her The Virgin of the Bathtub," said Mary Margaret.

"I can see why," said Theresa, looking at the all-white Madonna, surrounded by a white arch on a white marble base.

"I feel sick," said Betsy, turning around toward Theresa.

"Are you going to throw up?"

"I don't know. I just feel…" The color drained out of Betsy's face just before she fainted. Mary Margaret tried to catch her. Betsy slumped. Her weight caused Mary Margaret to stumble and they fell together. Betsy landed on top, hitting her head on the sharp corner of the marble base. Mary Margaret struggled to move the millstone of Betsy's weight. A warm liquid touched her face. Her eyes widened. Panic and horror overcame her. Blood gushed from a huge gash in the back of Betsy's head. Mary Margaret gasped out loud. She could not get up.

Theresa stood watching in shock after she heard the loud crack of Betsy's head hit, and the sound of her cry. She reached down to help.

A hush fell over the group, then screams pierced the silence. Sister Joseph ran toward the crowd. She saw Theresa holding Mary Margaret in her arms and Betsy covered in blood.

"Go get Father James. Have him call an ambulance and Dr. Puccini." Sister pulled off her veil and clamped it to the wound, then yelled at the children to step back. It was another shock to them to see the nun's white skull cap. Dr. Puccini and the ambulance arrived at the same time. It only took seconds for the doctor to realize Betsy was gone.

The rest of the day was a blur: the wail of the ambulance, the keening of the children, the shake of Dr. Puccini's head. But mostly, they would remember the blood, the way it spread, and the lifeless body of their friend Betsy, lying next to Mary Margaret. A heavy pall fell over the camp. Heavy as the gathering clouds that hung in the afternoon sky before unloading their contents in a drenching rain. A gully washer they called it. No one took shelter, they let the rain wash over them, washing away the day.

With only one week left until the end of the summer session, many of the campers went home the next day. Theresa had to stay until the weekend because her parents were out of town. Mary Margaret begged her father to let her stay. He cleaned her up, making sure she wasn't hurt. He talked to her for a long time.

"Daddy, it was awful. Why did Betsy die? She only hit her head. I don't understand." Mary Margaret said, tears streaming down her face. "I should have caught her."

"Sweetie, it's not your fault, it was just a terrible accident." Joe wiped her nose and tucked her hair behind her ears. "I think staying here with Theresa will be good for both of you."

He took her in his arms and whispered. "You're so brave, honey. You're my Piccola Stella. T'amo."

She watched with a heavy heart as his black Buick bounced down the rutted road, out of sight, but she knew she had to stay with Theresa.

Sister Joseph announced after a short service in the chapel, that Father Brennen would be available to counsel the remaining campers.

"I'm not going," Mary Margaret said, getting up from the pew. "I don't like that priest, but you go if you want to."

"I just feel so guilty. Do you think she fainted because of the bourbon?" Theresa said.

"No, of course not. It's Sister Joseph's fault making us stand in the hot sun so long," said Mary Margaret, remembering sweet Betsy laughing, her plump rosy cheeks, her round face surrounded by black curls. The image of Betsy also came into Theresa's head as Mary Margaret squeezed her into a hug. "I'm going to our hideout. I need to cry. Come there after you talk to Father Brennan."

A small air-conditioning unit grunted in the window of the office behind the chapel. Theresa was biting her fingernails when she entered. The priest motioned for her to take a chair across the room. He got up from his desk, bringing his notes, and sat on a stool facing her. It groaned slightly as he leaned forward and smiled at Theresa. His unruly gray eyebrows peaked in the middle, giving him a crazed look.

"Now, young lady, a terrible thing has happened. It seems to you the Lord has taken," he looked down at his notes, "Elizabeth, way too soon. You must bear in mind that God has a divine plan. It is not for us, as mere humans, to question His judgment."

"We called her Betsy, Father, not Elizabeth."

He moved in so close she could smell his alcohol breath. He put his hand on her thigh.

Theresa pushed away the chair. She wanted to leave but did not want to make a scene.

"I feel so guilty."

"Why, dear child, would you feel that way?"

"I looked at her, and her face was red. It was so hot out there. She was. It was my fault. I should have told someone." She sobbed into her hands.

Father took Theresa's hands away from her face. He placed them in her lap then made the sign of the cross.

"Let the Lord take away your guilt."

He pulled her to him by the shoulders and kissed her on the lips with his mouth open, his tongue against her clenched teeth. She wriggled free, wiping her mouth with her arm, over and over as she jumped up and ran, stumbling over the priest's feet. She rushed to find Mary Margaret.

Inside the shed, Mary Margaret was trying to prop up the broken chair.

"Holy Toledo, Mac, what happened? You look like you've been hit by a truck. Did that priest do something to you?"

"He put his hand on my leg and then kissed me. He kissed me on my mouth. I could feel his tongue pressing on my teeth." She stuck out her tongue, pointed her finger into her mouth, and made a gagging sound.

"That's gross. You know I never did like him. He used to spy on the girls when he'd come out to the beach."

A serious look crossed Mary Margaret's face. "You have to swear on a stack of Bibles that you will never tell anybody what I'm going to tell you."

"I swear, you know you can trust me."

"Well, for one thing, when I was younger, he'd come over to our house and grab me and tickle me. Once when my mama went into the kitchen, he put his mouth on my neck." Mary Margaret rubbed her neck as if to wipe off any remaining traces. "He's a creep."

"Ugh, why didn't you tell your mother?" Theresa said, rubbing her arm across her own mouth again.

"I didn't dare. But wait, it gets worse. Just before camp, he invited me and two of my friends, Pauline and Catherine, to go to Tybee with him. It was supposed to be a reward for good grades. One of his parishioners loaned him their beach cottage every year. While the girls were getting into their bathing suits in the maid's quarters, I went to the main cottage to use the bathroom. That's when I saw Father. He was peeking in the window where the girls were changing. He was rubbing himself down there." Mary Margaret looked toward her crotch.

"That is so gross. Did he see you?"

"He may have, but I snuck around the other way. Later, I tried to tell Anne, but she got mad. She said it was a sin to talk bad about a priest. She didn't even tell Daddy, or he would have done something. She didn't believe me. I wasn't making it up and what happened to you was real. Maybe we should tell somebody about him."

"Do you really think if we told it would be a sin against God?" Theresa said.

"I don't know. I'm in enough trouble with God, so I don't need any more sins. Sometimes, when I see Father Brennen in his robe saying Mass, I can't believe it even happened. Now, after what he did to you, I'll bet he does a lot of that kind of stuff. It just makes me feel sick."

"We'll keep this our secret. Let's get out of here. I'm glad it's almost time to go home." Theresa felt under the mattress for the flask. It was still over half full. They had not drunk that much after all. She took the flask down by the outhouse and hurled it into the river.

Five
Camp Villa Veronica, 1961

Theresa was on the top bunk reading *To Kill a Mockingbird,* listening for Mary Margaret's melodious voice with her two-syllable 'Hayee'. Outside, there were a lot of 'hi yas', shrieks, and 'glad to see yas', but none from Mary Margaret. Theresa had gotten there early, having come from Macon at midnight on the Nancy Hanks train the night before. Her grandmother's maid, Delia, met her at the station and they spent the night at Isle of Hope. Her grandparents were out of town. She hadn't bothered to unpack. She had Delia bring her to camp early, not wanting the other campers to see her dropped off by a maid.

The lunch bell rang. In the dining room, there were many unfamiliar faces. She asked around about Mary Margaret, but her inquiries were met with shrugs. The nuns were conspicuously missing, and no blessing was offered before lunch. When she got back to the cabin, Carol was bringing in a group of campers.

"This is your bunkmate this year," Carol said, indicating Theresa to a new camper.

"No, Mary Margaret is, just ask Sister Joseph."

"Sister Consuela fell last night, so the nuns won't be coming until later. I'm in charge."

"But Mary Margaret will be here soon and she's with me."

Carol looked at her with a sly grin. "Katie isn't coming, and neither is Mary Margaret."

"Oh, yes she is, I just had a letter from her last week. I know she is."

Carol ignored her and handed her a stack of sheets and towels and turned to pick up the clipboard. "Which one of you is Hannah?" She said. "You're over here with Theresa," suddenly the voice of authority.

Theresa snuck into the office and used the phone. No one answered at the Puccini residence. The new campers were at orientation, so Theresa went back to her bunk, still expecting to hear Mary Margaret any minute. She woke up to the sun coming in at a slant and the ominous sounds of the cicadas rising and falling. In the distance, she heard the dinner bell and the excited birdlike yelps of the campers pressing toward the mess hall. The scent was familiar, and the dinner was tasteless. She looked around the room and realized that she was the oldest one there. She felt she no longer belonged here. Her eyes were glued to the door as she chatted with her cabin mates, envying their first-night enthusiasm. She really didn't care where they were from, or why they had come.

Theresa declined the bonfire and went back to the cabin to reread Mary Margaret's last letter. In it, she mentioned how mad she was at one of her neighbors. She was a witch, and no one liked her. The letter ended by saying she had a scathingly brilliant idea and would tell her all about it when she saw her at camp on Saturday. *Where is she? Oh, no, I bet she got in trouble.*

The next day, she went through the motions of camp. After Mass and Sunday lunch, she went to the art room only to find the supplies limited and a sign *Only to Be Used Under Supervision.* Sister Joseph announced over the loudspeaker that all the campers were to assemble in the chapel at 4:30.

"Campers," began Sister Joseph, "it is with deep regret that I announce that Sister Consuela had a very bad fall on Friday and is in critical condition. Please join me in praying for her. As many of you know, she has been a beloved leader at this camp for years. Hail Mary, full of grace…"

Campers squirmed in their seats. The boys were punching one another. One was even so brazen as to shoot a spitball, which hit Theresa on the back of her head.

At bedtime, there was still no Mary Margaret. After tossing and turning with worry, Theresa succumbed to the whirring of the fan and the sounds of the summer night around her. She was dreaming about Mary Margaret, even hearing her voice.

"Mac, Mac, wake up. Come on. I've got your clothes, come on."

It wasn't a dream. It was Mary Margaret shaking her. "Come on," she whispered. She stumbled down the ladder following Mary Margaret, biting her tongue not to speak. She was certain that the thundering of her heart would wake the whole cabin.

Outside, Mary Margaret grabbed Theresa's hand, pulling her along. A rut in the parking lot caused her to fall, but she ignored her skinned knee. Soon they were out of sight of the cabins.

"Holy Toledo, Pucci, what in the name of God?"

"I stole the car," she said, pointing to the two-toned Chevy, parked at a rakish angle. "Get in, quit crying, you're not hurt, hurry up."

"You know how to drive?"

"My brother taught me a little." The car lurched forward. "Where's the reverse? I'll just ease up and turn the wheel really hard."

Theresa held her breath until Mary Margaret managed to get the car out of the parking lot and onto the road. Her watch read one o'clock.

"We're going to be in big trouble. Where are we going?"

"Tybee Beach. My family moved down there for the month. Oh, I've got so much to tell you."

The drive took about an hour. Fortunately, it was late, and very few drivers were on the road.

Mary Margaret kept veering into the other lane. Theresa looked at her in total disbelief.

"Have you lost your mind? We are going to be killed, in more ways than one." Mary Margaret looked at her. "As long as we stick together and swear never to tell, nothing should happen. Besides, I'm getting the hang of driving."

"I don't know, one of these days, one of these days…" Theresa said, shaking her head.

She felt like they drove forever. Every time they went over one of the bridges, Theresa held her breath. The tide was low and through the open window, the smell of the marsh permeated the air.

"Smells like rotten eggs."

"It's the smell of the marsh. I like it." Mary Margaret inhaled deeply. She pulled the car up next to a brown shingled beach cottage.

"Be careful not to slam the door," whispered Mary Margaret. A warm damp breeze, smelling salty like the ocean, unlike the putrid smell of the marsh, hit Theresa in the face. She quietly closed the car door and shuddered all over.

"Follow me," said Mary Margaret, as she climbed the wooden staircase to the main level of the house. Even before they settled into wicker chairs, she began her story.

"Remember when I wrote to you about that lady, Mrs. Horton, who was Catherine's neighbor? She's the one whose son could play in our houses, but we were not allowed to go into his. Can you believe they had this white carpet everywhere? She said we would mess it up. Catherine and I had this brilliant idea, well, I guess it was mine, to ransack her kitchen when she was not home."

"Ransack?" Theresa asked. "What in the world did you do?"

"Well, we took everything in her refrigerator and flung it all over the kitchen." Mary Margaret stood up and swept her hands in front of her. The ocean breeze was lifting her hair in the same direction as her hands. "Eggs, tea, milk, and whatever we could. We had a ball. I really wanted to pour stuff all over that white carpet, but just couldn't do it. Unfortunately, Mrs. Horton saw Catherine running out of her backyard and down the lane when she was coming back from the store. So, she called her mother and Catherine confessed and said that I was involved. I swear, that girl just has no spine. Then Mrs. Horton called my mother. I really did think I was going to die that night."

"Pucci, you have so much nerve. What did your mother do?"

"She drove me over and made me apologize and clean up the whole disgusting mess. I got screamed at, all the way there and all the way home. Thank God, Daddy was home when we got back, otherwise I would be dead."

Mary Margaret intended to take Theresa back to camp that night, but by the time she told her story, the sun was coming up over the ocean. The girls snuck in from the deck and climbed into a vacant bed in the back of the house. They hoped no one would notice them until they hatched a plan to get Theresa back to camp.

It was afternoon when Father James tromped over the sand dunes and found Mrs. Puccini under an umbrella with Nan and the twins. They were eating pimento cheese sandwiches. His sandy-colored hair was curling with the humidity and his handsome face was twisted into a scowl.

"Father James, what brings you to Tybee?"

"Theresa McDermott is missing from Camp Villa Veronica. Is Mary Margaret around? We wondered if she knew anything." The sun made his green eyes sparkle and he squinted against the glare.

"I didn't see her this morning. She was still in bed when I came down to the beach. You know how teenagers are."

She turned toward the ocean and shouted, "Come back in, Charlie, you're too far out. Father, Essie's up at the house. She'll find Mary Margaret. I'll get the others out of the water and be up in a minute. Do you mind bringing this one up to the house for me?"

Nan took Father's hand smearing pimento cheese all over it.

"Mary Margaret has been on restriction and hasn't left the house or used the phone all week. I'm sure she couldn't have had anything to do with it," said Anne. A feeling of irritation came over her as she wondered to herself how her daughter pulled it off.

Essie was making up beds upstairs when Father James found her and explained the situation.

"There's two still sleeping in that bed in the back. I'll check," said Essie.

"Miss Mary Margaret, what in the world? You gonna get yourself in a pile of trouble," Essie said, with her hands on her hips.

Mary Margaret and Theresa both jumped from a sound sleep. "Father James is here looking for you, Miss Theresa and your mama is looking for you, Missy. They's all worried."

Mrs. Puccini and Father James came into the room and saw the two girls crouched in the corner of the bed, both as white as the sheets they were pulling over their heads.

The Willinghams came to Tybee to get Theresa. She begged them not to make her go back to camp to get her things.

"Send Delia, she knows where my stuff is."

"No, ma'am, you have to face the nuns. Do you know how worried they were when they couldn't find you?" Her grandfather said. "You will tell us how you got out here."

Theresa looked down and pursed her lips and shook her head.

"Get in the car. And you better get your story straight before we get there," he said.

"It will be okay, darling," said her grandmother. "Just hold your shoulders back, and smile sweetly and tell them you are sorry."

The nuns were waiting at the camp. Mrs. Willingham held Theresa's hand. She bowed her head and quietly said, "I'm sorry."

Sister Fatima gave her a hug, "We were so worried."

Sister Joseph gave Sister Fatima a stern look and asked Theresa, "How did you get to Tybee?"

Theresa refused to answer, only shaking her head. "You know you won't be welcomed back here."

"Yes, Sister," said Theresa.

"She will be adequately punished. Now let us get her things," said Mr. Willingham.

Inside the cabin, Carol was packing her own things.

"I knew you girls were trouble from the start. Thanks a lot, Theresa. Now I'm in trouble because I didn't hear you sneak out."

Her eyes were swollen as she placed the rest of her stuff in her suitcase.

July 12, 1961
Dear Pucci,

I hate being back in Macon. It's day five of my restriction and I'm so bored I could scream. My parents keep hounding me to tell them how I got to the beach. I plead amnesia. They are making me go to Mrs. Edward's Etiquette School as punishment. Don't ask what that is. It will make you throw up. I can't have any phone calls and no one can come over. I've read two books, but I find it hard to keep my mind on them. I miss you so much and wish somehow, we could be together this summer.

Love,
Mac

Theresa heard a knock at the door, shoved the letter under her pillow, and grabbed her book.

"You're so pale and sad-looking. Why don't we go to a movie?" Elizabeth said.

"It's okay, Mama, I want to finish this book."

"Maybe you could call one of your friends to come over and swim. The pool hasn't been used in weeks."

For days, Elizabeth had tried to get Theresa to show some interest in something other than her books. She continued to sulk and rarely came out of her room. She wrote to Mary Margaret almost every day but was running out of things to tell her. Theresa visualized her on the beach or the porch swing, laughing with her sisters, and playing gin rummy with their friends at Tybee.

"Can I go to Grandmother's?" Theresa said. "I miss her."

"They're out of town, in San Francisco. In fact, we were supposed to be there as well."

"You didn't have to stay home. I could have stayed with Pearly."

"She's at her sister's."

"Why don't you let Mary Margaret come here? She wants to, we talked about it last year."

"Out of the question."

July 27, 1961
Dear Mac,

Daddy brought your letters in from town. I guess they had been there a while before he saw them. I forgot to give you our beach address. I think Anne steamed them open to see if she could find out how you got down here. They know I can't drive. She keeps threatening to keep me away from the beach if I don't tell. How can I, since I don't remember either? I'm supposed to be on restriction and not see my friends, but with all the confusion here, I just blend in. We're going home the day after tomorrow. I think they'll be stricter there. Maybe soon we can at least talk on the phone. I miss you too. xoxo, Pucci

Sunday, Theresa appeared downstairs with her hair uncombed and her hat askew. Her normally erect back was slumped, and her eyes were dull. In church, she sat back for the sermon lost in thought until the priest said, "Continue to ask and God will give it to you. Continue to search and you will find. Continue to knock and the door will open for you."

Theresa jerked to attention and sat up straight, listening.

"If you want your prayers answered, you must be specific," he continued.

The next morning, Theresa got up early and asked her mother to take her to Mass.

"Why the sudden interest in daily Mass?" Elizabeth, who made a habit of going every day she could ever since her conversion. The quiet simplicity of it gave her a serenity to deal with her inner demons.

"There's something I want to pray for," said Theresa. "I also want to go to confession so I can go to Communion on Sunday."

"Of course, darling, is there something you want to talk to me about? Are you ready to tell me what happened at camp?"

"Mama, please don't ask me that anymore. I just want to talk to the priest and start going back to Communion."

Theresa and Elizabeth had always had a close relationship. Theresa naively told her mother almost everything. She knew there was something that her mother didn't tell her. She heard her crying in her room. Whenever asked, she told Theresa that she'd understand one day. Theresa knew that her mother wanted to be a fashion designer and had gone to Parsons in New York. She had given up her career to marry George and move down here away from her Connecticut family.

Elizabeth didn't press Theresa. She was learning that if she left Theresa alone, she would eventually tell her everything, so she took her to Mass and Confession and listened outside her door until she heard the prayer.

Please, dear Lord, let me and Pucci be together again soon.

Six

"Mary Margaret is pinching me," whined Joel.

"Your stupid butt is on my side of the car," said Mary Margaret.

"Language, now hush. We're almost home," said Anne.

Anne Puccini pulled into the driveway with a car full of sandy, sunburned children and sour, wet beach towels.

Dr. Puccini, in a borrowed truck from one of his patients, followed with a load of beach equipment, the TV, and Essie.

A thick moldy smell assaulted Anne when she opened the back door.

"Joe, what's that terrible smell?"

Dr. Puccini had been commuting to the beach every day after work and on the weekends. "I think the house is just musty being closed up for a month."

The smell got worse as she moved into the house. She heard running water. The floor was slick in the kitchen and water was dripping from the ceiling.

They quickly found the source, the children's bathroom. Someone had left the water running in the sink.

"Dear Lord, what a mess," said Anne.

George McDermott came into the kitchen scratching his head.

"I don't know how those girls arranged this. Joe called and asked if Mary Margaret could stay with us for a while. They discovered a leak when they got home from the beach which caused extensive damage. They had to evacuate the house and are finding places for their children to stay until they can get back home."

"What did you tell him?" Elizabeth said, turning off the stove.

"Yes, of course, she can stay here. He also mentioned there may be a position coming up at St. Joseph's Hospital that I might be interested in."

"But George, if we give in, we'll never find out what happened."

"I think we may as well give up on that. I don't think they ever will tell us. They've been punished and they're both safe. That's the important thing. I'm hoping Joe will put in a good word for me at the hospital," he said, taking two glasses out of the cabinet. "It sounds like a wonderful opportunity. They're developing a practice that will specialize in surgery for cleft palate patients. I'll fix us a drink and we can tell Theresa the good news."

Theresa, just outside the door, heard the conversation. She made the sign of the cross, ran up to her room, and was lying on her bed reading when her parents knocked.

"Theresa, quit leaning over the track. The train will be here when it gets here. You could fall," said Elizabeth. "You know you still have to go to that class on Wednesdays. It's part of your punishment and the deal for letting Mary Margaret come."

"I know, I just wish she could go with me."

"They were full and you're halfway through. She'll be fine on her own."

"I see the train's headlight, it's almost here."

First the whistle, then the screeching of the brakes as the train ground to a halt with a gust of hot air.

"There she is, I can see her in the window," said Theresa, jumping up and down. Mary Margaret leaped from the train embracing both Theresa and her mother.

"I didn't even unpack from the beach," she said, pointing to her suitcase and laundry bag. "They turned off our water."

"Don't worry, darling. Pearly will wash your things."

The girls skipped along the platform leaving Mrs. McDermott to arrange a porter for the luggage.

Mary Margaret's mouth dropped open when they drove up the steep driveway to the McDermott's large stucco house. It looked like an Italian villa she had seen in one of her father's books. Theresa's mother was glamorous and her father, though a bit gruff, was a charmer. He was tall and well-built with a square jaw and long face. In Mary Margaret's eyes, they were perfect.

The first few days the girls were model children; swimming in the morning, playing cards in the afternoon, and helping in the kitchen. Mrs. McDermott invited Theresa's friends to a Coke party to introduce them to Mary Margaret. She and Pearly made watercress and cucumber finger sandwiches. At the bakery, she bought petit fours decorated with pink flowers with green leaves in fondant icing. Elizabeth had the bakery slice a loaf of bread horizontally to make her famous peanut butter and Vienna sausage roll-ups. The Coca-Cola Company brought out an ice chest filled with six-ounce bottles of Coke.

Ten girls arrived wearing flowery Villager sundresses and Capezio flats. They smiled at Mary Margaret and said how pleased they were to meet her.

"We just loved Savannah when our Girl Scout troop took a field trip to the Juliette Gordon Low house," said one of the girls. "We toured a lot of the squares with big statues and heard the stories about all those famous people."

"It's like an enchanted place with all that Spanish moss, all those quaint row houses, and that spooky cemetery," said Frances.

They all gathered around the table enjoying the refreshments and continued to chat.

"I heard a story about some square across from a courthouse that housed a jail. Evidently, long ago they used to hang prisoners in a huge oak tree in front of that building. They say now that moss will not grow on that tree at all. Is this true, Mary Margaret?" Another girl asked.

Mary Margaret remembered the story and nodded. She added that the moss would not grow only after an innocent woman was hung and the tree became haunted. Theresa looked at her and wondered if she was lying.

"The Pirate's House Restaurant was the best. I missed Theresa so much when she was at camp, she's my best friend," said Frances. "We've been friends since we were two."

Mary Margaret felt a pang of jealousy. She was quiet while the others chatted, only answering the questions she was asked directly.

"Is it true you stole a car?" Frances asked.

"I just borrowed it. It's my family's."

"That a hoot. Theresa also said you told her about the facts of life and that ya'll saw the counselor doing it."

The girls went into the bath house to change into their suits. After a swim, they stretched out on towels in the sun.

Theresa realized that Mary Margaret wasn't around and went to look for her. She found her in the music room crouched down beside the piano. She squatted beside her.

"What's wrong?"

"Your friends all seem so grown-up talking about their training bras. Once they put on bathing suits, I realized I was the only one still flat-chested, and they are all younger. I don't like Frances."

"Why not? She's my best friend. I mean at school."

"She's a prude and wouldn't put on her suit. She said she couldn't go to the pool because her aunt was visiting. The others were giggling about Aunt Ida coming to visit."

"Who is she? Like I'm supposed to know."

Theresa laughed. "It's your period, and it's just our code for it. Mine started a couple of months ago but come again. I was going to tell you at camp."

"Just quit telling Frances all our personal stuff." Mary Margaret bolted up and fled the room.

Outside, the girls were gathering their things.

"Tell your friend we just loved meeting her."

"Yeah," said another, cramming a petit-four into her mouth. "I loved Savannah. That homemade ice cream at Leopoldo's was the best. I'd go back just for the Tutti Frutti."

Theresa waved goodbye as the girls piled into their mother's cars.

Upstairs, Mary Margaret was stretched across the bed, her back rising and falling. She couldn't be crying. She never cried.

"Holy Toledo, Pucci, what's wrong?"

"I'm six months older than y'all and don't have boobs. I haven't even started yet. I never heard it called Aunt Ida. I feel so dumb and out of place."

Later Mary Margaret busied herself sweeping the patio, ignoring Theresa, who couldn't do anything to bring May Margaret out of her bad mood.

"It's not my fault, Pucci," she said, picking up a pleated wrapper from one of the petit fours and placing it in the trash pile. "Why are you mad at me? I didn't do anything."

"I know, but you didn't tell me your friends would all be dressed up in their flats and sundresses. Here I was in my shorts and Keds," she said, going back to her sweeping.

"I'm sorry I didn't know they would dress like that. I've been on restriction and haven't seen them all summer. The restriction was your fault. And, in case you didn't notice, I have on shorts too."

By late afternoon the next day, the girls had not spoken. Theresa became concerned when she saw Mary Margaret sitting on the bed reading a book. She never read books.

"Hey, Pucci, what are you doing?" Theresa said when she entered the room. "Are you actually reading a book? You, a book?" She was hoping to make her laugh and change her mood. Mary Margaret shot her a bird.

"Hey, I've a great idea for a scheme. Come on, you'll love it."

Mary Margaret perked up and put the book down. "You, a scheme?"

Theresa headed down to the den. Mary Margaret followed.

"Okay, close the door and be sure Mama and Pearlie aren't lurking." Theresa picked up the phone and motioned for Mary Margaret to come over and listen in. She dialed a random number. Both girls had the receiver up to their ears.

"Hello," Theresa cleared her throat. "This is Arnold's Appliance calling. There have been a number of issues with our refrigerators. Can you tell me if yours is running?"

"Well, I think it is, let me go check," the woman answered.

Mary Margaret looked at Theresa, narrowed her eyes, and said in a whisper. "What's this about?"

"Shhh...just wait," she said with a smirk.

"Why yes, I just checked and it's running," the lady replied.

"Well, you better go catch it!" Theresa said. Then she hung up the phone.

"No way." Mary Margaret looked at Theresa and howled. "I love it. I can't believe you did that. I'm so proud of you."

"Don't be impressed. Frances taught me."

"Mac, who else can we call?"

Later that afternoon, Elizabeth asked the girls if they wanted to join her to see the movie *A Summer Place*. They quickly changed, put on some mascara, and met Elizabeth in the car. Every time Mary Margaret thought about the scheme, she would look at Theresa and they would grin. Toward the end of the movie, Mary Margaret's hand, grimy with salt and butter, sought Theresa's, sticky from Milk Duds.

"I'm in love," she whispered.
"Troy Donahue?"
"Yeah."

On Wednesday, while Theresa went to her etiquette class, Theresa's mother took Mary Margaret shopping. She had noticed that the only clothes the child brought were her beach clothes. Elizabeth liked the girl, her devious spunk, and her independent spirit, lacking in most teenage girls. She had been surprised at her sudden lack of self-confidence at the party when she normally had so much. Maybe it was her faded beach clothes which were on the verge of being too small.

In the Lulabelle boutique, Mary Margaret walked past the racks of Villager dresses to the skirts and blouses. She liked the first one she tried on. The pleated skirt was cerulean blue with a coordinated striped blouse. Together they selected a belt and navy ballet flats. Elizabeth was surprised. It wasn't like shopping with Theresa who tried on everything and still wasn't happy. It usually ended in tears. Mary Margaret was bright and fun. It was clear to Elizabeth why Theresa was so drawn to her.

Mary Margaret was also taken with Mrs. McDermott. She put on her most charming self, keenly observing everything around her, hoping Elizabeth would find her amusing. She quickly made her decisions as she'd learned to do when shopping with her mother, or she wouldn't get anything. She tried to pay but was told she was being treated. She loved Elizabeth and imagined a world where she could be her daughter, the only child.

The next day, Frances invited the girls to have lunch at Idle Hour Country Club. The Tudor-style clubhouse reminded Mary Margaret of a haunted mansion she had read about in a novel. She looked around every corner as if something was going to pop out and grab her. When Frances came through the door, Mary Margaret jumped behind Theresa.

"Pucci, what in the world?"

"I'm sorry," she told the girls about the spooky story.

"Oh, don't worry," said Frances, giving each of the girls a hug. "There are some skeletons, but they're all in the closets." She laughed.

They entered a small vestibule and were greeted by a young hostess. "Right this way, Miss Wright. I have a table for you by the window overlooking the golf course."

"Frances' father is the chairman of the board. She knows all of the club's secrets," Theresa whispered to Mary Margaret.

They were handed menus. "The best thing here is the club sandwich," said Frances, setting her menu aside.

"What is it?" Mary Margaret asked.

"It's made with three slices of bread, turkey, ham, bacon, lettuce, and tomato. They only make them at clubs."

"That sounds great. I'll have one."

"Make that three," said Theresa. "Now, Frances, tell us about the skeletons in the closet."

"See that man over there with the blond wearing that beehive hairdo?"

"Dr. Brush? He's my dentist. I think he had to be one because of his name," said Theresa, giggling at her joke.

"That's funny. Well, that woman with him is his receptionist. They come here every Thursday."

"So, after all, she works with him."

"Yeah, but watch under the table. They think no one can see."

"Oh my God. She just lifted his pants leg with the toe of her high heel all the while chewing her food and looking at the plate," said Mary Margaret. They broke into a fit of laughter. The waiter walked up and cleared his throat. They placed their order.

While they ate their sandwiches. Frances who went to public school regaled them with stories about her classmates. They dipped their French fries in Catsup and kept the waiter running back for more.

"If only they'd put the bottle on the table instead of these tiny bowls," said Mary Margaret. Theresa and Frances looked at her like she was from Mars. She blushed and quickly added, "I was just kidding. This sandwich is delicious."

After lunch, Theresa and Mary Margaret headed to the pool. Frances was still entertaining her aunt Ida, so she declined and went home.

"I think I like Frances after all. She told some really funny jokes and knew lots of juicy gossip. I love it she taught you a scheme. What's in there?" Mary Margaret asked, pointing toward a dimly lit room.

"It's the men's bar. Girls are not allowed."

"Look, Mac, there's no one in there. Come on, let's go see. Oh, are those slot machines?"

"No, we can't. Come on, let's go to the pool."

Mary Margaret charged ahead into the room. A long bar crossed the room horizontally. Behind it, an up-light illuminated myriad-colored bottles on glass shelves that were reflected in a mirrored wall. Paneled dark wood walls faced a row of one-armed bandits, which glowed eerily across the room.

A movement behind the bar caused Theresa to grab Mary Margaret. It was only them reflected in the mirror. They laughed. Mary Margaret produced a dime from her skirt pocket and slipped it into the machine.

"What now, Mac?"

"Pull the arm down."

"Wow, look at all that fruit. I got two cherries. Do I get a prize?"

"No, you need three across, come on."

"Wait, I've got another dime," Mary Margaret said, inserting the coin. The cylinder in the machine rolled around hesitating slightly on two cherries then another fell into place. Bells rang, and dimes poured out. "Hot diggidy dog."

"Not so loud. Geez, look at all those dimes."

"What are you girls doing in here?" A deep voice from behind the bar asked.

The girls looked up to see an imposing man in a white jacket. His dark, shiny face glowed in the reflected light.

"Calvin, hi, we were just…" said Theresa, pushing Mary Margaret toward the door.

"Well, you may as well take your winnings," said Calvin, handing them a couple of paper cups to put the dimes in. "I'd better not catch you in here again, Miss McDermott."

They were still giggling when they got to the pool. Under the umbrella, at a table away from the occupied ones, they poured out the dimes.

"Wow, twenty dollars," said Mary Margaret.

"I'm thirsty, let's order Humphrey Specials with extra cherries."

After their swim, Mrs. McDermott picked them up, delivering some bad news.

"Sister Consuela died this morning. We'll have to go to the Rosary tomorrow evening."

"Mama, she must have been a hundred. She was very sweet, but do we have to?"

"Of course, you do."

"Could we at least go to the afternoon service so we can watch Alfred Hitchcock?"

The next day, they rode the bus to the convent. They got off in front of a bakery. The smell of recently fried doughnuts lured them in. Mary Margaret pulled out four dimes to pay. They sat on a bench and laughed at each other's sugar mustaches.

"These are good, almost as good as Libers, back home," said Mary Margaret, licking her fingers and pressing more of the warm glazed dough into her mouth. "I think we should get a drink," she mumbled through her over-full mouth, pointing to the little store across the street.

She pulled out a couple more dimes. They went in and bought Cokes.

When they got to the convent, they walked down the long dark hall, their footsteps echoing despite the worn, red carpet.

"I wonder where the Rosary will be," whispered Theresa. "Let's go into that room. There's a coffin in there. Where is everyone?"

"Look, it's Sister Consuela," said Mary Margaret, reaching into the coffin and touching the dead nun's hand.

"Ooh, it's cold and feels like wax. Let's get out of here."

"Girls, can I help you with something?" A very large nun looming in the doorway said. She looked like she could eat them both alive, at one time.

"Where's the Rosary? We were just paying our respects to Sister Consuela. We knew her at camp," said Mary Margaret.

"You missed the Rosary. It was over fifteen minutes ago, but if you like, I can say it with you two now." Her face softened.

"No, thank you, Sister. We just said our prayers," said Theresa, feeling rather brave with Mary Margaret by her side, "we need to get home and do our chores."

Theresa had trouble keeping up with Mary Margaret's long strides as they hurried to the bus stop.

"Do our chores, ha. Saint Theresa, you're getting good," said Mary Margaret, handing the bus driver three dimes.

That night, Dr. McDermott announced that the Puccinis were back in their house.

He would take the girls to Savannah on Sunday. He had an interview at St. Joseph's Hospital the next day.

"Mary Margaret's parents agreed that since you girls have been so good here, you will be allowed to stay together for two weeks at the Puccini's. Mrs. McDermott and I will join your grandparents in California. Be warned that we expect you girls to be on your best behavior," he said.

"Yay, Daddy," said Theresa, grabbing Mary Margaret by the arm and leading her in a do-si-do around the kitchen.

"Girls," yelled Elizabeth. "Y'all better behave. No shenanigans while you're there."

Seven

Huge live oaks lined the streets of the Puccini's neighborhood. Their branches, green with resurrection ferns reached across the street like arms trying to touch each other. A gaggle of children came rushing down the steps of the wraparound porch, while others came from neighboring yards, shouting, "Theresa, Theresa," Mary Margaret was behind them laughing as the little girls clung to Theresa.

"These children, they're not all part of your family, are they?"

"No, those two, live next door, and those three live across the street. Remember my twin brothers, Joel and Frank, and my sisters, Jeanne and Nan. Charlie's here somewhere, and the older girls are traveling with friends. Come on, let's go inside."

Jeanne and Nan followed as Mary Margaret started up the porch steps and shooed the other children away.

"I love all these children," said Theresa, her eyes darting around.

"Come on up to my room," said Mary Margaret. She kicked aside a couple of toys in the front hall. "Okay, Jeanne and Nan, leave her alone."

Nan, dragging Theresa's duffle bag behind her, suddenly stopped and unzipped it.

"Get out of there, that's not yours," yelled Mary Margaret.

"Did she bring us presents?"

Theresa covered her mouth, wishing she had thought of that.

"Mind your manners, girls." Mary Margaret grabbed the bag and headed up the steps.

A tall boy with sandy-colored curls covering one of his brown eyes stood in the doorway of a bedroom. "Hi, Theresa. I'm Charlie," he said.

Theresa felt her heart flip a little, "Hey, I'm Theresa," she said, looking down with a shy smile. They all started laughing.

"In here," said Mary Margaret. "Geez, you're acting weird."

"Pucci, you didn't tell me your brother was so cute."

"Charlie? You have got to be kidding. Here's my bed. We'll pull out the mattress underneath, or you can sleep in the top bunk with me. There's a mattress under every bed in case someone wants to spend the night. Our friends are always crashing here." The cluttered room had chairs draped with clothes. Baskets of toys and books were in the corners.

"All three girls sleep in here?"

"We do. The boys have their own room. The older girls share and then our parents have a big room across from this one."

The days tumbled past in a blur of activity. Anne Puccini and their maid Essie were constantly running the washing machine or cooking. Mrs. Puccini, always busy, kept a cigarette and a cup of coffee going, while a parade of children came and went. Charlie and his friends used the garage apartment in the back as a clubhouse. Sometimes his friends climbed the huge live oak next to it and tried to peek in the girl's bedroom.

One afternoon, the house was quiet. Theresa was lying on her bed finishing *The Scarlet Letter*. Mary Margaret rushed in from her job of sweeping her neighbor's sidewalk.

"I have a scathingly brilliant idea."

"Pucci, I want to finish this book. It's so good. The last scheme you had, almost put us in jail."

"Holy Toledo, Mac, lighten up," Mary Margaret said.

Theresa closed the book, turned over, and sat up. "Okay, what is it?"

Mary Margaret told Theresa about her neighbor Mrs. Henderson. "She's always yelling at us to stay off her property. Let's roll her yard." Theresa had no idea what rolling a yard was, but she knew it could not be good. She remembered she had promised her parents not to get into mischief.

"After supper, as soon as it gets dark, we'll slip out. I'll get everything ready while you finish your book. I'll show you what to do."

At the dinner table, Charlie and Theresa kept eyeing each other. Theresa was nervous. Excitement was gurgling up in her stomach. She was concerned about whatever it was Mary Margaret was planning and she couldn't keep her eyes off of Charlie.

"You're not eating, Theresa. Is anything wrong?" Anne said.

"She has cramps, Mama. She's fine. May we please be excused?" Mary Margaret said.

Theresa turned a deep shade of red. She stood up and picked up her plate.

"Just leave that. It's Jeanne's turn to clear," said Anne.

Charlie rushed over and pulled out Theresa's chair.

"Wanna go to the movies tonight with me and my friend Ben? We're going to see West Side Story," Charlie asked.

"Er, I'd love to but…"

"We have plans," said Mary Margaret, pulling Theresa away from Charlie. Out of earshot of the others, she whispered, "We have to do it tonight because there's no moon. As soon as it gets dark, we'll go. Meanwhile, let's watch The Twilight Zone. Mama and Daddy are taking the kids to the drive-in. I'll tell Anne you don't feel well so we can stay home."

The house was suddenly quiet. Mary Margaret went into the kitchen, popped some corn, and heated sugar and butter until it turned into caramel. She poured it over the popcorn. Theresa and Mary Margaret settled on the floor in front of the TV.

"I just love it when I'm the only one home. Mac, you're so lucky to be an only child."

"I don't know. I think it's really fun having a big family."

"Look, getting dark. Let's go."

"I want to see the end of the show, or we'll never know what happens."

"Who cares? Come on."

Mary Margaret grabbed a bag by the back door, leaving Theresa to follow. In the dark outside, fireflies blinked against the lawns. Mary Margaret pointed to a house, three doors away, across the street.

"That's the Henderson's. We're going to their backyard."

At the gate, Mary Margaret reached through and slid the latch over. It fell with a clang. The girls jumped into the air then grabbed each other. They waited silently, but nothing happened. Mary Margaret tried the gate. It wouldn't open.

"See how mean they are, they're always trying to keep us out of their yard."

"Let's go home," said Theresa, backing away.

Mary Margaret reached in and slid her hand along the post until she felt a hook latch. The gate opened as she released it, "They put up that hook just to keep me out."

Inside, she handed Theresa several rolls of toilet paper. She threw the bag behind a bush, unrolled sheets of toilet paper, and threw it over the trees and bushes.

"Come on, Mac. Try it."

Soon the backyard was transformed into a winter scene.

"This is crazy but really fun," Theresa said, as she sent the end of a roll spiraling into the huge magnolia tree. "Got any more?"

The next morning, they got up early and watched Mr. Henderson pull toilet paper from the trees, while Mrs. Henderson screamed at him. "I swear to God, I just know it was that kid, Ralphie. Just because I wouldn't let him climb the magnolia tree. I'm calling his mother," Mrs. Henderson said.

"Don't you feel bad about getting Ralphie into trouble?" Theresa asked.

"You've got to be kidding, that no good Ralphie getting into trouble? I love it," Mary Margaret grinned.

After breakfast, they went upstairs to make up their beds. Jeanne was screaming from the bathroom. "Somebody, bring me some toilet paper, quick. Where's all the toilet paper?"

The next day, Anne asked Charlie if he would go to the grocery store for her. "Charlie, can Mac and I go too?" Mary Margaret asked.

"I guess so," he said. "Go ahead and get your stuff and go to the bathroom. Let's get going."

"I've got shotgun," Mary Margaret yelled. She bolted down the stairs and ran to the car leaving Theresa standing on the porch.

"No way, Jose," Charlie said. "Theresa's company and she gets the front seat. You get in the back."

Mary Margaret gave Charlie her typical stare, pursing her lips and narrowing her left eye. He glared back.

Although Theresa felt awkward sitting up front, she liked the idea of Charlie looking out for her. Mary Margaret sat and sulked until they got to the A&P.

"What all does Mama want?" Mary Margaret asked. She rolled the cart through the aisles grabbing some Corn Flakes and Cracker Jacks, her father's favorites. "I got Daddy's. Charlie, let's get some whipped cream."

"You pay for it separately or Mama will know," he said, placing the groceries on the checkout counter.

"Hand me the whipped cream," Charlie said. Mary Margaret rooted around in the bags next to her on the back seat.

"Voila." She took the cap off, squirted some in her mouth, and passed it to Charlie. He did the same.

"This is one of our secrets we do. Anne would kill us. Here, try it, Mac."

After Theresa took a squirt, she handed the can back to Mary Margaret. She tapped Theresa on the shoulder, tilted her head toward Charlie, and gave her that mischievous look. She wondered what that was about. As soon as the car stopped at a light, Mary Margaret took the whipped cream and squirted it on Charlie's head.

"Goddamn it, Mary Margaret." Charlie pulled the car over, grabbed the can, and reached for Mary Margaret in the back seat. She tried to wiggle free and fight him off, to no avail. She was covered. The two of them sat back and laughed using the only thing they could find to clean off.

"You two are nuts," Theresa said. She loved watching the closeness of the two. It made her sad that she would never have this in her life.

Charlie continued his drive downtown.

"Hey, let's take a minute and show Mac my new school. It's not far. Then we can show her some of Savannah."

"I can't believe all these rows of beautiful old buildings. They look so sad. Someone should fix them up," said Theresa, aiming her camera. "Stop, Charlie. I want to take some pictures."

"Lady Astor called Savannah a beautiful lady with a dirty face. There's the cathedral, next to my school," said Mary Margaret pointing to the multi-steepled church.

"See that house over there," said Charlie, punching in the cigarette lighter on the dashboard. "It's haunted. A workman who was remodeling the house was thrown down the staircase by a mysterious force and killed."

"Yeah, and people who lived there heard noises every night that sounded like chains being dragged across the cellar floor," Mary Margaret chimed in. "They used to keep slaves down there. A girl at school used to live there, she heard it. Charlie put out that cigarette. You can't smoke in Mama's car. She'll kill us."

He turned around and blew smoke into his sister's face.

"Here's my school," said Mary Margaret pointing to a large gray building.

"Look at that wrought iron fence. Is that really your school? I hope they don't lock you in."

"They should," said Charlie.

"Wait, I have a scathingly brilliant idea," said Mary Margaret.

Charlie and Theresa looked at each other and rolled their eyes.

"Just move the car around the corner," said Mary Margaret, as she reached into the grocery bag next to her on the back seat. Keep the car running. "We'll be right back."

"Come on, Mac, this will be even more fun than the Henderson's."

She handed Theresa a dozen eggs as she moved toward the gate of the convent. She reached through the iron posts and hurled an egg toward the glass-paned door.

"No," said Theresa. "They'll kill us for sure. It's daylight, someone may see us."

As if overcome by a demon force, she reached in and pulled out a smooth cool egg. She threw it, feeling satisfaction as it splattered against the door, the yellow dripping down.

"Hurry," said Mary Margaret. She grabbed a couple of Theresa's eggs.

When all the eggs were gone, they raced back to the car. Charlie inched the car away from them, making both run faster and faster to catch up to him. They were so out of breath that their hearts raced. When they jumped in the car, Theresa almost passed out. She looked back and screamed. She thought she saw a nun flying toward them, her black veil floating behind her.

"It's only a shadow of the Spanish moss and your vivid imagination," said Mary Margaret. "Now, we'll have to go back to the store and get more eggs. Anne really will kill us, if we show up without them. Oh, and some more paper towels."

As a reward for getting the groceries, Anne promised Charlie he could take his friend Ben and the girls to the drive-in movie to see *The Guns of Navarone*. When they picked up Ben, Mary Margaret said she wanted to drive. Charlie jumped into the back seat with Theresa. Mary Margaret slipped under the wheel while Ben sat shotgun. The car jerked away from the curb. Ben, who had more patience than Charlie, coached Mary Margaret.

"Ease up on the clutch and press the gas pedal, slowly."

They were all laughing hysterically when the car choked down. They made it to the drive-in without incident until she hit the speaker. "Quit laughing at me." She jumped out of the car. "I'm going to get popcorn."

Ben slid over and corrected the car.

"Go with her," said Charlie. He winked and handed him a dollar.

In the middle of the newsreel, Charlie put his arm around Theresa. She jumped slightly, then looked down. He reached up and turned her face toward him and kissed her on the mouth. She held her mouth hard against his. He pulled back and smiled at her.

"Relax."

She did and felt the pleasure of her first kiss. Her whole body tingled. She kissed him back.

Outside the car, the unmistakable shriek of Mary Margaret caused them to fly apart.

"Here's the popcorn. Ben's coming with the Cokes. I don't want to drive anymore so get back in the front, Charlie."

Since the drive-in, Mary Margaret had given Theresa the silent treatment. She was her friend and Charlie was taking over. That next day, Mary Margaret came in from her job sweeping her neighbor's porch and found Charlie and Theresa in the living room playing *Heart and Soul* on the piano. Nan and Theresa were singing at the top of their lungs. Charlie kept messing up the notes and when Theresa reached over to help him, she accidently knocked him off the bench. As he was sliding, he grabbed her by the arm and they both tumbled to the floor. Nan jumped on both of them. They all laughed hysterically. Mary Margaret watched from the doorway. She was fuming.

Charlie spotted her. "Hey, come help me. Get these two off of me."

Mary Margaret just glared at them. "You go to hell, Charlie Puccini. And the rest of you too."

"Hey, watch it, young lady."

Everyone turned to see Mrs. Puccini standing on the stair landing.

"You talk like that again and I'll wash your mouth out with Octagon soap."

"I'm sure by now you've acquired a taste for it," Charlie said getting up from the floor. He took Theresa's hand and pulled her to standing. "Nothing like a good swig of gasoline." They all started laughing again.

Mary Margaret stormed out of the front door.

When Theresa's parents called and told her that it was time to come home, she was ready. She had tried to see Charlie alone, but it never worked out. Somebody was always around. The night before she was leaving, she and Mary Margaret were on the porch.

"I saw you kissing Charlie."

"I wanted to tell you about it, but you've been so moody. Why? We've talked about what our first kiss would be like so many times."

"But, Mac, Charlie? Ugh."

"Pucci, I really like him. It was actually great. You could have kissed Ben."

"Ben only sees me as Charlie's plain sister. He would never think of me that way. You might as well forget Charlie. He chases all the girls. I've seen him. That's why he does what I tell him to do. He's afraid I'll tell."

"You're just jealous," said Theresa, sniffing and wiping her sleeve across her face. "I'm glad I'm going home."

Theresa's train was leaving early the next morning. She and Anne were at the kitchen counter, having a cup of coffee. Jeanne and Nan were eating cereal at the breakfast table.

"Please don't go, Theresa. Who'll play Go Fish with me?" Jeanne said. Nan grabbed her around the legs. Her crying started Theresa's tears. She was going to miss being a part of this family. She hugged Jeanne and lifted Nan up, kissing her on the cheek. Mary Margaret hadn't gotten up, and Charlie was nowhere to be seen.

Dr. Puccini came in with Theresa's suitcase, "Come on, honey. We don't want to be late."

The train pulled out of the Grand station, leaving behind the elegant brick buildings, giving way to tumble-down shacks surrounded by a variety of junk and old cars on blocks. Theresa stared blankly out of the window. Her tears mimicked the raindrops outside. Soon snowy fields of cotton appeared, then row after row of corn stalks turning brown in the late August heat.

"Can I buy you a cup of coffee and cheer you up a bit?" A deep husky voice said. Theresa turned in her seat and saw a six-foot figure swaying gently with the motion of the train. At first, she thought it was a friend of her father's, then realized he was much younger but older than she was. The sun-streaked-haired, dark-eyed stranger had a boyish look about him. His face was open and kind as he grinned down at her.

"Okay," she said, following him into the club car.

"My name is Monty Hamilton," he said. pointing to an empty place. "Let's sit there."

They settled at the table and ordered coffee.

"I'm on my way to Atlanta for my freshman year at Georgia Tech. I couldn't bear to see you so sad. You remind me of my younger sister, Rose. I miss her already. Now, tell me why you're so sad."

"Oh, I feel silly. I'm Theresa McDermott. I just left my best friend in the world, and she's not speaking to me. I also fell in love, but he doesn't love me. I'm going home to Macon. I just spent two weeks in Savannah. Are you from Savannah?"

"No, we live in New York but have a summer place on an island called Isle of Hope. Have you been there?"

"Yes, my grandparents just bought a house on the bluff. I love it."

"Me too. I could spend all day on the river. My parents gave me a Sailfish."

"What's that?"

"It's a small sailboat. I hated for the summer to be over. Next summer, I'll take you for a sail."

The train clattered along the track. Outside the window, the landscape blurred by. Fully charged with caffeine, they talked and talked and were shocked when the conductor called out, "May-con, next stop May-con," emphasizing the second syllable.

He helped her with her luggage and promised they would get together next summer, so Theresa could meet his little sister.

"My grandfather's name is Oliver Willingham. I'm sure he's in the phonebook. Good luck at school," she shouted over her shoulder as she descended the steps.

At first, she didn't see Frances standing behind Elizabeth, who was smothering Theresa with hugs.

"Frances, you came."

"We've missed you so much," said Elizabeth.

"Mama, I was only gone two weeks, and you were in California one of them."

"Who was that good-looking guy behind you, waving?" Frances asked.

"Oh, just someone I met on the train. His family has a house on the Isle of Hope. He has a sister around my age."

Frances chatted non-stop, her voice echoing in the marble lobby of the terminal. News of their Macon friends had a certain sameness, as compared to what she had experienced in Savannah.

Summer was almost over. Pearly brought out a tray of cucumber sandwiches for Theresa's friends who were over swimming.

"I've got a surprise for you, Miss Theresa," she said. She reached into her apron pocket and pulled out two letters postmarked Savannah.

Theresa's heart skipped when she saw one was from Charlie and the other from Mary Margaret. "Please put them in the hall, so they won't get wet. I'll read them later."

"Okay, but don't you come in that house dripping wet, you hear."

Theresa thought her friends would never leave. When they finally did, she retreated to her room. She was apprehensive about what the letters might say.

Charlie's letter was short. She could barely make out his scrawl. He was sorry not to have said goodbye. He enjoyed meeting her and looked forward to seeing her again.

Mary Margaret's was long and friendly, the tone not implying anything amiss; her aunt Ida had finally come, she got a training bra, and her uniform was cool, especially when she turned it at the waist to make it shorter. Their favorite nun from camp, Sister Fatima, had been transferred to Saint Bernadette's. Next week, they were going to start high school and she couldn't wait. She was in trouble again. This time sneaking to see Psycho with Pauline, even though they were both told they could not. Mary Margaret got caught when she went to take a shower that night and got shampoo in her eyes. She got scared and started screaming. Her father rushed to the bathroom door and pounded on it asking what was wrong. She cried out she was scared that Norman Bates was going to come and get her. She would never take a shower again.

Theresa wrote back with her news; she hated her navy gabardine uniform, and they weren't allowed to wear saddle oxfords, which were all the rage. She met an adorable guy on the train, on his way to college. He spent his summers at Isle of Hope. Glad to know about Psycho. She wanted to see it, but not now.

The best news of all, she and her family were coming to Savannah for Thanksgiving.

Eight

Late Wednesday afternoon, the McDermotts dropped Theresa off at Isle of Hope before heading to the hospital where the doctor had another interview. Her grandparents were out shopping for Thanksgiving dinner. Theresa settled into the porch swing to read *The Brothers Karamazov*. A car door slammed, and someone shrieked. She looked up but didn't recognize the couple coming up the walkway.

"Mac, Mac," shouted Mary Margaret.

"Oh my God, Pucci, you look so grown-up. I love your new hairdo. Hey, Charlie," she said, flinging her arms around the two of them. "You've had a haircut too," she said, running her fingers along his scalp.

"Yeah, I had to get it buzzed for school," he said, as they filed into the kitchen.

Delia, coming in the back door, humming to herself, stopped short when she saw Charlie Puccini. His six-foot body was in a plank, leaning against the sink. He was smoking a cigarette. Mary Margaret and Theresa were sitting at the tin-topped table smoking and drinking Cokes.

"You kids will sure get in trouble with your grandmother. Smoking, now get your sorry selves on out of here. I've got lots of work to do to get ready for Thanksgiving dinner."

She pushed Charlie aside and dumped the vegetables she had just brought from the garden, into the sink. She brushed her hands together to remove the loose soil before heading back out of the door for another load.

After being exiled to the porch, the three plopped down in wicker rockers. Charlie and Theresa couldn't take their eyes off each other. Mary Margaret launched into a soliloquy about her new school.

"I was elected class president but got suspended and kicked off of student council when I wouldn't rat on Pauline for smoking. Daddy picked me up because Anne was at a meeting. Can you imagine? I didn't think he had any idea where I went to school. When he asked me why I didn't just tell Sister, I told him I was not a ratfink. He smiled. The nuns don't understand why I'm not a model student like my sisters. Sister Hope made me kneel on the ground, and when my hem didn't touch, she ripped it out. Anne was furious. I couldn't use the phone for a week. And Sister Hope is always on me about my hair. We aren't supposed to use hairspray or tuck our hair behind our ears. Well, I'm always in trouble for that. And you two aren't even listening, are you?"

"Hmm, yeah, I just realized I'm supposed to pick up Ben," said Charlie.

"Why don't you go get him and bring him out here?" Mary Margaret asked. "I've got stuff to tell Theresa."

Charlie ambled down the walk to his car, stealing looks at Theresa over his shoulder.

"Maybe the four of us can go to the movies tonight," said Theresa.

"I can't. We're having our Thanksgiving dinner tonight because tomorrow, St. Thomas' School is playing Savannah High at one o'clock. Let's get together on Friday."

"I haven't gotten a chance to tell you, Pucci, but we're going to Paris for Christmas. Why don't you come with us? It'll be so much fun. The Atlanta Art Association will be taking a group in May so Mama's checking out some restaurants in Paris. She's helping her friend from Atlanta plan the trip."

"Wow! I've always wanted to go to Paris."

Friday evening Dr. and Mrs. Puccini were invited to the Willingham's for dinner. Mary Margaret came with her parents. The girls rushed upstairs to Theresa's room while the adults went out on the porch for cocktails.

"Mac, I can't believe your room." Mary Margaret looked around at the four-poster double bed that had a thick quilted coverlet. The bed skirt and draperies were custom-made in a rich blue and white toile print. She ran her hand up the smooth mahogany post noting the deeply carved rice pattern. "You're so lucky to be an only child."

"You're lucky to have such a big family. I loved being at your house with all the craziness. I was bored silly when I got home, and so upset when I thought you were mad at me."

Theresa plopped down on the bed, stuffing a fluffy pillow under her head. Mary Margaret did the same. They faced each other.

"I'm so bummed, my parents won't let me go to Paris with you. They want me home with the family."

"Maybe we could talk them into it."

"Anne says there are too many children to let each one go on a vacation. I swear I hate everybody."

"No, you don't. Maybe I can talk them into it. After all, I need someone to hang out with. I can promise them I'll keep you out of trouble. The room will be free since we already have to pay for it."

"Oh, si vous plait," said Mary Margaret, sitting up and clapping her hands together in prayer position.

"Oui, oui, Mademoiselle."

From downstairs, Theresa's father was whistling.

"Theresa, you and Mary Margaret come down," Dr. McDermott called. "We have something to tell you."

"See, I'll bet they are going to let you go after all."

The girls rushed into the living room.

"What are you going to tell us? What is it?" Theresa said.

"Let's go to the table, Delia's already dished up the gumbo," said Elizabeth.

George looked around the table. The girls' eyes were wide with expectation.

Mary Margaret's were dark underneath, where her mascara had smeared. He raised his glass.

"Here's to the beginning of our new life, right here in our beloved Savannah."

"What?" The girls said in unison.

"Your father has accepted a position at St. Joseph's Hospital," said Dr. Puccini.

The girls looked at each other and squealed.

"My new job will be starting in January after we get back from the Paris trip," said Dr. McDermott.

"Can't I go to Paris?" Mary Margaret looked longingly at her parents. Anne shook her head.

"We're looking at houses tomorrow. Theresa can start Saint Bernadette's after the Christmas break. Sister Hope assured us that transferring would be no problem," said Elizabeth.

"You mean you've known about this and didn't tell me?" Theresa said. "That's not fair. Did she know?" She pointed to Mary Margaret who shook her head.

"We were still negotiating with the hospital. We wanted to be sure," said Elizabeth.

Delia brought out floating islands and the conversation split to the adults and girls each having their own conversations.

"So, who was the cute guy you met on the train? You never did tell me," Mary Margaret said.

"His name is Monty Hamilton." The room got quiet.

"What about Monty Hamilton?" Mrs. Willingham asked, suddenly interested in the girl's conversation.

"He's just some guy I met on the train. He said his family comes to Isle of Hope in the summer."

"His father is Montgomery Hamilton," said Mr. Willingham. "They have a compound at the end of Bluff Drive. You can't see much from the street, but I've heard it's quite an impressive property. His father owns a manufacturing plant in upstate New York and has quite a few holdings in the city. His mother's family is in the wine business in Italy."

"He was really nice and has a younger sister my age. He's going to take me sailing next summer," said Theresa.

"They're huge donors at St. Joseph's," said Dr. Puccini, "I think they come in the winter too and have house parties on Jekyll and Ossabaw Islands. Some kind of millionaire's club."

After lots of boozy goodbyes and hugs, the Puccinis drove off. Elizabeth found Theresa on the porch swing, crying.

"What's wrong, honey? I thought you would be so happy."

"What about my school and my friends? Pucci has all her own friends and her family."

Elizabeth sat down and pulled Theresa into her lap stroking her hair. The swing creaked rhythmically in tune with the surrounding night sounds and Theresa's sobs.

"It's going to be wonderful being close to Nana and Papa. The job your father has taken will be such gratifying work for him. He'll be working with cleft palate patients and accident victims, not just women wanting to be more beautiful. His talents were wasted in Macon. The pay is better too."

"Oh, Mama, I hope you're right. I do want to be closer to Nana and Papa. I know Mary Margaret won't let me down."

Across town, Mary Margaret was also having second thoughts. *Would she have to share Pauline and Catherine? Maybe they would like Theresa better and prefer going to her house with her private room and bath, not sleeping on a mattress on the floor. What if Theresa was a killjoy in some of their adventures? Sister Hope would certainly like her better. Ben might even try to date her. Surely Charlie would.*

December 5, 1961
Dear Mac,

I saw your mother today going into your new house. I wish you had come with her. She let me take a tour. It's fabulous. I love that huge room. It's like a ballroom. Boy, we'll be able to have some fun sleepovers there. I'm so excited your house is only two blocks from ours. She told me about all the farewell parties your friends are having for you. It must make you feel sad, but the excitement of leaving for Paris may make up for it. We are so thrilled you will be coming here.

Did I tell you about this new girl named Bunny? She moved here in the fall. You will like her. Pauline and Catherine are so impressed with her that they don't talk about anything else. Her parents are as rich as Croesus, and let her do whatever she wants. She has a walk-in closet where all her Villager dresses are in one section, and under them, are racks of shoes. I can't wait for you to meet her. They all are looking forward to you coming to St Bernadette's. Have fun on your trip and send me lots of postcards. Joyeux Noel, bring me something French.

XOXOXO,
Pucci

Postcards to Mary Margaret from Theresa:
December 1961

Paris is everything I ever dreamed it would be and more. Today we cruised the Seine in a Bateaux Mouche at twilight and dined on board. They gave us blankets to wrap up in. Claudette and I have had such fun together. She is my mother's younger cousin so glamorous and she lives here. I told her about you. She can't wait for me to bring you to visit her.

December 21, 1961

The Eiffel Tower, and the Louvre Museum, I never imagined the Mona Lisa was so small.

The Luxembourg Gardens are gorgeous, but the Jeu de Paume was my favorite with all the wonderful Impressionist paintings. I ate snails last night. Ugh! I'm so tired.

December 1961

Today we went shopping. Mama bought me a bottle of Caleche at Hermes. Wait till you smell it, I'll never wear anything else. She also bought me a Jean Patou black dress. She says you never know when you'll need a black dress. It can be dressed up or down. It has a matching jacket. Imagine a black dress. I feel so grown-up. Claudette took me to meet some of her friends. They are artists and live in a loft. It reminded me of a scene from La Boheme.

December 26, 1961

We went to midnight Mass at Notre Dame. I never felt the presence of God so strongly. It moved me to tears. We ate Christmas dinner at the Grand Hotel. Seven courses. I thought I would pop. I wish you were here. I can only imagine what fun we would have sitting in a cafe and talking about all the beautiful clothes. There are lots of mink coats that get thrown casually over a chair when the sun comes out.

December 27, 1961

I'm nervous about coming home and having to move. The men here look you up and down. They are very bold about it especially when I'm with Claudette. She says it is normal, but it makes me feel uncomfortable. Mama is dragging me to way too many furniture stores. She wants to furnish the house with genuine French provincial furniture, not the imitation stuff we find at home. I can't wait for you to see what I am bringing you. See you very soon.

Nine

Savannah 1962

Theresa kissed her father goodbye in front of Saint Bernadette's. She waved and walked over to the wrought iron gate in front of the looming gray building. The gate was locked. She peered through the intricate ironwork, looking for any traces of the eggs they had thrown last summer, but the facade was spotless.

Where was everybody? She sat down on a nearby bench, her stomach in knots. A large woman who smelled of Juicy Fruit gum sat down next to Theresa and placed several overstuffed bags beside her.

"You catchin' the bus?"

"No, I'm waiting for someone," said Theresa.

The bus pulled up, and two girls wearing uniforms got off.

Theresa stood and smoothed down her navy gabardine skirt, her uniform from Macon. She followed the girls around the corner where students were everywhere, coming out of every nook and cranny. The cacophony rose and fell as classmates reunited after the Christmas break. Mary Margaret was nowhere to be seen. A tall platinum blond stepped out of a long black car. The crowd split and let her go to the front of the line. They called her Bunny.

A door opened and a bell rang. Of course, this is the school. She had been envisioning going to class in the convent. Inside, the hall was long with a polished terrazzo floor. Lockers clanked open and banged shut. Theresa found the bathroom. Among the smells of urine, menstruating women, and hairspray, a melee of girls rushed in and out of stalls. Another bell rang. Like ants the students scurried through various doors until she stood alone, pressing her books against her chest. The exterior door opened, and a disheveled Mary Margaret rushed toward Theresa.

"Oh, Mac, I'm so sorry. Charlie brought me and he forgot a book, so we had to go back home. Sister Hope's office is the last door on the right. She'll give you your schedule. I'm late," Mary Margaret said, running toward her homeroom. "I'll see you in class."

Theresa's knock on the office door echoed through the hall.

"Come in," said Sister Hope. Theresa slowly opened the door. The nun sat behind a large wooden desk stacked high with piles of papers, "Well, come on in, I don't have all day." Light filtering in through the Venetian blinds exposed dust mites in the stale air. "Well, Miss McDermott, I see you have not complied with the uniform for this school," said Sister. She looked up and squinted at Theresa from behind her wire-framed glasses. Her gray eyes were as cold as stone.

"I'm so sorry, Sister. My mother forgot to order it. She's still in Macon, packing up to move. My grandmother will take me shopping today."

"I understand that you and Mary Margaret Puccini are friends from camp. Her sisters were model students, but she challenges me almost every day. Don't be influenced by her. I'd best put you in a different homeroom," said Sister Hope. She handed Theresa an index card. "Your schedule. I'm sure some of the other girls can help you find your way." She looked down at her papers and began to write.

Theresa didn't see Mary Margaret again until lunchtime. She had saved Theresa a place at the table with Pauline, Catherine, and Bunny. Catherine and Pauline were shooting questions at Theresa, but Bunny ignored her. After a few minutes, she got up and left.

"She likes to be the center of attention," said Catherine. "I think she's mad that we didn't compliment her on her new John Romain pocketbook."

"Wasn't it fabulous?" Pauline said. She drank her last swallow of milk. "I wish I had one." She grabbed her tray and rushed to catch up with Bunny.

That afternoon, Mary Margaret met Theresa and showed her how to get to study hall. It was in the basement of the convent, through a breezeway.

"You'll love this, we can sneak out, and there's a Seven-Eleven across the street. The seniors are supposed to be the class monitors, but they sneak out too, so they don't tell," Mary Margaret said. "I'm so glad you are coming home with me this afternoon."

Mrs. Puccini came to pick them up from school. Theresa climbed in the back of her four-door yellow Buick.

"Thanks, Mrs. Puccini, this is pretty roomy back here. What are those plastic tubes in the rear window?"

"They're air-conditioning vents, very important for our summers here. I talked to your grandmother, and she and I agreed that you could stay with us during the week until your mother gets here. I can alter one of the girl's uniforms, so it fits you," she said. "I'll run you out to your grandmother's, so you can get your things."

At the Puccini's, Nan came flying down the banister, landing in Theresa's arms.

"Look how you've grown," said Theresa. She tousled Nan's hair.

"We can sleep in the big girl's room since they are away at college. We just can't touch their stuff," said Mary Margaret. She hauled Theresa's suitcase up the steps.

Theresa felt suddenly shy when Charlie stepped out of the boy's bedroom. "Hey, you," he said. He smiled and winked at her.

Mary Margaret grabbed Theresa, who was melting on the spot, and pulled her into the bedroom.

"I think you should stay away from Charlie, at least until you're older. He has lots of girlfriends. Besides, you're here to be with me."

Theresa found her new school more challenging in some subjects and easier in others. She was doing well and fitting in with most of the girls except Bunny, who still ignored her.

Mary Margaret tried to get Theresa to sneak out of the study hall. She refused; she wanted to get her homework done. That gave her freedom in the afternoons to explore the neighborhood and to help her mother unpack.

The McDermott's house was becoming a showplace. Located in Ardsley Park, a neighborhood developed in the early 1900s when residents began to leave the historic district for suburban living. The main street, Abercorn, was divided with a median clustered with trees and lush bushes. Every several blocks small green parks mimicked the downtown squares that Savannah was renowned for. Each park was surrounded by large imposing homes. Because those coveted houses stayed in families for generations, it was fortuitous the owner died leaving no heirs and the McDermotts were able to purchase it. The kitchen and bathrooms were remodeled, the floors refinished, and all rooms painted. The large room over the garage had been dubbed the ballroom.

When the movers arrived in February, the neighbors gathered around to watch the enormous van reveal its contents.

Mary Margaret began spending more and more time at Theresa's. Now that the twins were getting older it was even more chaotic at the Puccini's. To sit in the family room and try to watch a TV was almost impossible with the boys always tussling and Jeanne and Nan claiming the best seats. She didn't think her parents would mind or even notice for that matter. Just last week her father had scolded a child sitting on the porch for not being in the house for supper.

"But Dr. Puccini, I don't live here. I live down the street."

Theresa and Mary Margaret could spread out in the McDermott's den with its paneled walls, parquet wood floors, and high ceiling coffers. They loved to lie on the cozy Heriz rug or sit in the twin green leather wing chairs with matching ottomans.

"I just love the way your mother decorates," Mary Margaret said. "Maybe she could give Anne some tips."

"Until the younger children grow up, Pucci, they'd only wreck it. I think she does a great job considering."

"Okay, girls, you run upstairs and play, I have a show I want to watch." Elizabeth came in the den, turned on the TV, then settled in her chair.

"But we wanted to watch the Beverly Hillbillies. It comes on in a minute," said Theresa.

"Sorry, but Mrs. Kennedy has redecorated the White House and is giving a televised tour. Also, I can't wait to see what she is wearing. George, it's about to start. Would you please mix us drinks, darling?" Elizabeth looked toward the bar built into one wall. "Fix something elegant. We're going to the White House. If you two want to watch you can, just be quiet."

"No, thanks, we'll just go up to my room and listen to some records."

"Theresa, before you go, please change the channel, I don't feel like getting up. Oh, and Sweetie, you may need to adjust the rabbit ears."

Mary Margaret plopped down on Theresa's bed. She looked around the room admiring her peach carpet and white walls.

"I love your room. It reminds me of a Dreamsickle."

"Cool, that's my favorite ice cream bar."

"Anne doesn't like the Kennedys."

"Pucci. Why not? My parents think he's great. He's Catholic."

"I don't really know. I once heard Daddy say he was doing a great job as president and Anne totally disagreed. She said he was nothing, but a fanny patter."

"Fanny patter, what's that?" Theresa asked.

"You know, a man that pats ladies behinds." Mary Margaret turned over on the bed and patted her rear end. "But she thinks Jackie is the best-dressed First Lady. She's so sophisticated."

"Geez, I hope not he's not like that. You want to listen to *Judy's Turn to Cry?*" Theresa took the 45-record out of its sleeve, slipped in a converter disk, and put it on her record player. Mary Margaret jumped up and grabbed Theresa's hair brush. She held it like a microphone, pranced around the room, and started singing the words to the song.

"Lordy, Pooch, you need singing lessons." Theresa grabbed her other brush and joined in.

In March, Theresa planned a sleepover in the ballroom.

"This is perfect for your party," said Mary Margaret, looking around the large room. "We can spread our bedrolls over there and dance over here by the record player. I'm so glad your mother hasn't put a lot of furniture in here. Let's keep it small. You definitely need to invite Bunny. She's so much fun, and everyone likes her."

"Pucci, there's just something about Bunny that's not right," Theresa said. "You know she still snubs me."

"Oh, Mac, you're being too sensitive. She's just jealous of our friendship. You'll like her once you get to know her. She's so funny and generous. Did I show you the Madras shirt she gave me? She gave Catherine a silver bracelet."

"Sounds like she's trying to buy, you two."

"Maybe you're the one who's jealous."

"Pucci."

"You know I'm just kidding. You're so much prettier and nicer and a lot less spoiled."

After Bunny was invited to the spend-the-night party, she couldn't do enough nice things for Theresa. One afternoon, she invited the girls to come over for Cokes.

"I think you should include Marnie," Bunny said to Theresa. "She's such a nice girl. Her family doesn't have much, and it will mean so much to her. I'll tell her."

"I really like Marnie. Hmm...I didn't know that Bunny did," Mary Margaret said to Theresa, on the way home.

"Which one is Marnie? I was embarrassed to tell Bunny I didn't know."

"The girl who usually sits in the back. She'd be pretty if she would just fix herself. I don't think they have much money. They live on the other side of town. Anne would say the wrong side of the tracks."

"Oh, I know now, the one who always gets A's and knows the answers in class. She's really sweet."

"She'll be thrilled to come. She wants to fit in."

"I wonder if Bunny is up to something."

"Now, why would you say that? I thought you were beginning to like her."

"I don't know. It's just a feeling I have."

Behind Theresa and Mary Margaret's back, Bunny assigned the other girls to bring eggs, makeup, beer, and a bikini. She told Marnie they were initiating her into a special sorority.

Marnie arrived first. When Mrs. McDermott opened the door, she saw a sweaty disheveled girl looking up in awe at the pediment over the door.

"Come in. You must be Marnie. I'm Mrs. McDermott."

"Yes, ma'am."

"I bet Theresa forgot to tell you to bring a sleeping bag. Don't worry, we have extras. I'll show you where you girls will be sleeping."

"Thank you, ma'am," she said, her brown eyes darted around like a frightened deer. Elizabeth led her into a huge room. She looked around for a place to hide the brown paper bag with her things in it.

"Did you walk?" Elizabeth asked.

"Just from Abercorn. I was dropped off," she said. She crumpled her bus ticket in her hand and hid it in her pocket.

"I think I hear the others. They're upstairs in the room at the end of the hall. Make yourself at home."

Dr. McDermott grilled hamburgers for the girls. While they ate, Elizabeth entertained them with jokes and funny stories. After dinner, she gave each one a goody bag containing candy bars, samples of French perfume, and makeup. The girls retreated to the ballroom and spread out their sleeping bags.

"I love your mother. She's so funny and beautiful. You are so lucky," Catherine said, dabbing some Je Raviens on her wrist. "This smells so much better than Jungle Gardenia."

Theresa nudged Mary Margaret and winked. They both knew that was the perfume Bunny wore. Bunny looked down, throwing her gift onto her sleeping bag, unopened.

"Let's get started," she said.

They took turns putting makeup on and plaiting each other's hair. Bunny pulled up a chair next to a little table. She handed the bikini to Marnie to go change into and told her they were going to do a fashion show.

"I don't know about this," said Marnie, looking at the scanty suit.

"Go on," said Bunny. "It is part of the initiation, we've all done it."

Theresa was in the corner sorting through some 45s and the others were shouting out their favorite songs for her to play.

"Mac, take off that Elvis Presley, nobody likes him anymore. Let's just play Beatles." In an aside, she whispered to Theresa. "What the hell is Bunny doing?"

"I like Chubby Checker," said Pauline, twisting her hips.

When Marnie came out of the bathroom, Bunny whistled. Marnie felt silly and could see there was no sign of a fashion show. Bunny blindfolded her and led her to the chair.

Theresa grabbed Mary Margaret's arm and pulled her ear close to her mouth. "I don't like this. What's she gonna do now?"

"I have no idea but let's get this stuff off of our faces."

"Open up," said Bunny, cracking a raw egg directly into Marnie's mouth, then handing her a glass of beer to wash it down. Marnie spit out the beer all over Bunny. In the meantime, the other girls had taken out their braids and wiped their faces clean.

Bunny led Marnie down the street to the Seven-Eleven. She was still blindfolded, wearing the bikini. The girls followed. When they got there, she was told to remove her blindfold.

"Now go in, and ask the clerk for some extra-large rubbers," said Bunny, looking at the others for encouragement. Their mouths dropped open as she walked in. They watched through the plate glass window and saw him point to the door and heard him scream for her to get out.

Outside, the girls were giggling. Marnie realized they were making fun of her.

"Did you really ask him for rubbers?" Bunny asked, turning to the others, and twirling her finger around in front of her ear. "Cuckoo."

"There is no sorority, is there?" Marnie said. She felt humiliated and embarrassed. She put her head down and started to run in the wrong direction. Theresa and Mary Margaret realized she had no idea how to get back to the house. They took Marnie by her goose-bump-covered arms and led her back.

When they got to the house, Marnie pulled away and went inside to change into her clothes. She came out, looked at everyone with tears in her eyes, and started out of the door.

Theresa yelled, "Please don't go."

Mary Margaret ran past Theresa, Marnie turned, "How could you? I thought you were my friend. Just leave me alone."

Mary Margaret started after her but tripped. When she got up, Bunny caught up with her and held her arm. "Just let her go."

By the time Mary Margaret wriggled free, Marnie was gone.

"Bunny, I can't believe you're so cruel and you talked us into going along with you."

"So, what?" Bunny said and marched back into the house.

When the others were finally asleep, Mary Margaret whispered to Theresa. "Did you see how hurt Marnie looked?"

"I feel awful, I'll never invite Bunny back to my house. I don't care what any of y'all say, there is something wrong with her. She's mean," Theresa said.

The next morning, Elizabeth came into the ballroom with a tray of orange juice. She shook Theresa, "Where's Marnie?"

Mary Margaret rolled over and looked up at Elizabeth, "She had to leave early."

"But the bedroll and blanket I got for her hasn't been touched."

Mary Margaret glanced over at Theresa for an answer.

"I don't know, Mama."

The other girls were stirring.

"Pearly's serving breakfast downstairs," said Elizabeth.

While everyone was heading to the table, Bunny gathered her things and slipped out of the back door.

Around the table, the girls were bleary-eyed and quiet.

"I demand to know what happened. There's a sticky mess on the parquet floor, a bathing suit in the trash can, and one of you is missing. Did Marnie walk home last night? She could have been killed or worse," said Elizabeth, looking around the table. "And where's Bunny?"

"Oh, she had to be somewhere this morning. She said to thank you," said Catherine.

Mary Margaret bit off a piece of bacon and then pushed the scrambled eggs around on her plate. "I feel terrible. I'm gonna call Marnie. What if something happened?"

Mary Margaret ran to the phone and before she could say much, Marnie hung up on her.

After Catherine and Pauline left, Theresa reiterated to her mother a little of what happened, leaving out the Seven-Eleven part. "I really don't like anyone right now, especially myself. Can I go to my room now?"

"I know I'm disgusted with the whole mess. Let's go upstairs and get some sleep," said Mary Margaret.

"Not until you both promise to apologize to that girl." They nodded and got up from the table.

In the cafeteria on Monday, Bunny joined Catherine, Mary Margaret, and Pauline at their usual table. Theresa left when she saw Bunny coming their way. The others looked down while she went on about Marnie being a baby and no fun at all. Bunny continued to rant as the others got up from the table one by one. They deposited their half-eaten lunches on the conveyor belt.

The next weekend, Mary Margaret went over to Theresa's to spend the night.

"Modeling classes? I could never be a model, I'm not tall enough, but you'd be perfect," Theresa said. She rolled over and put a bottle of Paint the Town Pink fingernail polish on the bedside table.

"It'll teach us posture and how to walk and all," said Mary Margaret. "It says so in this handout I got. We'll learn how to talk to boys, even how to paint our nails without making a mess like you just did." She handed the brochure to Theresa.

"When Frances and I went to Charm School in Macon at the YWCA. The teacher hit us between the shoulder blades and made us walk with a book on our heads. Listen to this," said Theresa, reading from the pamphlet. "To be a girl means more than just not being a boy. Learn to be more than feminine and then be proud of being a girl and proud of being yourself. A boy will notice if you have something special about you. Maybe it's the way you tilt your head, or your eyes are bright, or your special laugh. Your charm is to make a man feel like a man."

"Oh, hogwash to that," said Mary Margaret. "However, we'll get to be in a fashion show at the end. Let's do it."

"I'll think about it. Speaking of boys, Pucci, what's Charlie up to?"

"Oh, he's busy. Come on, let's go down to Central Pharmacy and get a cherry Coke. But clean that mess off of your fingernails first."

Central Pharmacy was the hub of the neighborhood. In addition to the prescription department located in the back of the store, they had personal items, cosmetics, and even a few groceries. A checkerboard of black and white tiles spelled out the name Central Pharmacy on the floor of the front entry. A gray Formica counter ran along the right-hand wall. Stainless-steel swivel stools with red vinyl cushions were usually full of teenagers sipping sodas or eating grilled cheese sandwiches. They were grilled to perfection, mashed almost flat, but the bread remained crispy.

"Let's split some fries to go with our Cokes," Mary Margaret said. "Why are you tilting your head so funny?"

"I want that man to notice me."

"Oh, I wonder who that is," said Mary Margaret, swiveling the stool to get a better look. "He's awfully handsome. I wonder if he's a movie star."

Theresa giggled a little too loud.

The man, square-jawed, and clean-shaven was impeccably dressed in a crisp white shirt, plaid bow tie and a blue cashmere sweater casually thrown over his shoulders. He was looking around when the checkout girl came up to him.

"May I help you, sir?"

"I'm Dr. Houston, I came to pick up a prescription. I'm new to the neighborhood, just admiring the beautiful woodwork behind the bar."

"The prescriptions are in the back, let me know if you need anything else." He turned to the two girls who were staring and nodded.

"Wow, I think he saw us. I guess we better sign up for that modeling class after all," said Theresa, turning back to take a sip of her drink.

On Wednesday afternoons, the day physicians had off, they started going to Central, hoping Dr. Houston would show up. When the modeling class began on that day, they had to give up their pursuit. Levy's department store had a special room in the back where the class met. There were fifteen girls, not all from St. Bernadette's.

"Pucci, I didn't know Bunny was going to be here."

"Me either. Where?"

"She's over there trying to talk to Pauline and Catherine. They're ignoring her," Theresa said. "They haven't spoken to Bunny since the incident with Marnie. Oh look, here comes our instructor."

"Mac, I didn't know she'd be so young. She looks like a model."

The tips for making themselves attractive using makeup correctly and styling their hair were practical. The girls enjoyed experimenting with the cosmetic samples the store provided and the individual advice the teacher gave them. She showed them how to make a face mask out of oatmeal to exfoliate their skin and brought high heels to let them practice walking. Theresa felt taller and more confident. She was looking forward to being in the fashion show. Everyone's family would be invited.

At the end of the session, a saleswoman wheeled in racks of clothes for the girls to model. Like locusts they swarmed on the clothes, grabbing the pieces they wanted to create an outfit. In the large dressing room, Mary Margaret and Theresa noticed Bunny sneak a dress into her bag as she was leaving.

"Did you see that?" Mary Margaret said to Theresa, "She just stole that dress. That's awful."

"I told you she was bad news, Pucci."

"I know, I know. Please don't tell me you told me so. She had me fooled," said Mary Margaret.

"I can see how y'all were all taken in with her good looks and charm," said Theresa. "She knows how to flatter people to get them to do stuff. How she ever convinced the nuns that she was a natural platinum blond, so she wouldn't get in trouble for dying her hair, I'll never know. However, I did tell you so."

Mary Margaret cupped her hand and whispered to Theresa, "I'll tell you something she did that I really feel bad about. One time I saw her steal someone's wallet in study hall and didn't say anything about it. I'm sorry; I never trusted your instincts about that girl. I told Anne about Marnie at the pajama party, and she insisted I apologize to her, but I chickened out. I was afraid I'd be Bunny's next victim."

Mary Margaret and Theresa were disappointed Bunny's parents did not come to the fashion show. They wanted to check them out and see what they were like.

"Pucci, look at Bunny standing over there by herself. She looks sad that everyone's parents are here gushing, and she has no one. Maybe that's why she's so awful. Maybe we should…"

"No way, Mac, don't even think about being nice. I will never trust her."

Ten

Later, on a warm Saturday afternoon in March, Theresa was spending the night at the Puccini's. She and Mary Margaret went to Central to get a hamburger for supper. They were finishing when Dr. Houston came in.

They followed him out, staying a good distance behind. It was just turning dark. Under his sharply pressed pants, shiny brown Weejuns propelled him straight ahead. He turned down Washington Avenue and started up the sidewalk of a large yellow brick house, stopping to pick up a leaf from the perfectly manicured lawn.

"That's my favorite house, those columns remind me of Tara," whispered Mary Margaret.

They hid behind a crape myrtle bush.

"Look at that red Mercedes convertible in the driveway. I wonder if he's single."

"It's a really big house for one person, Pucci."

In the street, a green truck slowed down and backfired. The girls jumped and retreated behind another bush.

"Let's get out of here," said Theresa.

"No, wait, the truck's backing up. It's pulling in the driveway, behind the red car." A tall dark-haired young man got out. He took a pack of cigarettes from the rolled-up sleeve of his white undershirt, smoothed out the sleeve then put on a navy Nehru-style shirt. Before heading up the sidewalk, he slicked back his long greasy hair with a comb from his jeans pocket. They crouched down and ran up behind a closer bush. They watched the man as he approached the house. Dr. Houston opened the door a crack, then wider. He looked around, then placed a hand on the man's shoulder, and beckoned him inside.

It was getting dark, so the girls returned to the Puccini's.

The next morning on the way to church, they noticed the truck still in the driveway. They were listening to Mary Margaret's parents in the front seat.

"Joe, isn't that where that new OB/GYN lives?" Anne asked.

"Yes, it is. I think we should have a get-together and introduce him and the McDermotts to some of the other doctors in the neighborhood."

"That's a great idea. Let's do it soon."

Mary Margaret and Theresa were nudging each other in the backseat. Jeanne was holding Nan in her lap. "What's so funny, you two?"

"Nothing," said Mary Margaret, straightening Nan's hat.

Theresa and Mary Margaret went into the older girls' room and rummaged through their closet until they found the perfect dresses to wear to the party.

"We'll be in trouble if anyone finds out we were in here, but they have all the pretty party clothes. There's some makeup on the dressing table," Mary Margaret said, holding up a blue taffeta dress.

"Is there any blue eye shadow? Remember how they showed us in modeling class to put it on? It'll really bring out your blue eyes especially now that you're wearing mascara."

Mary Margaret blinked after applying the mascara.

"Now you look like a raccoon. Let me put the eye shadow on you or you'll look like a hurt one."

"Oh crap, I'm not very good at this."

Theresa carefully removed the smudges under Mary Margaret's eyes and reapplied the eye makeup.

"It's perfect. Let me try the green dress. Won't your mother recognize their clothes?" Theresa asked.

"No, she's so preoccupied supervising Essie making the crab cakes, she won't notice."

"How's this sound? I'm so pleased to make your acquaintance, Dr. Houston. My name is Theresa."

"Just say pleased to meet you and drop the curtsy, for God's sake."

They finished their makeup with a little rouge and some lipstick and went downstairs to meet their idol. The McDermotts had just arrived when the girls walked down the steps.

"Theresa, go back upstairs now and wipe that stuff off your face, or I'm taking you home. You too, Mary Margaret, y'all look like clowns," Elizabeth said, turning toward the kitchen to find Anne.

Mary Margaret stuck out her tongue before they trudged up the steps. After blotting off a little of the lipstick, they sat on the top step and watched as the guests arrived. As soon as they saw John Gray Houston, they ran down to greet him. "What's that smell?" Theresa asked, wriggling up her nose.

"It's Evening in Paris. I found it in the dresser."

He was standing at the front door next to the Puccinis and the McDermotts. Theresa held out her hand which he took into both of his. "Aren't you a lovely, young lady? I can certainly tell whose daughter you are," he said, looking at Elizabeth and smiling.

"This is Pucci. I mean Mary Margaret."

"Hello," said Mary Margaret. "So very pleased to make your acquaintance." She gave a little curtsy, "That's a beautiful red convertible you have."

"Why don't you girls come over one Saturday, and I'll take you for a ride? I've seen you both at the Central Pharmacy. Don't you just love their hamburgers?"

Other guests were coming in the door, trying to meet Dr. Houston. Theresa and Mary Margaret went into the dining room and nibbled their way around the table. They nodded and spoke politely to the guests.

Theresa whispered to Mary Margaret, "Are my stocking seams straight?" She turned, trying to look at the back of her legs.

"No, I guess we better go upstairs and fix them."

The girls bolted upstairs.

"Fix my stockings, Pucci."

"No, let's change. I just said that so we could get out of there. Unzip me."

They noticed the volume from below become louder and louder as the drinks flowed. When things got quiet the girls went downstairs to get a snack. The McDermotts and the Puccinis were sitting together in the den. All the others had gone.

"Wait," said Mary Margaret with her fingers to her lips, she motioned for Theresa to be quiet and come closer to the den door.

"It was a lovely party," Elizabeth said, taking off her shoes.

"John Gray really is a dandy. I just love the way he dresses. I don't care if what you say is true, Joe, I like him," Anne said, lighting a cigarette.

"All I can say is that he's a wonderful doctor, and his patients love him. I hope it doesn't come out, or they'll fire him," said Joe.

"Well, I've only told you, and maybe I'm wrong, but I can't imagine why a young man would be coming out of his house at six o'clock on a Monday morning," George said.

"We saw that old green truck there last Sunday on the way to church. I think the girls saw it too. You know they are fascinated by him. Did you notice how they had fixed themselves up tonight?"

They all laughed. Mary Margaret and Theresa looked at each other wide-eyed then ducked into the kitchen.

"I'm hungry, let's get something to eat." Mary Margaret rummaged through a cabinet and pulled out a large can. "What about this?"

"Chef Boyardee spaghetti, yay. See if you have any with meatballs."

"Yes, here's some."

Mary Margaret dumped it in a pan and heated it up. "Daddy thinks spaghetti in a can is barbaric, being Italian and all. It's the only kind Nan will eat so he just deals with it. Oh, and Charlie's pizza in a box, it makes him crazy."

The next weekend, the girls stayed at the McDermott's. Mary Margaret threw some of Theresa's stuffed animals on the floor and nestled herself among the pillows.

"Mac, why don't we go over and ask John Gray for a ride in the convertible tomorrow?"

"Okay, but what do you think it is that could get him fired, Pucci?"

"I don't know. Maybe they don't like his friend in the truck. Maybe he's a crook and Dr. Houston's harboring a criminal."

"You and your imagination. I'll bet that guy's just doing some work around his house."

"I don't know, Mac, he looked pretty shady."

The chime of the doorbell echoed within the entrance hall. They waited at the door, but nobody came.

"Mac, he has to be home, his car is here. Ring it again."

"No, Pucci, I don't want to bother him. Maybe he's napping."

"It's kinda late for that," Mary Margaret said, reaching past Theresa and pressing it again. "Boy, that's an impressive sound, no way he couldn't hear it if he was in there. Maybe he's at Central. Let's go get a Coke."

"Isn't that the green truck in the garage?" Theresa said as they walked away.

"It sure is. Maybe they'll both be at Central. We can meet the fugitive."

On the way home, they walked past the doctor's house again. The green truck was still in the garage. It was beginning to get dark, so they decided to peek in the window from the patio to see what might be going on. They found a small table to stand on and placed it behind the azaleas. Mary Margaret pushed Theresa up onto the table. She peered inside and drew in a sharp quick breath.

"Holy Moly. You won't believe this. They're kissing."

"Who? Let me look," she said, pushing Theresa off. "Oh my God, it's John Gray and the fugitive. He's a queer."

"That must be what our parents were talking about. How did they know? We can't ever tell a soul. We don't want him to get fired."

"That is so gross," said Mary Margaret, jumping off the table. Inside the light went off. The girls stumbled home in the dark.

"I can't believe what we just saw. We can't say anything, not even to your mother, Pucci. It's just not right, two men kissing."

"There goes my dream. I was kinda hoping he liked younger women."

"Oh, geez, I doubt he likes girls." Mary Margaret plopped down on Theresa's bed. "You know how sometimes we tickle each other's backs before we go to sleep? I would never want to kiss you on the mouth. It's just disgusting."

"Women don't do that, do they?"

"I don't think so. I can't even imagine how men do it."

Eleven

Mary Margaret and Theresa were on the floor in her room playing Monopoly.

"You make me sick. Here's all my money," said Theresa, when she landed on Park Place. She threw her last one-hundred-dollar bill at Mary Margaret. "You get all the good ones, you cheated. Next time, I'll be the race car. I'm going to get a Coke."

"You're just depressed your mother's leaving tomorrow," said Mary Margaret, picking up the race car and Scottie dog and putting them back in the box along with the money and deeds. "I wish Anne would do something exciting like this instead of all that boring volunteer stuff she does."

"Yeah, you're right, I'm feeling a little sorry for myself."

The tour, sponsored by the Atlanta Art Association, commemorated a newly launched Air France airplane and included the art capitals of Europe. After studying art at Parsons in New York where she met and married George, Elizabeth gave up her plans for a career and followed him back to his home in Georgia. Her dream was to see the artworks she had studied.

In Theresa's parents' bedroom, clothes littered the beds and chairs. A pile of Hermes scarves was spread out on the chaise longue.

"Mama, you're like a teenager, I can't remember seeing you this excited before, ever."

"I wish you and your father were going too. I'm just a little bit nervous. What if the group doesn't like the restaurant we picked out when we were there in December?" Elizabeth said.

"What's not to like about La Tour d'Argent? Dad and I thought it was great."

"Me too, but these people are Atlanta's elite."

"Why don't you take this suit?" Mary Margaret said, picking up a brown tweed jacket. "You could also wear the jacket with that beige skirt and silk blouse. Oh, and this scarf."

"That's a great idea," said Elizabeth, folding the blouse and putting it into the suitcase. "Would one of you girls get my train case from the closet, please?"

"Don't forget these," said Theresa, handing Elizabeth a folder containing clippings from House Beautiful and House and Garden magazines. She had plans to buy more furnishings for the house, which the neighbors had already dubbed 'Le Chateau'.

"I can't believe you'll be gone a whole month. When Daddy comes over to meet you, Mrs. Puccini said I could stay with them until school's out. Then Pucci and I can go stay at grandmother's until you get home," said Theresa.

"Okay, but be sure to help Anne. Take her some of those casseroles from the freezer. I'm sure you and Daddy won't eat them all. Pearly's been cooking for a week."

"Knock, knock," Dr. McDermott called. "Man, on the hall."

Elizabeth slipped on her yellow Chinese kimono and wrapped the sash around her waist.

"Come in, darling, the girls were helping me finish up my packing."

"I've brought you a dressing drink," said George, handing her a scotch and water. "I'll go down and read the afternoon paper until y'all are ready. Coming with us, Mary Margaret?" He looked around the room at the piles of clothes.

"No thanks, Dr. McDermott. Mama said I couldn't. This is a goodbye celebration and should just be family, although I do love the Boar's Head. We went there once for Mama's birthday."

"You're more than welcome to come. I'll be downstairs," he said. "Theresa, shouldn't you change?"

Theresa followed her father out.

"Darling, you are family," said Elizabeth, caressing Mary Margaret's cheek. "You've been a sister to Theresa and a daughter to us. You know I always wanted more children. Let me call your mother, maybe she'll reconsider."

"You always make me feel so special. I wish I were your daughter, but I know I'm not. I'll just finish hanging up these clothes you're not taking," she said, and began busying herself with the task.

She peeked back at Elizabeth pulling on her navy skirt. Her dark hair hung down in a smooth wave and framed her pale perfect face.

Mary Margaret walked over to Mrs. McDermott's dressing table and was looking at the jars of makeup.

"Sit down," Elizabeth said. "I'll put some rouge on your cheeks and powder on your nose. I'll call your mother. We'd really like for you to join us for dinner. I'm sure Theresa has something you can wear."

The house seemed large and empty with Elizabeth gone. Pearly had gone back to Macon to get the rest of her things. After her six-month trial, she had decided to move to Savannah and would be living with Delia in the cottage behind the Willingham's.

Theresa felt she had to stay home with her daddy and not go running off with Mary Margaret. He came home from his new job exhausted. She greeted him with his house shoes, a bourbon and water, and the evening press. She dutifully heated up a casserole every night for their dinner. Afterward, they watched The Price Is Right then went up to their rooms to study or read.

"Daddy, too bad you had to work and couldn't go with Mama. At least, you'll be meeting her, and you can fly back together."

"I'll be working Saturday and Sunday to get as much done as I can before I leave. There's a new procedure the French have perfected that I've arranged to observe, so the hospital is anxious for me to go," he said, taking a sip of his drink. "My work here is really important."

"Will you still be doing plastic surgery?"

"Yes, but I'm specializing in repairing cleft lips and palates. It's so rewarding, seeing those children smile."

"Daddy, did Mama tell you about the fight we had just before she left?"

"She mentioned it. I think she understood that you've been under pressure lately with her leaving, and that mean girl at school is always trying to bully you and Mary Margaret. She said you asked her something about queers?"

"Yeah, well she told me what I needed to know about that," she said, blushing. "When I got the invitation for the Mother-Daughter Tea at the Lafayette Club, I realized she wasn't going to be here. I had a little meltdown and said some things I regret. Anyway, I wrote this letter for you to take to her." She handed him a pink envelope with hearts drawn all over it.

"I know it will mean a lot," he said, tucking the letter under his arm. "Good night, Sweetie," he paused as if to say something else.

Theresa waited. When he didn't say anything else, she went over to him and put her arms around him. She sensed a certain sadness. "I'm gonna miss you. Seems like Mama's been gone forever."

"Yes, these three weeks have dragged without her. We'll be back in a week. You'll be busy finishing up school. I know you and Mary Margaret have lots of plans, and Nana and Granddaddy can't wait for you to visit."

The green Imperial pulled out of the driveway. Mary Margaret and Theresa waved from the sidewalk.

"Come on, Mac, let's go get your things. We have to pick out some clothes for our last day at school. We don't have to wear our uniforms." Theresa stood where she was, still waving.

"Come on, Mac, where are you going?" Her eyes followed Theresa who was walking toward the barely visible car. "Mac. Come on."

Theresa stopped and turned. Tears were running down her cheeks. "Pucci, I need to stay home. Daddy promised to call from a pay phone at the Atlanta airport, so I know he got there safely. I'll come over later. Is it okay if I bring a couple of my stuffed animals?"

"Okay, but don't be too long."

Theresa went back inside, packed, and then went into her parents' room. She lay down on the bed near the telephone, taking in her father's scent. She examined their wedding photograph on his bedside table. *I do look like Mother.* When she answered the phone, she saw the pink envelope and her heart sank.

"Daddy, you forgot the letter. What...? I can hardly hear you. You sound so far away. Is that your flight they're announcing? I love you, tell Mama I love her too and I'm really sorry for what I said. Please don't forget."

Oliver picked the girls up at St. Bernadette's on the last day of school.

"Phew, what's that smell?"

"Sorry, Granddaddy, we cleaned out our lockers."

"We'll stop at your houses so you can leave that stuff and get your weekend things. Nana and Delia are preparing a feast," he said, pulling out just as a car full of screaming girls almost hit him.

At the Willingham's, the girls dropped their things in Theresa's room and met Oliver at the dock to see his new boat.

"Want to go for a quick spin while the sun is setting?"

"Sure, I'll go get Nana."

"No, she doesn't like boats, besides she just had her hair set. But we'd better not be late for dinner."

The dining room table was set with fine china napkins.

"George left his car at the airport. They'll be tired when they fly in from New York, so they're going to spend the night in Atlanta and be home late Monday," said Oliver, pulling out the dining room chair.

Mary Margaret's mouth was full with her fourth roll. "I love your rolls. You need to teach my Essie how to make these," she said, looking up at Delia.

"That's Miss Elizabeth's recipe. They're called Wilkes County rolls. Don't ask me why. She taught Pearly and me," said Delia.

Mrs. Willingham frowned at Mary Margaret who was slurping her okra soup and motioned for Delia to move on. The next course was fried chicken and creamed corn. Mary Margaret looked at Mrs. Willingham, wondering if it was okay to pick up her drumstick.

"Nana allows us to pick up fried chicken with our fingers. Delia, you make the best," said Theresa.

"Told ya'll it taste better cooked on that wood-burning stove," Delia said, grinning so wide that you could see the sparkle from one of her gold teeth.

A foghorn blast caused the girls to run out on the porch to watch a barge navigate the turn in the river.

"Girls, you didn't ask to be excused," Mrs. Willingham shouted after them.

Mary Margaret was up early the next morning, gazing out of the window. "The river is so beautiful. Let's go take a walk."

"Just let me sleep a little longer," said Theresa. "You just about wore me out yesterday."

"It was fun though poking around Wormsloe. Hard to believe one old lady lives alone on that beautiful property. I loved finding that old tabby fort remains. Must be from the Revolutionary War."

"I love the mile-long oak-lined driveway. It's been used in several movies."

"It's already eight o'clock, and I have so many things I want us to do today," said Mary Margaret.

"I should have known Granddaddy would make us put up the boat."

"Yum, I smell bacon, I'll bet Delia's cooking breakfast."

"Yeah, she likes to make a special one when I'm here. Wait until you try her French toast." Theresa sat up in bed rubbing her eyes. "We shouldn't have stayed up so late with one of your bright ideas."

"Do you think your granddaddy will still be mad? He was really angry when he caught us trying to take the bateau out in the middle of the night."

"He's picking up Pearly at the bus station and bringing her here, then heading for the golf course. If he wins, he'll be in a better mood and not mention it. He gave us a pretty good cussing-out."

"It's a good thing he didn't come out sooner when we were skinny-dipping. That water was so cold and we lit up."

"That was the phosphorus in the water. I can't believe he heard us. They were sound asleep in their bedroom in the back of the house when we snuck out. That's kinda scary."

The day was warm, the sky was blue, and felt near. Mary Margaret sprinted down the bluff.

Theresa yelled, "Slow down, Pucci. I've never known you to be in such a hurry to go to church."

"Let's go look at the turtles and get a peach ice cream cone at Barbee's Pavilion instead."

"Pucci, we have to go to Mass; besides, you just stuffed yourself on French toast. How can you even think of food?"

"Always room for ice cream. We can't go to Communion anyway, since we ate breakfast. I'm so glad your grandmother isn't Catholic. Let's just skip church. We can go back and sunbathe on the dock. Maybe your granddaddy will let us take the bateau to go crabbing this afternoon."

"No, come on. We don't want to go to hell. It's bad enough we can't go to Communion. We'll get ice cream after church. You'll love the little chapel."

"Mac, who will ever know?"

"God will know."

"Oh geez, we're probably going to hell anyway," said Mary Margaret, pushing Theresa in the direction of the Pavilion. Theresa rolled her eyes, took the lace mantilla off her head, and stuffed it in her pocket.

"Let's walk out on the dock and look at the water."

"No, Mac, let's get ice cream first."

"Why aren't you girls in church?" Mr. Barbee said.

"We went to five-thirty Mass yesterday at the cathedral," lied Mary Margaret. "We'll have two double peach cones please."

"This is the best peach ice cream," said Theresa, licking the top scoop.

"Yep, Mac, but boy those turtles sure do stink."

"You know they make tortoise soup out of those putrid things. It's world-famous. I'm not about to eat any, but my daddy loves it."

"Is that Delia running toward us?" Mary Margaret said, sucking in a mouthful of ice cream.

"It is. She's motioning for us to come."

"We must be in trouble. I guess your grandfather is still mad about the bateau."

"Miss Theresa, Miss Mary Margaret, you girls get back to the house at once," Delia yelled. "I ran all the way to the church. Why ain't you there?" She turned and ran back toward the house as fast as her short legs and generous girth would allow, looking back to make sure the girls were following.

"Oh God, we must be in big trouble from the way Delia looked. Now they know we didn't go to church."

"I've got to quit listening to you." Theresa stopped and pointed. "Look, is that your father's car in our driveway? I wonder if something's wrong."

The foyer of the Willingham's house was dark. A mournful wail came from the dining room. Illuminated in front of the window were the silhouettes of Delia and Pearly with their arms around each other. A door closed in an upstairs bedroom. Mary Margaret looked up to see a figure in the galley above the hall.

"Daddy?" Mary Margaret said.

Dr. Puccini put his fingers to his lips and came downstairs. He hugged Theresa and motioned for Delia to take her up to her grandmother.

"Let's go, Mary Margaret. Pearly packed your bag," said Joe, picking up her suitcase guiding her to the front door.

"But Daddy. Where are we going?"

"Please, Mary Margaret. I'll explain outside," Dr. Puccini said.

They were almost to the car when Mary Margaret heard Theresa scream.

Mary Margaret stopped and grabbed her father's arm. "What's going on? Please tell me. Did something happen? Is it Mrs. Willingham?" Her voice became louder and louder.

He dropped the suitcase and took his daughter in his arms. "No, Honey, she's fine." He squatted down to her eye level and told her what happened.

Her hands went up to her mouth. She gasped and hugged him tighter. "I've got to go to Mac." She raced back into the house and up the foyer stairs.

Heavy curtains had been pulled shut against the harsh noon light in Sara's bedroom. Theresa, in her grandmother's embrace, sat up. Mrs. Willingham reached out to Mary Margaret, who came over and held them both. All three quietly sobbed. After a while, Delia whispered to the girls to leave, so that Mrs. Willingham could rest.

Once Theresa's bedroom door was closed, she let loose and wailed. "No, no, Pucci. It can't be true, it can't be."

"I'm so sorry. I'm so sorry, Mac. If only we could go back to yesterday when everything was so perfect."

Pearly answered the door when Anne arrived. They just looked at each other and sadly shook their heads. Without words, Pearly took her to Theresa's room where both girls were on the bed crying. Mary Margaret jumped up and ran to her mother, hugging her hard. They both went over to Theresa. Anne pulled her up to a sitting position and caressed her tear-stained cheek.

"I feel so alone, Mrs. Puccini."

"I know you do, honey," she said. "But you'll always have us."

Earlier that morning, after Mass at Sacred Heart, Dr. Puccini opened the car door for the children, who ran into the house tearing off their church clothes. The phone was ringing.

"Anne, get the phone," he yelled.

"Joe, I think it's Delia, but I couldn't understand a word she said. She sounds upset," said Anne, handing him the telephone.

"Delia, tell me, what's wrong?" He said, grasping Anne's arm. "I'll get there as soon as I can. Go find the girls."

"Joe, what's going on? You look like you've seen a ghost."

Joe struggled to make eye contact. He pulled her into his arms and told her the terrible news. "I'm going out to the Willinghams. Get the children settled and come as soon as you can," he said.

Anne was reluctant to leave his embrace but knew he had to go. "I'll be right there. Dear God, I don't know how the girls are going to deal with this."

Joe went to the Golf Club to find Oliver, hoping he had not heard about the crash. The golfers were standing around shaking their heads in disbelief listening to a news flash on the radio. Oliver saw Joe and collapsed against the bar. Joe pulled him to standing.

"Joe, Joe, please, don't tell me," Oliver cried, holding himself up by the bar. "Was it the plane Elizabeth and George were on?"

Joe's face was a dead giveaway. He grabbed Oliver before he collapsed again.

"Oh, my God. Sara, does she know?"

"Delia called me after the police came. I went to your house and gave Sara something to calm her. Mary Margaret is there with Theresa, and Anne should be there by now. I'm so sorry." Joe put his arm around his shoulder and led Oliver to the car.

Twelve

It was front-page news all over the world. The Orly plane crash was the worst air disaster in the history of aviation. Air France Flight 007 crashed off the end of the airport runway after an aborted take-off attempt. The city of Atlanta was stunned to lose so many of its prominent citizens.

In the two weeks, it took to return the remains and before they could have a funeral, the family barely had time to breathe. The phone rang off the hook. Pearly and Delia spent most of their time managing the food brought over by well-wishers, most of which ended up in the garbage. Mary Margaret stayed at the Willingham's to be there for Theresa. Sara refused to come out of her room even when her sister Fiona arrived. Oliver mostly stood around scratching his head and getting in everyone's way.

Fiona's presence seemed to calm Oliver and snap him out of his confusion. He went about finalizing the funeral arrangements. He and Fiona took long walks beside the river, taking turns trying to console Sara and coax her to eat.

Theresa was standing in the hall with her mouth and eyes wide open, clutching the telephone when Mary Margaret came in with yet another flower arrangement she found on the porch.

"Mac, what's wrong? More bad news?"

"No, Pucci, you won't believe this. I just hung up from talking to the president."

"The president? The president of what?"

"The President of the United States. He called to offer his condolences. I spoke with Jackie too. She really does have that whispery voice. They were so kind. The President of the United States."

Theresa clutched the receiver to her chest before gently hanging up the phone. She ran up the steps in a daze and flung herself across the bed. Her exhilaration turned to sorrow before she fell into an exhausted sleep.

She slept through the late afternoon into the night. At midnight, she screamed in her sleep. Mary Margaret gently shook her.

"Wake up, Mac, I'm here. It's okay."

"No, it's not okay, it'll never be okay. It was too horrible, the fire. It was so hot," she sobbed.

"It was just a dream. You're okay, I'm with you. Do you want to tell me about it?"

"Mama and Daddy were on the plane talking about how great the trip was. They had champagne. All around them, everyone was making toasts. They were so happy and excited, all talking at once. The plane throttled picking up speed. There was a lurch and champagne bubbles were floating all over the inside of the plane. Daddy grabbed Mama and hugged her. Fire engulfed the cabin. I heard a piercing scream. It was my mother."

Mary Margaret just sat there and held her hand.

On another night, Theresa shook Mary Margaret awake.

"Did you see her?" Theresa asked.

"Who, Mac?"

"My mother. I felt her cool soft hand on my forehead and smelled her perfume. She was here, Pucci."

Mary Margaret sat up looking around the room. A light danced across the floor and onto the wall. The movement caught her eye and she shivered. "I think the breeze is moving the trees, throwing shadows on the wall from the full moon."

"She was bathed in moonlight, but she was real. I know she was. I felt her." Mary Margaret turned on the lamp beside the bed.

"Pucci, you know that time I almost drowned at camp? I didn't want to wake up. It felt so peaceful, but I felt you pulling on me, and I saw a vision of my mother. She was beckoning me to come back. I should have told you that when Betsy died. It made me feel better knowing she was in that peaceful place. Now I hope Mama and Daddy are there too."

Theresa refused to go back to her home. Mary Margaret and Anne went there to get Theresa's clothes. Soon the closet at her grandmother's house was overflowing.

"What will I wear to the funeral, Pucci?"

"Here's the black dress you got in Paris. What about wearing this?" Mary Margaret said, rubbing the dress against the back of her hand. "I love this fabric."

"It's crepe de chine. Have you seen my black heels? I'll never get all my stuff organized," said Theresa, taking the dress from Mary Margaret. "Do you think she had a premonition, getting me this dress?"

"She always wanted everything to be perfect for you. Oh, Mac. It's just not fair," she said, taking Theresa into her arms.

Theresa slipped the dress over her head.

"Oh dear, it's too big. You've got to start eating again, Mac," Mary Margaret said, pinching the extra fabric at the waist. "Anne can take it in for you."

In the misting rain, a steady stream of cars, lights on, proceeded through town and down the narrow unpaved lanes in Bonaventure cemetery. The large crowd of mourners tramped through the mud to stand on the grassy graves of the dead around the tent. Umbrellas closed when the rain stopped. A man in a black suit passed out fans as the heat from the wet earth rose and enveloped the already damp, hot visitors.

A priest from Macon officiated with Father James. The two priests stood in front of the two coffins, the two holes, and two piles of black earth. A tent covered the few remaining relatives, the Willingham's best friends, and the Puccinis. Pearly, Essie, and Delia were in the front row, keening, rocking back and forth. Next to them, Theresa sat erect, stone-faced between her grandparents, clasping their hands. Fiona, on the other side of Oliver, held his hand.

They're cold, no they're hot, no they're not there, they are nothing, no more, burned, gone, oh Mama, oh Daddy. It's my fault. I didn't love you enough. I envied Pucci, her big family and now there's only me. Hail Mary, full of grace, the Lord...

The black limousine pulled away. "Stop," Theresa yelled from the back when she noticed the pink envelope on the seat. She jumped out of the stopped vehicle and flew to where the men were lowering the coffins. She tossed the envelope with the unread letter into her mother's grave.

Mary Margaret came up behind her and threw in a red rose.

The last time I saw you was at the restaurant the night before you left. You were so lovely and elegant. You made me a part of your family. You were such a beautiful lady, who loved me like a daughter. It hurts to think of you in that awful box on that cold ground. I didn't get a chance to ask you if I could call you Mama Mac.

The two watched as if in a trance as clods of red earth began to rain down over the coffins.

At the house, Essie set the table with an impressive assortment of funeral food from finger sandwiches to pecan tassies. Theresa came down the steps after redoing her hair and makeup. The guests in the hall quieted as she descended.

"Looks just like Elizabeth," whispered one guest. "Such poise, it's so sad. The poor child, an orphan."

"At least, she has Oliver and Sara," said another, stuffing a deviled egg into her mouth.

"Can you believe this spread? These southerners sure know how to cook. Try one of these rolls with tenderloin," said her husband, moving on to the platter of fried chicken.

"Isn't that Sara's sister? She certainly is an odd duck. Imagine showing up at a funeral in that mini skirt."

"What about those platform shoes? I hope she doesn't fall off them like a friend of mine's daughter did."

"It certainly isn't an age-appropriate outfit. I guess she and Sara are okay after all that happened between them."

"My God, Mac, you look like a model," Mary Margaret whispered. "That dress really looks great with your dark hair and blue eyes. I could never wear black with this pale skin and reddish hair."

"Oh, Pucci, I hope you never have to wear black."

"Who is that good-looking guy over by the sideboard?" Mary Margaret ran her fingers through her hair and shrugged slightly.

Theresa turned. "Oh, it's Monty Hamilton; that must be his sister. Remember I told you about meeting him on the train last summer? That seems like a million years ago."

Theresa gave them a little wave. Monty saw her and guided his sister through the guests to where she and Mary Margaret were standing.

"Hi, I'm Montgomery Hamilton and this is my sister Rose. My parents asked me to stop by and pay their respects to the family." He scanned Theresa, wondering who this beautiful girl was. She looked familiar.

Theresa looked into his brown eyes and rugged face. "Remember me? I'm Theresa, we met on the train a year ago. This is my friend Mary Margaret Puccini."

"Oh, of course, you look so grown-up. I didn't recognize you. I'm so sorry about your parents. I don't even know what to say."

Charlie came over and put his arm around Theresa. "Hi, I'm Charlie Puccini." There were introductions all around. Her grandmother pulled Theresa away.

"You've got to meet my good friends from Connecticut," she said, indicating the lady in the tan wool suit who was cramming another egg in her mouth.

Theresa's head was spinning by the time all the guests left. She and Mary Margaret retreated to her room and changed into casual clothes.

"Let's go for a walk on the bluff. I need to clear my head. Geez, all those people."

"Mac, I noticed that necklace. Is it new?"

"It was Mama's. I know it's silly, but it helps me keep it together," she said, fingering the gold cross.

"It's not at all silly. You're so brave. You know we're going to Tybee in July. Anne wants you to come and stay with us. What do you say? Maybe it will help take your mind off things."

"I would love to, but I'll have to ask my parents. No, I mean my grandparents, I guess they're in charge now," she said, touching the cross.

Thirteen

Theresa looked up from her book at the endless blue sky. She framed the beach scape in the rectangle she formed with her thumbs and index fingers, imagining putting it down on canvas. A mix of ultramarine blue, maybe a tiny dab of violet, not much white, which might flatten the clarity of the color. Behind her, Jeanne was being dressed down by Mary Margaret for kicking sand onto her blanket. Theresa felt herself relax and drift off as warmth from the sand, the brilliance of the day, and the carefree squeals, heard over the roar of the ocean, released some of the tension Theresa still held since the accident.

"Hey, girls," said Catherine, carefully laying out her beach towel. Dark glasses hid her eyes, swollen from crying. She sat down and rubbed a mixture of baby oil and iodine on her arms and legs. "Will somebody rub some on my back?" She held up a bottle.

"I swear, I don't know about this baby oil stuff," said Mary Margaret, spreading some on Catherine's back. "You and Mac get golden brown, and I just get red like a lobster, then end up with a bunch of freckles."

"Look at that lady over there walking down the beach," said Jeanne, pointing with her thumb.

"I can't believe she has on a two-piece bathing suit with that big belly," said Theresa.

The girls continued to comment on everyone who walked by.

"Catherine, you're awfully quiet. Is something wrong? You don't seem like your usual self," said Mary Margaret.

"It's my parents, they're always yelling at each other. Mama accuses Daddy of drinking and playing cards all the time. I have to be home early today because she's going out, too," said Catherine.

"Oh, not again. I thought they worked things out from the last time," said Mary Margaret.

"Sometimes I hate my parents. No, not sometimes, all of the time."

"At least, you have parents," Theresa said, fingering the cross.

"Oh my God, I'm sorry, I'm so sorry I said that. You're right." Crimson splotches crept over Catherine's face. "How could I be so insensitive?" She walked over to Theresa and put her arms around her.

"I'm sorry, Catherine. I know you didn't mean to hurt me. I shouldn't have said that."

"Sometimes I just don't think before I speak. Please forgive me."

"Hey, here comes Pauline. I wonder what she's grinning about," said Mary Margaret, as she pulled Cokes from the scotch plaid cooler and passed them around.

"Yoo-hoo everybody. Guess what? My mother's going to town for a meeting tonight. She said I could invite y'all over to spend the night. We can make pizzas and go out on the beach," said Pauline.

"Well, I can't go," said Catherine, clenching her fists. "I've got to babysit."

"Oh no, can't you get out of it?"

"I wish," said Catherine, getting up and walking down to the ocean.

They told Pauline what was going on.

"We'll be there, okay, Mac?" Mary Margaret said, lifting her bottle in the air as if to toast. "Hey, I have a brilliant idea."

"Oh no. What?" Theresa said. She rolled her eyes and placed her hand over her heart. "Let's dress up and go down to the Front."

"The Front? The place where all those bars are? Your mother tells us to stay away from there. She always says, 'They're not our kind of people'."

"But Mac, aren't you curious about what 'those kind of people' are like?"

"I'm game," said Pauline.

Pauline's house was contemporary with floor-to-ceiling glass windows in the living room, overlooking the beach. The large kitchen was separated from the dining area with a granite-covered island that had stools for casual meals. Her mother, owner of a successful real estate firm, designed and built the house. It was unlike most Tybee cottages that only had several bedrooms and one or two bathrooms, shared by all with a large wraparound porch where everyone gathered, hoping to catch a cool breeze from the ocean. This house with central air-conditioning was special. In the huge master suite, complete with a dressing room and walk-in closet, the girls were examining the things on Mrs. Brown's dressing table.

"Your mother's beautiful," said Theresa, picking up a photo of Pauline's parents. "Where's your father?"

"He's traveling for work."

"Look at all these fun cosmetics. Your mother really takes good care of herself. Won't she be mad if we use her stuff?" Mary Margaret asked.

"No, she lets my sister and me try on her makeup all the time."

"What's this stuff in the can?" Mary Margaret said. She picked it up, took off the top, and sprayed some in her hand. "Geez, it's so sticky."

"Oh, that's her lacquer hair spray." Pauline took the can and sprayed some on her hair. She let it dry for a minute then shook her head. "See, your hair never moves. Now you know why Mama's beehive always stays in place."

"Is that one of those vibrating exerciser belts?" Theresa asked. She pointed to a machine in the corner of the bedroom. "I've seen them in magazines. How does it work? I want to try it."

"Me too," Mary Margaret chimed in.

Theresa went first. Pauline placed her on the machine platform. "Here, take this big belt and put it across your stomach. Now lean forward." She turned on the machine and it started vibrating.

"Oh my God. This is a gas," Theresa said.

After several minutes, Pauline turned the machine off. "Okay y'all, let's get ready for the Front before my mama gets home. We can do this later."

Theresa stepped off the machine and walked over to the full-length mirror. She turned to the side and pressed her two hands to her stomach. "So, what do you think? It looks flatter, doesn't it?"

Mary Margaret and Pauline looked at each other and laughed.

The girls walked from Pauline's to Sixteenth Street. The sidewalks were crowded with people of all ages. Some were licking ice cream cones or eating corn dogs. Outside one shop, onlookers watched a machine pulling saltwater taffy.

"What if somebody sees us?" Theresa said.

"You think they'll recognize us, with all this makeup and these outfits? You look good in that blond wig. How do you think I look as a brunette? That pancake makeup covered my freckles," said Mary Margaret.

"Your boobs look real. That tissue did the trick. I just hope my mother doesn't find out you wore one of her bras," said Pauline.

Inside the Novelty Bar, the air was thick with smoke and smelled of spilled whiskey and sour beer. When their eyes adjusted to the dim light, they found a table in a corner where they could watch the activity at the bar.

"Is that girl at the bar the one we saw in that neon orange bikini?" Theresa said.

"I think so," said Pauline, "look, I think she's trying to pick up that man."

"I can't make out what he's saying; it's so noisy in here."

"Did anyone bring cigarettes?" Theresa asked.

"Here," said Pauline, handing them each a Winston. After rummaging through her purse, she shook her head, "Sorry, I don't have any matches."

"Allow me," said a man at the next table. A clump of greasy hair hung over his left eye as he leaned over with his lighter. His tattooed right arm reached to light Theresa's cigarette, while his left hand touched her thigh just under her skirt. She jumped up.

"Let's get out of here," she said. "That guy's a creep."

Down the street, at Clifton's Bar, they opened the door and were greeted by a tall man in a blue leisure suit. His muscles bulged against the polyester fabric. When he asked for their IDs, they turned around and walked as fast as they could toward the corner.

"Phew, that was close. Is my wig straight?"

"No, Pucci, yours is cockeyed."

Mary Margaret straightened her hair and pulled down on her short skirt. Her eyes widened, "Isn't that Father Dreamboat in that two-toned Impala?"

"Yes," said Pauline. "I've seen him get in that car at church."

"Who's Father Dreamboat?" Theresa asked.

"He's Father Robert. We used to call him that 'cause he's so handsome. What's he doing down at the beach driving around, not wearing his collar? He's turning onto Butler, let's follow him."

The traffic on Butler Avenue was moving at a snail's pace. Walking along the sidewalk, the girls kept his car in sight. They followed until he backed into a parking place near the Sands Motel. The girls ducked behind some bushes and watched him get out of his car. His gate was cautious as he scoped the area.

"What in the world is he doing?" Pauline whispered, "It looks like he's making sure nobody sees him."

He knocked on a door on the first floor of the motel. The door opened swiftly. A woman stepped slightly out of the doorway, hugged him, and the two kissed. The three girls were struggling to see who it was.

"Who was that? I couldn't see," Theresa asked.

"Jesus Christ, I think it's Catherine's mother," said Pauline.

"I know it is, I recognize that sundress." Mary Margaret looked at the two girls in disbelief.

"Oh, Pucci, are you sure? This is awful. It makes me sick. I know Catherine has been upset about things at home," Theresa said. "She would die if she knew about this."

They headed straight back to Pauline's, changed and washed off all the makeup, and walked to the beach. The moon came up as the three sat huddled on a blanket, their innocence stripped away.

"Y'all, we can't say a word, no matter what. Anne would never believe Father Robert would do this. She thinks that priest hung the moon." She pointed to the sky. "She volunteers for a program that he started for orphans after school."

"I want to throw up. I've been to confession with that man. He's the one who should be confessing," said Pauline.

"You know, Catherine confided in me that her mother had been going to Father Robert for marriage counseling," said Theresa, gathering a lump of wet sand and throwing it. "Who can you trust?"

The next day, Mary Margaret squinted as she crossed the dune, trying to see who was toweling off under their umbrella. He was handsome with a shock of dark hair hanging wet over his face. His muscles were well developed, but his waist was slim.

"Ben. I didn't know you were coming down today," said Mary Margaret. "Where's Charlie?"

"He and Theresa walked down to the pier."

"Here, sit down," he said, patting the end of a beach towel.

Their eyes met for a moment. Ben couldn't believe that this was Charlie's little sister. She looked so grown-up. He checked out her figure. It wasn't the boyish shape he remembered. She looked at him wondering if this was really Charlie's nerdy friend, Ben.

He smiled a warm broad smile that made Mary Margaret feel fluttery inside.

They started talking nervously at first, then became so engrossed in their conversation that they didn't even notice Charlie and Theresa approach.

"Hey, Buddy, come on, let's go for a swim," said Charlie. Ben pulled Mary Margaret up off the towel. "Come with us."

They spent the afternoon crabbing, then later, Essie boiled their catch. They feasted on boiled crabs, potato salad, coleslaw, and watermelon. Mrs. Puccini was taking Essie back into town to visit her mother, while she and Dr. Puccini dined with friends at Johnny Harris'.

"Charlie, you're in charge. Get the boys in and don't let anyone go back out on the beach. Make sure the little ones get to bed by eight. We'll be late coming back."

"I'll make sure he does," said Theresa, scooping up Nan in her arms.

Essie came in carrying bags of leftovers to take to her mother. "Now you children stay out of my kitchen. I better not come back here tomorrow and find a mess in there."

Mary Margaret and Ben were playing a game of Russian Bank on the porch. They looked up and waved to Anne and Essie as they started down the steps.

The Puccini children, all bronzed from the sun, were beginning to get bored with being at the beach. Endless games of Crazy Eights, Spit in the Ocean, and Old Maids were failing to amuse them. Jeanne yelled back to the others that their mother's car was out of the driveway. After much cajoling, the little girls talked Charlie into taking them to ride the Ferris wheel.

"Okay, but don't tell Mama and Daddy. They don't like the Front. We would all get in trouble."

Theresa got in the car with Charlie and the children. Ben and Mary Margaret volunteered to walk via the beach since the car was full.

Ben helped Mary Margaret across the dune, then looked up. "The sky is unbelievable tonight, it's so clear. That one is Cassiopeia." He pointed to a constellation.

"I only recognize the big dipper," she said, sitting down on the edge of the dune. "Come sit. Tell me more."

"That one is Orion, the hunter, see his belt?"

But Mary Margaret was staring at Ben. His brown eyes looked black and deep. She wanted to touch his sun-streaked brown curls. He reached over and pulled her to him and kissed her awkwardly on the side of her mouth before finding the right spot.

"I've never been kissed before," she whispered.

"Really? I can't imagine why. Let's make up for lost time."

With each kiss, they moved closer and closer until they both gasped for air.

"We can't do this," she said, catching her breath. "Our parents would never approve, and Charlie…"

Ben was breathing hard. "Yeah, I guess you're right," he said, but gently grabbed her behind the neck and pulled her face back to his. "The hell with Charlie."

For the moment, she abandoned any concerns and let herself be thrilled by the danger of it.

Mary Margaret's heart beat so hard she could barely breathe. Now she understood what Theresa meant when she talked about how Charlie's kisses paralyzed her. When his hands touched her breast, it made her tingle. She yearned for more.

Someone walked down the beach and shone a light in their direction. Ben stood up brushing the sand from his shorts. He pulled Mary Margaret up.

"I guess we should go meet the others. They'll be wondering where we are," she said. He squeezed her hand, and they ran down the beach toward the ocean. They kicked off their shoes and splashed in the surf.

Charlie and Theresa were sneaking kisses in the Ferris wheel car behind the children. When they got off, they spotted Ben and Mary Margaret. They all rode the merry-go-round and ate ice cream cones before returning to the house. The little children went to bed, and the others found spots in front of the TV. Someone popped corn, so everything looked normal when the parents came in. That night as Mary Margaret was falling asleep, she shivered at the thought of Ben's touch.

Oliver came down to Tybee to pick up Theresa. Anne invited him in for coffee while Mary Margaret and Theresa went up to pack her things.

"Pucci, thank you for having me. I actually felt normal some of the time, then I'd feel guilty about it. I dread going back and feeling such waves of sadness seeing my grandparents so bereaved. I have to try and be upbeat for them all the time. It takes everything in me not to be the one shutting myself in my room and staying in bed all day."

"I could see you struggling, Mac, but you were such a good sport. Please don't shut yourself away. Come to me when you feel sad. I'll always listen."

The two sat on the bed and cried until all their tears were gone and Oliver stuck his head in the door. "We need to go now, sweet Theresa. Your grandmother is waiting."

After Theresa returned to her grandparents, she stayed close to home feeling guilty about her respite at the beach. Oliver had started taking comfort in the bottle, adding to Sara's stress. Theresa spent her days sorting through boxes. Pearly brought a few at a time over from the house. Among the boxes was a small painted cedar chest filled with baby clothes.

"Nana, who was GWM?" Theresa asked, holding up a monogrammed sailor suit. "Look at all these precious clothes."

Sara picked up a small blue hand-knitted sweater. She pressed it to her face inhaling the scent. Carefully choosing her words, "You had a brother, George Winston McDermott. We called him Winnie. He died when he was two. Your mother planned to tell you about him when you were older and would understand."

A wave of sadness came over Theresa. The small garment suddenly felt heavy.

"Why didn't she tell me? I thought we were so close." Theresa felt betrayed, not only by her parents and her grandparents but by her older brother's death. He could have been protective like Charlie is to Mary Margaret. She wouldn't be alone now. She wanted to pull the details out of her grandmother's head, not bothering with the words sugarcoating the truth.

"I know you are hurt, darling. Part of your mother never got over Winnie's death."

"How did he die?"

"He had a disease, Cystic Fibrosis. He was the only one who survived."

"What do you mean only one?"

"Two other babies weren't full term. When you were born, it was a miracle you didn't have the disease. Your parents didn't want the sad shadow of the others hanging over you, that's why they never said anything. They feared you may have the gene."

Looking at Theresa's horrified expression, Sara knew she had said it all wrong. She and Elizabeth had gone over how to tell Theresa at least a million times, and here she had just blurted it out.

"I might be carrying a disease that I could pass on to my children?" She said in a panicked tone. "Should I not have babies?"

"Honey, I can't answer that."

Theresa sat back on her heels and turned to stone. Her body refused to soften to her grandmother's arms around her.

A feeling in Mary Margaret's stomach told her that something was wrong. Theresa's voice, usually so clear and melodious, resonated flat and slightly slurred over the phone. Never had she sounded so down. Mary Margaret threw a few things into her overnight bag, jotted off a note to Anne, and raced to the bus stop. Out of breath when she reached the Willingham's, she plopped into a chair on the porch and waited for someone to answer the door. After a few minutes, she knocked again, then walked around back to see if there were any cars.

From a storage shed, she heard someone whimpering.

"Mac? What are you doing out here?"

"You came," said Theresa. She knelt in a small space among stacks of boxes.

"I knew something was wrong. What's the matter? Whose clothes are these?" She picked up a small blue linen Eton suit.

"They were my brother's," said Theresa, holding a pair of denim overalls.

"Your brother's?"

Mary Margaret listened while Theresa relayed what her grandmother had told her earlier. "Can you believe my mother never told me? He died when he was two. He would be a year older than Charlie. She didn't even love me enough to tell me."

"Of course, she did, Mac, she loved you too much to tell you. She just didn't want you to have to feel her hurt. It's really hot out here. Let's get a drink and go sit on the porch." She pulled Theresa up and carefully replaced the clothes in the cedar chest.

The sun was beginning to set and cast a fiery display over the river, the effect dramatized by the reflection in the water.

"Pucci, I just can't imagine not having children. I really wanted a big family like yours."

"Mac, things are always changing in medicine. Besides, you don't really know if you have the gene."

Later upstairs, Theresa came out of the bathroom waving her toothbrush. "I forgot to tell you, Sister Fatima and Father Robert came to see me."

"Tell me, but first go rinse that toothpaste off your mouth," said Mary Margaret, looking up from her *Seventeen* magazine. They settled on the floor with their backs against the bed.

"I loved seeing her. I ran up and gave her a hug, Father Robert tried to hug me. It gave me the creeps, thinking about Catherine's mother. I really do need to talk to someone." Theresa looked over at Mary Margaret. She took a wad of string out of her pocket and started winding it through her fingers to play Cats Cradle. After looping it several times to create the number eight, she handed it to Mary Margaret for her to continue the game.

"I've had such misgivings about God since the accident. Now thinking about that baby boy, God seems even more unfair. To think how my parents suffered over the loss. Some days, I don't even believe there is a God. But I don't want to talk to that priest. He told me how much he had enjoyed meeting my mother and how beautiful she was. I wanted to run from the room. I excused myself and got Delia to bring in some drinks."

"It still makes my skin crawl when I think about seeing that man kiss Catherine's mother at the beach."

Theresa got up and went to the window, "I look at the sunset over the river and want to believe in something greater than us. But nature doesn't care how I feel. It just goes on, doing its thing as if nothing ever happened."

"Maybe you could talk to Sister Fatima, privately at school." Mary Margaret continued to loop the string through her fingers.

"I dread going back to school. Everyone will stare and feel sorry for me. I won't know how to handle it. Almost everyone in the class came to the funeral."

"Bunny didn't. You probably didn't want her there anyway. I'm not looking forward to being in class with her. I wonder who she'll pick on this year?"

"Last year, that new girl quit after she found notes on her locker. One of them read 'she lost all her charm when she lifted her arm. Use deodorant'."

"That was outright mean, but she did sorta smell bad."

Just before school started, Theresa and Mary Margaret took Marnie to lunch at the Pirate's House.

"Marnie, I saw you at my parents' funeral, I just wanted to thank you for coming," Theresa said.

"I felt so bad about your parents. Your mother was so sweet the night of…"

"That's what we wanted to talk to you about," Mary Margaret said. She looked at Theresa who nodded slightly. "Theresa and I felt awful about participating in that horrible night. We didn't know it would go so far."

"I knew it was mostly Bunny," said Marnie. She bit her bottom lip and looked in the direction of the door.

"Yes, but we didn't stop her. We've wanted to apologize ever since. We just couldn't get up the nerve because we didn't want to be on Bunny's hit list. Mary Margaret and I promised my mother that we would tell you how sorry we were so…"

"How could we let such a mean girl influence us so much? We never meant to hurt you," Mary Margaret interrupted.

"Will you be our friend?" Theresa asked, passing Marnie a box with a small gold charm engraved with all three names.

She opened the box, covered her heart with her hand, and smiled. Theresa put her hand flat on the table, Mary Margaret covered it, and Marnie followed suit. They vowed never to let Bunny intimidate them again.

"Y'all really are the Dynamo Duo."

"What?" Theresa and Mary Margaret looked at each other with question-mark eyes.

"Didn't you know, that's what they call ya'll at school?"

Fourteen

Bunny was holding court in the school hall on the first day of class. She glanced up at Theresa and Mary Margaret before returning to her audience. The two slipped by and went to find their lockers.

"Look, a whole new group of victims," said Mary Margaret. "Let's take these two next to each other." She put in some books and slammed the metal door.

Theresa stood frozen, staring into her locker.

"Come on, Mac, we're already late for class. You have to face them sometime. Just remember that they mean well."

They slipped into the back of the classroom, taking the last two desks.

The entire class turned and looked at them. A murmur spread through the room. Theresa felt her face burning. Mary Margaret's hand on her shoulder kept her from running out of the room.

Sister Fatima stopped writing on the board and faced the students' "Girls, quiet, please."

The first few days of classes were tough for Theresa. Her classmates weren't sure what to say; some were overly friendly, some just moved away, and others showered her with sympathetic words. By the end of the first day, Theresa thought she would scream if one more well-meaning person came up to her and offered condolences.

Are they really sorry? Do they know how I feel? How do they know that my parents are with God, in a better place? They all say the same stupid things.

The first couple of weeks were fraught with feelings like this from Theresa, but in time, things at school felt normal again.

After school, Pauline, Catherine, Mary Margaret, Theresa, and Marnie would get together, finish their homework, then go to Central or hang out, usually at Mary Margaret's house. They experimented with new makeup, listened to records, and practiced the Mashed Potato and the Watusi.

One morning, in the study hall, Mary Margaret, Theresa, Catherine, and Pauline were whispering in the back. "Haven't you ever wondered what the nuns wear under their habits?" Mary Margaret asked.

"They're women, they probably wear what all our mothers wear," said Pauline, and then looked regretfully at Theresa.

"My mother wears red or black bikini panties," said Catherine. The other girls looked at each other and raised their eyebrows.

"I've got a great idea. Why don't we find out?" Mary Margaret said, her mouth curled up. Theresa recognized that mischievous smile. "We could sneak into the convent and plunder though one of the nun's drawers."

"You've lost it this time, Pucci."

"Come on, Mac, you need a little pick-me-up. Mary Margaret jumped up from her chair and started flailing her arms, describing her plan."

"I double-dog-dare you," said a voice behind them. Bunny stepped out of the cloak room.

Mary Margaret looked around. "You don't believe we'll do it. Do you?"

Bunny came forward and leaned in toward her. She narrowed her eyes. "You wouldn't have the nerve."

"Just you wait," Mary Margaret said, feeling like she wanted to punch Bunny in her face.

"You'll have to have proof," said Bunny.

The next Tuesday, after Chorale practice, Mary Margaret gathered her partners in crime. They had invited Marnie to join them. The girls protested the idea at first but finally agreed to go along with her scheme. They hid in the shadows of the hall as the ten nuns filed into the chapel.

Mary Margaret handed Theresa a Polaroid camera, "Here, Mac, you take the pictures. Pauline, you stay behind and watch the chapel. Whistle if any one of the nuns leaves early."

"This makes my stomach hurt," said Catherine.

"Your stomach always hurts. Why don't you just guard the kitchen door in case the cook comes out? Come on, Mac, let's take the back stairs," she said, pointing down the hall. "Marnie, you watch the front ones."

The narrow stairway was dark, and the boards creaked with every step. The plastered walls with pealing beige paint felt cold to the touch. When they got to the top and rounded the corner, they could smell that scent that all nuns. *Was it patchouli?* Hues from the stained-glass windows danced along the walls of the long hall of closed doors creating colorful mosaics. The eerie silence gave Theresa chill-bumps.

"Pucci, let's get out of here. This gives me the creeps. Nothing's going to be unlocked," said Theresa, after they tried several doors.

"No, let's try one more," Mary Margaret said, pointing down the hall. "Voila, this one isn't locked."

The room was spare inside. A white chenille spread covered the narrow bed.

Mary Margaret pointed to the crucifix hanging above the iron headboard. "God, I'll bet there's one of those over every Catholic's bed," she said, picking up a photograph from the bureau. "Look, it's Sister Fatima with her family. Jesus Christ, she's so young and beautiful. How could they let their daughter become a nun? What a waste."

The top drawer was slightly open. Mary Margaret rummaged through it. She found a pair of white cotton drawers and held them up.

"I can't believe Fatima wears old lady underwear. They look like my daddy's boxer shorts."

"I'll take the picture," said Theresa, backing up into a small table. A book crashed to the floor.

"Geez, Mac. You f...ing scared me."

Theresa clutched the camera to her chest. "God, I almost had a heart attack."

Mary Margaret reached to pick up the table. "Look, something fell out."

It was a photograph of a young couple. A woman with red wavy hair in a yellow print dress stood next to a young man in an ill-fitting suit.

"It's Fatima. It says May 1946. That's the year before I was born. I thought she was older. Here, I'm going to hold up the undies with the picture of her with her family. Now take the photo."

The Polaroid clicked and ejected the picture.

"Pucci, let's go."

"Geez, the picture's blurred and you cut me off."

"I know, my hands were shaking."

"Go ahead, take another. Wait, be sure to get me in it this time. Just to prove to that dumb-ass Bunny we were here."

Somewhere a bell was ringing. She snapped another picture before they raced down the steps into the back hallway where Marnie was on watch.

"Come on, let's go get the others."

"Did y'all get a picture? Let me see it." Marnie reached over, took the picture from Mary Margaret, and shook her head. "Wow, y'all got balls. We better go, I thought I heard someone."

"Hold up there, you three." A nun standing in the doorway called out to the girls who had started to run. Mary Margaret stopped on a dime. Theresa and Marnie slammed into her.

"Sister Martina, hey. It's me, Mary Margaret Puccini. You know, from camp. My father, Dr. Puccini, takes care of y'all." She cocked her head and smiled. "Oh, and this is Theresa McDermott. Remember, your best art student." Mary Margaret pulled her around in front. Theresa was livid and kicked her in the shin.

Sister tilted her head and squinted, trying to recognize her. "Ah, yes, the trouble maker. And just where have you been and what are you up to?"

"We were looking for the chapel. Someone said it was back here," Marnie replied. The two looked at her and cracked a smile.

"Well, it's not. It's on the parlor floor. I'll escort you, follow me. You will be just in time to say the ten sets of the Rosary with the other sisters."

They followed the nun to the chapel.

"This is worse than being punished by Sister Hope," whispered Mary Margaret to Theresa, who covered her mouth, suppressing a giggle. Inside the dimly lit chapel, they filed into a pew noticing that Pauline and Catherine were just across the aisle. They looked back at Mary Margaret. Catherine squinted at her while Pauline mouthed, "You owe us."

The next week, Study Hall was abuzz with talk of Saint Thomas Military School's Commissioning dance. All the girls at St. Bernadette's hoped for an invitation. Charlie had already invited Theresa. Mary Margaret planned to double-date hoping Ben would invite her. She had refused an invitation from Ted Grant, certain that Ben would call.

"Who's this Ted Grant that asked you to the dance?" Theresa asked.

"Mac, you're not going to believe this. Ted and his family just moved in three doors down from us. I ran into him at Central and mentioned that he looked familiar. He stared at me with a wicked smile then lifted his eyebrows and said, 'I'll show you mine if you show me yours'. Remember that time at camp when some of the boys took off their pants, thinking I would take off mine, and I grabbed theirs and ran? Well, it was him. I was so embarrassed, and now he's asked me to the dance."

"Oh no, Pucci," Theresa covered her mouth with her hand suppressing a little squeal. "Ted was really cute. Maybe you should go with him since you haven't heard from Ben."

"I don't want to. Don't you dare say a word that could get back to Anne. She says you have to go with the first person who asks you or it's rude. I want to go with Ben and I know he's gonna ask me. He's probably just getting up the nerve."

All summer Mary Margaret had been head-over-heels in love with Ben. They snuck out to the garage apartment and made out a few times when he allegedly came to visit Charlie. They went to the drive-in with Charlie and Theresa. When they started making out in the front seat, Ben and Mary Margaret kissed too. Later, when Charlie walked Theresa to the door, they started laughing.

"Those two really think they're fooling us," Charlie said, opening the door for Theresa.

"Yeah, ever since the beach," said Theresa. "I think they're afraid your parents wouldn't approve because of their rule about the girls not dating before they're sixteen."

"Gosh, I think it's great to see Ben act normal. I was really concerned about that boy. I was afraid he was a queer. He better not cross the line with my sister." He leaned over and gave Theresa a kiss.

It had been a week, and Mary Margaret still hadn't heard from Ben. Every time her phone rang, her heart skipped a beat. She just knew he was going to invite her.

One day at school, two of the older girls were in the locker room chatting about the Commissioning Dance. Theresa and Mary Margaret looked up when they overheard one of them talking about who was taking whom. "Patty McAfee is going with Ben O'Brien. They've been dating."

The words felt like a dagger through Mary Margaret's heart. She felt sick to her stomach and completely betrayed. One look at Theresa and tears welled up in her eyes. She ran out, afraid she would make a scene. Theresa found her in the stairwell, crying.

"Pucci, I'm so sorry. I didn't know for sure he was going to ask her. Charlie said something."

"You knew? You knew, and you didn't tell me?" Mary Margaret cried even louder. "I don't understand. Why is he taking her and not me? I love Ben," she said, brushing off her tears and wiping her nose with the back of her hand. "We've been close and he said things that made me think he really cared."

"Why didn't you tell me how you felt, Pucci? I knew you liked him and sometimes you two kissed, but I had no idea it was that serious."

"Obviously, it wasn't for him. He made me feel special. I didn't say anything to you or anybody, because I wanted to keep it a secret. I was afraid you might let it slip to Charlie and he might tell my parents. Anne would be furious since I'm not sixteen yet."

"Pucci, I didn't know any of that. If I did, I would have told you. Please don't be mad at me. Why don't you call Ben and find out? Get him to explain."

It took Mary Margaret days to get the nerve to call. She almost hung up when Mrs. O'Brien answered. Her voice quivered when she asked for Ben.

"I'm calling for my brother," she lied.

When Ben came to the phone, nothing came out of her mouth.

"Mary Margaret? Mama said you were calling me for Charlie. What do you want?"

She blurted out, "Are you really taking Patty McAfee to the dance?"

"Yes, why?"

"What about me? What about this summer? I thought we would be going together. You said you really cared for me." Her voice cracked.

"Mary Margaret, I do care for you, and your whole family. What happened this summer was just a thing. You said you couldn't date until you were sixteen. Your parents would have a fit. I couldn't ask you to the dance. I'm sorry, but I thought you knew that."

Mary Margaret hung up the phone. She went up to her room and grabbed Maddie, the doll Theresa brought her from Paris, then went into the bathroom, turned on the shower, sat on the toilet, and sobbed.

Joe walked into the room where a piece of fabric was flying through Anne's sewing machine.

"Stop that racket; I want to talk to you."

"But Joe, I have to finish this dress for the Medical Auxiliary party this weekend."

"I need to talk to you."

"Okay, what?" She turned to face him, pins sticking out of the sides of her mouth.

"Take those things out of your mouth before you swallow them and choke to death. What's this about you telling Mary Margaret she can't have a Sweet Sixteen birthday party?"

"The other girls didn't have any such nonsense. Why should she be special?"

"Well, you know she is."

"We shouldn't treat her that way."

"We're in a better financial position to do it now. Also, I was so proud of the maturity she showed and the support she gave to Theresa when her parents died. And she didn't get to go to the Commissioning Dance. I think we should do it."

"I guess she's been talking to you behind my back."

"No, but I did find this on my desk." He pulled a sheet cut from a magazine of a party with Mary Margaret's face pasted on the guest of honor and Sweet Sixteen in a heart above her head.

"I swear, I can't fight city hall." Anne turned back to her sewing.

"Mama, look at this." Mary Margaret dashed into the kitchen and stood at the breakfast table where her mother was drinking a cup of coffee, a smoking a cigarette while making her weekly grocery list.

Anne put down her ball point pen and glanced up. Mary Margaret pushed a magazine page in front of her mother, showing a model in a multi-colored sheath mini dress with tall white boots. She struck the pose of the model, putting her hands on her hips and her right foot slightly in front. "It would be perfect for my party. You could probably make the dress."

"Absolutely not. There are plenty of party dresses in the older girls' closet," said Anne, returning her gaze toward her list. "Go ask Essie if we need flour."

Mary Margaret stood there for another minute opening her mouth to speak but nothing came out.

"Well, go on. And ask Essie." Anne flicked the back of her hand in her daughter's direction. "You better quit while you're ahead. At least, you're having this party."

Mary Margaret knew better than to press her luck. She picked a blue raw-silk dress which she accessorized with a wide black belt and black pumps. Her excitement built as they designed and sent out over a hundred invitations. They chose pigs in a blanket, finger sandwiches, chips with onion-soup dip, and shrimp paste on crackers for the menu. Her father arranged for a popular local disc jockey to play the music.

Mary Margaret changed her mind four times about which dress to wear. On the day of the party, she decided to go with her original plan. She dressed carefully. She studied her reflection in the mirror, ran the comb through her hair one more time, and added a touch of Aqua Net before joining her sister downstairs to pile in the car with her mother.

The Desoto Hotel was the perfect venue with its large ball rooms designed with blue velvet drapes, exquisite chandeliers, and big palm trees. Mary Margaret was delighted when she entered the room and saw the tie-dyed crepe paper streamers, balloons, and flowers her sister Joan had used to decorate. She felt like the belle of the ball. All of her friends rushed up to greet her and showered her with gifts. The music started playing and the party began.

"Mac, look over there," she whispered and pointed across the room. "It's Bunny. Who the hell invited her?"

"Probably herself."

"Look, there's Ben with Charlie." Mary Margaret felt a pang in her heart.

The room filled with scents of cheap perfume and aftershave. The girls migrated to a wall of lined up chairs waiting for someone to ask them to dance. Before long, the boys began picking off the girls and the dance floor filled.

A few girls made their way to the ladies' room lest they be called 'wallflowers' because no one asked them to dance. Theresa, breathless from jitter bugging with Charlie went to get a cup of punch.

"Mrs. Pucci, this is the best party ever."

"Theresa, have you seen Mary Margaret? I can't find her. Nobody's seen her in a while."

"I'll go look. She's probably in the ladies' room."

"My God, Pucci, what are you doing out here? Everyone's wondering where you are."

Mary Margaret had her hands on the iron rail of the porch and was gazing out toward Bull Street. A chilly breeze fluffed her hair and she shivered, clutching her bare arms.

"Tell me what's wrong? You've been so looking forward to your Sweet Sixteen party," Theresa said, putting her arm around Mary Margaret.

"Just listen, Mac, it's Skeeter Davis singing *The End of The World*. As far as I'm concerned it is the end of my world." She wiped tears from her eyes. "Not only has that horrible Bunny crashed my party, but she's dancing with Ben. I thought I was over him until I saw him tonight. Listen to that song. I could be singing it."

"Come on, Pucci, pull yourself together, this is your night, don't let that ruin it for you. I promise you Ben doesn't care one iota for Bunny. She wants you to be upset," Theresa said, reaching into her tan clutch, handing Mary Margaret a tissue. "Let's go to the bathroom and fix your makeup."

Mary Margaret thought back to early in the evening when her parents had given her a gold charm bracelet. She hadn't expected anything more than the party. She looked at Mac; so pretty in her green sheath minidress and tall tan boots, so brave, such a good friend. Mary Margaret's life was good. She had loving, generous parents, she needed to be brave.

Theresa coaxed Mary Margaret back to the party. The disc jockey was playing *Let's Twist Again*. There were her parents on the dance floor doing the twist.

She turned to Theresa. "Oh, dear God."

Theresa laughed and took her hand. "Come on, Pucci, let's twist. Pretend it's last summer. It'll make you feel better."

Pauline, Marnie, and Catherine joined them. The lights went out. A line of waiters carrying sparklers accompanied the cake and the whole room sang Happy Birthday.

The girls entered the Puccini house with armloads of presents. They piled them next to the stack the parents had already brought in. They all kicked off their shoes and sat around Mary Margaret. Saving theirs for last, they handed her the gifts one by one.

"This one is from your good friend Bunny," said Catherine.

Mary Margaret shot her a bird then took the gift with two fingers as if it was tainted.

"What happened with Bunny? She was gone when I came back. I was planning on telling her off."

"You don't want to know," said Pauline.

"Yes, I do. Just tell me."

"Your father saw Bunny spike the punch. He was across the room. By the time he made his way over there, Ted Grant had drunk three cups and was acting tipsy. He was dancing with Bunny, so your father just danced them across the room and showed them the door," said Catherine.

"I can't believe I missed it," said Mary Margaret, undoing the ribbon on the elaborately wrapped package. Inside was a bottle of My Sin perfume. The room got very quiet.

"That stuff is really expensive," said Theresa.

"I'll bet she stole it," said Catherine. "Do you think she's sending a message?"

"Here, open mine," said Theresa, handing her a large box.

"Shoes?" Mary Margaret said tearing into the box finding another box inside, then another until she got down to the last one, a tiny box. Inside was a gold heart-shaped charm engraved with Pucci on the front and Mac on the back. "How did you know? Anne must have told you."

She wiggled her arm showing off the bracelet. Theresa nodded.

The others laughed as she opened their charms, which contained a peace sign from Catherine, a number sixteen from Pauline, and a school logo from Marnie.

"To think I almost let Bunny and Ben ruin my evening," said Mary Margaret.

She smiled to cover up a deep sadness inside, a disappointment, that with all she had gotten, it failed to make her completely happy.

The day before school was over for the Thanksgiving holidays, Bunny came up to Mary Margaret in the hallway. "So, where is the picture?" She asked smugly. "I bet you didn't do it. You thought I'd forgotten, didn't you? You act like you have so much nerve, but at heart, you're just a coward."

Mary Margaret was enraged. She looked down the hall, then reached into her purse and produced the Polaroid of her holding up the nun's underwear with the photograph of Sister Fatima and her family. Bunny snatched it right out of her hand and ran down the hall. Mary Margaret started after her. Bunny turned the corner just before Sister Hope came out of her office.

"Miss Puccini, where are you off to in such a hurry?" Sister Hope said.

"She took something from me."

"Who?"

Hate gurgled up in Mary Margaret's throat. She checked herself before the name came out. "Bunn…but Sister, I'm so sorry, I left a book I needed in my locker. I was going to get it. Please forgive me. I hope you have a wonderful Thanksgiving. We have so much to be thankful for. Maybe I don't need that book after all. Thank you, Sister."

Sister Hope rolled her eyes, "Remember, we don't run in the school."

Mary Margaret scurried off.

A couple of days later, Bunny called Mary Margaret and told her she would show the photo to Sister Hope if she didn't fix her up with Charlie.

"Are you crazy? You know Charlie dates Theresa. She would kill me."

"Now, I wouldn't want to do anything to split up the infamous Dynamo Duo. But those two don't go steady. And, I'm sure he would like me. You know I won't hesitate to show Sister that picture."

"No, I'm not doing it," said Mary Margaret.

"Look, you better come with Charlie to the Triple-X tonight. I'll just chat with him a little. No harm done. Seven? See you there. If not, I'll have a little talk with Sister Hope." The line went dead on the other end. Mary Margaret shot a bird at the receiver before hanging it up.

Charlie was easily persuaded to go with her to the Triple-X. He was looking for something to do since Theresa and his friend Ben were both gone for the holidays. Mary Margaret drove. It was an unusually warm and balmy night for November. She pressed the button on the speaker box and ordered two hamburgers, French fries, and Cokes.

The drive-in restaurant was crowded with young people, some out of their cars, mingling with their friends. A transistor radio was blaring.

"You know our favorite waiter Rufus was fired," Mary Margaret said. She pushed the seat back to make more room for her food.

"Fired, Jesus, why?"

"He was selling liquor to underage minors and got caught." Mary Margaret glanced over to see Charlie's reaction figuring he was probably one of the guilty ones.

"Oh, that's too bad." He turned his head and looked out of the window. He became silent.

"I don't guess you happen to be one of them?"

"I'm not the only one. We were just trying to help him out. We always gave him a big tip."

"Well, y'all really helped him out. Now he doesn't have a job. Oh hell, here comes Bunny."

She wandered over to the Puccini's car and leaned into the open window on Charlie's side, her low-cut dress revealed a generous cleavage.

"Hi, Mary Margaret," she said, leaning over Charlie and wiggling her fingers. "Where's your twin?"

"My twin?"

"Yeah, the one you call Mac. You know, number two of the Dynamo Duo. Mind if I slip in?" Bunny opened the door and slid in next to Charlie. Her platinum blond hair was pulled back into a high ponytail which swung back and forth brushing against Charlie's cheek as she wriggled into the seat. Her short skirt hiked up and got Charlie's attention. A disgusted Mary Margaret jumped out of the car.

"You can slide over, Charlie, I'm getting out. Call me when the food comes," she said.

Pauline, Marnie, and Catherine waved from a few cars down. Mary Margaret walked over to join them.

"Is that Bunny with Charlie?" Catherine asked.

"Yes, she's blackmailing me with that Polaroid picture. Can I ride home with you? I just can't get back in that car. She makes me sick."

"What about Charlie?" Pauline asked.

"He can take care of himself. I guess that's part of her plan."

"Did you get the picture back?"

"No, Geez. I can't do it in front of Charlie. Theresa can't find out about them being together. What am I going to do?" Mary Margaret sighed deeply.

Theresa did find out. It was all over school, and Bunny was eating it up. She told everyone about how Mary Margaret had set her up with Charlie and that they were dating. Theresa was beside herself but didn't have the energy to confront Mary Margaret. She was emotionally bereft from Thanksgiving in Macon. Her parent's friends had hosted a reception which felt like a replay of the funeral. The thing that was really draining her was being the glue for her grandparents, his drinking, and her emptiness.

Theresa avoided Mary Margaret, eating lunch alone and riding the bus home instead of hitching a ride from a friend. Mary Margaret felt stupid and guilty about being blackmailed. Not getting that picture back plagued her. She tried to explain it to Theresa, who wouldn't listen. She tried everything she could to reach out to her. Mary Margaret was furious with Charlie for continuing to take Bunny out. Of course, she knew what they were doing. All she could do was to give Theresa time.

Midterm exams were coming up. Mary Margaret got another call from Bunny. "Yeah, I forgot to give you the picture. Listen, I have one more itsy-bitsy favor to ask, then I promise I'll give you back the evidence. I've been so busy going out with Charlie and Christmas shopping I haven't had a chance to study. I want you to steal a copy of the history final for me?"

"Bunny, are you crazy?"

"Come on, Pucci, I need it. I would hate to have to show the picture to Sister."

"Don't you ever call me Pucci again," Mary Margaret said, clutching her stomach. "I'll see what I can do."

Mary Margaret couldn't stand it anymore. She needed her friend. On the last day of school before the Christmas holidays, she raced out to Isle of Hope in hopes of catching Theresa after she got off the bus from school. Theresa was shocked but glad to see her.

"We have to talk. I have so much to tell you, and I just can't stand for you to be mad at me. I feel like half of me has been cut off," Mary Margaret said.

"I'm not mad, I'm just…I don't know, it's everything. I feel alone and scared. It's almost Christmas and the thought of it without my parents is unbearable. In the beginning, I could face each day by pretending that they were on one of their trips and that they'd be back soon, but it's not working anymore. They were always here for Christmas. Daddy got the biggest kick out of stringing lights everywhere. They're never coming back. And now this thing with Bunny and Charlie?"

"You're not alone, you have me and always will," Mary Margaret said, opening her arms.

Theresa hesitated, then went sobbing into the arms of her friend, just as the bus pulled off and enveloped them in a cloud of exhaust.

"I've had a lot going on with me too, Mac. Charlie and I don't talk and now this bitch Bunny, she's blackmailing me."

Theresa followed Mary Margaret to her car. "Blackmailing, what do you mean?"

"It's a long story. I'm staying over because what I have to tell you will take all night, so I brought my clothes." She grabbed her overnight bag and the two headed up the porch steps.

"Oh, Miss Mary Margaret, we so glad to see you," said Delia. "Miss Theresa, she been missing you. You know, Pearly decided to stay here and work with me instead of going back to Macon. She driving Dr. McDermott's old Imperial and done gone to the store. Miss Theresa, she'd rather ride the bus than have Pearly come fetch her from school."

Mary Margaret gave Delia a hug. "I've missed y'all too. Okay if I grab a couple of Cokes?"

"Sure can, I'll bring ya'll some Christmas cookies I just baked. Mrs. Willingham resting, so y'all be quiet now."

The girls settled in the den near the Christmas tree. Delia brought in their snack and lit the fire. Exiting the room, she began singing Joy to the World. The girls laughed when they heard Pearly back in the kitchen join her.

"Where to start?" Mary Margaret asked, biting off Santa's head. "Why don't you start by telling me about Macon?"

"No, it's too sad. Tell me about Bunny."

She told Theresa about Bunny snatching the photograph and blackmailing her. Then how she had come on to Charlie. She was sure he was just dating Bunny to have sex. She found condoms in his room.

"I had to steal a test for her out of Sister Hope's office. Sister came in while I was looking for it. I ducked behind that huge armoire thing she has. Pauline was standing watch and called her back out to see about the toilet, which was stopped up in the girl's bathroom."

"Did you get the test?"

"I did, but I swear, I almost wet my pants. Either Bunny is really stupid or really smart. She only made a C on the exam."

Sara Willingham heard singing from the kitchen and laughter from the den, "Who's here?" She asked Delia.

"It's Miss Mary Margaret, she in there with Miss Theresa," said Delia.

"Lord, we hadn't heard that child laugh in six months. It sure sounds good," Pearly said, turning to the stove and stirring the gumbo.

When Mrs. Willingham returned to the kitchen, Pearly and Delia had their heads together.

"Okay now, what are you two plotting?"

"Pearly was just saying, you know those recipes you done cut out from House and Garden and Goomay magazines? She'd like to try them."

"But, they're party recipes."

"Yas, ma'am." The two sheepishly cut their eyes over to Sara.

"You think we should have a party, don't you?"

"Yas, ma'am," said Delia, tilting her head toward the den.

"I can't believe so many people are coming. I was afraid everyone would already have plans for Christmas Eve," said Mrs. Willingham, taking a handful of red camellias from Delia and arranging them in the silver bowl on the table. "Everything looks delicious and smells even better. You and Pearly better not leave me and go into the catering business."

"Miss Theresa sure is excited. She done changed clothes at least five times," said Pearly.

"I'm glad y'all thought of doing this."

"The Hamiltons have just arrived. Theresa took their coats," said Oliver, gesturing for Sara to come into the entrance hall.

Theresa glided through the party with a grace and elegance not unlike her mother's. More than a few times, Sara glanced at her across the room and for a brief moment, thought it was Elizabeth. Feeling more alive than she had in months, she was excited about her granddaughter's future, watching the admiration in people's eyes, especially those of Monty Hamilton. Of course, he was too old for Theresa, but he certainly was handsome and well-heeled.

Charlie and Mary Margaret walked over to where Monty and Theresa were talking.

"Monty, this is Mary Margaret Puccini and her brother Charles, I believe you met her at the reception after the funeral."

"Pleased to see you again," said Monty, extending his hand.

Charlie was shifting his weight from foot to foot as the group laughed and chatted. Theresa and Mary Margaret were flirting with Monty. Charlie pulled Theresa aside, "We need to talk," he whispered.

Theresa looked at him with narrowed eyes, then turned back to the group. Charlie tried again, to pull her aside.

"I don't think she wants to go with you," said Monty.

"How do you know?" Charlie said, shoving Monty's shoulder. Monty put down his drink and raised a tight-fisted arm.

"Stop it y'all," yelled Theresa. She then turned and flew up the stairs. The front door slammed as Charlie left in a huff.

Mary Margaret found Theresa face down on her bed, her shoulders rising and falling. She sat down beside her. "It's okay, Mac. Charlie left."

Theresa sat up. She was laughing hysterically. Mary Margaret started laughing too.

"I'm only fifteen and already men are fighting over me. It was like a scene from Anna Karenina," said Theresa, drawing in a breath.

Downstairs the guests were leaving. "How will I get home? Charlie left," said Mary Margaret.

They walked out on the porch. "Take Mother's car, Pooch. No one is driving it these days."

Charlie pulled up and stepped out of his car carrying a dozen red roses. The girls nudged each other and giggled.

"Let's go to midnight Mass," he said.

The next day at the Puccini's, Pearly, and Delia were helping Essie prepare Christmas dinner.

"Who all's we feedin'?" Delia asked.

"There's the Puccinis, the Willinghams, Father Robert, Father James, and that do-funny doctor, that live around the corner. I don't know who all else. She told me sixteen," said Essie, opening the oven and basting the turkey.

Charlie and Theresa were on the porch swing. He presented her with a mustard seed pendant on a gold chain and a promise never to see Bunny again. He leaned in close and nuzzled her neck, then pulled her face toward his.

"No, you can't kiss me. The priests are in there," she said.

Ben bounded up the steps. He and Charlie exchanged some words and gifts before Ben rushed back down the steps into a waiting car.

Mary Margaret came out on the porch. "Was that Ben? Did he ask about me?"

"No, why would he? His brother was waiting. He had to get back to his family."

"He barely spoke to me," said Theresa.

Mary Margaret sighed and went back into the house, slamming the door.

"Oh great, look who's coming up the walk. It's your girlfriend, Bunny, bringing you a present," Theresa snapped. The door banged behind her as she went into the house.

Charlie stood and put his hands on his hips. "What are you doing here? I thought I made it clear that I didn't want to ever see you again," he said. Bunny threw the package in the bushes, ran down the walk, and scratched off in her new pale blue Thunderbird.

Pearly turned to Essie, "This place a zoo. The little uns fighting over the toys, that door keep slamming, Miss Mary Margaret's lower lip gone touch the floor, she pouting so, Miss Theresa all huffy. I can't wait to get back home. Let's get this here meal on the table."

Pearly and Essie were bringing in bowls of steaming vegetables while Nan ran through the house ringing the dinner bell.

"This table looks like something out of Goomay magazine," said Pearly.

"Yeah, Miss Anne done brought out all the good china and those flowers are a picture unto themselves."

The guests gathered around the table. Nan and Jeanne were shoving each other trying to sit in the same seat. Father James quieted everyone.

"In the name of the Father, the Son, and the Holy Ghost," he said, dramatically crossing himself. He said the blessing, elaborating at the end. He blessed; the children, the guests, and those no longer with us. He thanked; the Lord, the hosts, and the Pope.

"That food gone get cold if that priest don't change stop yacking and I'm gone drop this here turkey," whispered Essie from the door.

Finally, all were seated. Essie placed the turkey in front of Dr. Puccini to carve. Everyone helped themselves to stuffing, sweet potatoes, butter beans, and Delia's famous rolls. Mary Margaret was lost in thought. She looked around the table.

I could never be like my mother; managing eight children, doing volunteer work and always put together. Maybe if I could be that way, she wouldn't be so hard on me and she'd like me better. Will I ever find a man like Daddy? He has the deepest brown eyes and Anne's are as blue as Nan's baby dolls'. I wonder why I'm the only one with her eyes and the others have his.

That sour look on Theresa's face is not becoming. She's glaring at Charlie, who's staring at his plate like a sad puppy. Father James and Dr. Houston sure are deep in conversation. Two handsome men, what a waste for both. Hmm. What could Father Robert and Anne be laughing about? I still wonder about him and Catherine's mother. The Willinghams are quiet, probably sad about their first Christmas without Elizabeth and George.

"Mary Margaret, where are you?" Anne asked. "You seemed so far away. Wasn't that your friend Bunny bringing you a gift earlier?"

"I don't know, I didn't see her. I was in the house. Ask Charlie, she used to be his girlfriend."

Fifteen

January 1963

Back at school, Bunny was low-keyed, often missing class and seldom seen elsewhere. The whole class was whispering about how sallow her skin was and how tired she looked.

Mary Margaret and Theresa knew that Bunny was stalking Charlie. They had seen her cruising by the Puccini's and the Willingham's in her Thunderbird. On New Year's Eve, Mrs. Puccini found her in the garage apartment passed out. She was dressed up. An empty bottle of wine was next to her.

Ben and Charlie were with Theresa and Mary Margaret out at the Willingham's to celebrate and watch the fireworks at Barbee's. Mrs. Puccini called and asked that Charlie come home at once.

The four of them helped get Bunny sobered up. Charlie took her home and Ben followed in the Thunderbird. Theresa and Mary Margaret explained to Anne that Bunny had been stalking Charlie. In the past, no one had ever pushed Bunny away. Charlie telling her he was not interested, made her want him even more. She was relentless and determined he would be hers.

"That dress she had on was beautiful. I looked at it at Lady Janes and it was $250.00," said Mary Margaret.

"I love the layers of red and gray chiffon. Too bad she threw up all over it."

"They called the dress fire and smoke. Did you notice her false eyelashes?"

"Yeah, I bet she really looked good when she first went out. Kinda pitiful with one lash half way off. I couldn't help but feel sorry for her," said Theresa, picking up a party whistle and blowing it. Happy New Year! Here's to 1963.

Theresa opened a paper bag that was taped to her locker at school and screamed. Sister Hope heard her from the hall and demanded to see the contents of the bag. Her eyes widened when she peered into the brown sack.

"My office at once. I understand you are dating Charlie Puccini," she said, holding out the bag and rattling it. "Is this something that you need?"

"But Sister, they're not mine. Someone put them there."

"Who?"

"I don't know. It was just a prank."

"I demand that you tell me. Was it Mary Margaret Puccini? Sounds like something she would do."

"No, no, she's my best friend. She wouldn't do that. Sister, someone is putting mean notes on lockers, especially mine. No one has ever seen who is doing it."

Theresa wanted to get out of there, it was getting late and the office had become dark, the stale air, oppressive. The nun was in her face with her sour breath. The scent of starch was masking that other scent she couldn't quite identify. Her cold gray eyes were staring into Theresa's. *Mary Margaret must wonder where I am. Should I just rat on Bunny so Sister Hope will let me go?*

"I know you know who it is. Tell me," the nun demanded.

Just as Theresa began to speak, there was a knock at the door. "Go on," she said, her habit rustling as she walked across the room, but Theresa remained silent.

"Why Mary Margaret Puccini, you seem to have a sixth sense. Maybe you can shed some light on these," she said, picking up the bag with two fingers holding it out with a look of disgust on her face. "These were left on Miss McDermott's locker. Any idea who might have done this?"

Mary Margaret peered into the bag. "What are these?"

"You know perfectly well. They're condoms."

Mary Margaret put her hands in the air. "What are they for?" She said, with a puzzled look on her face. "I've never seen condoms before in my life, honest, Sister." She crossed her fingers behind her back.

The nun blushed. "I'm going to get to the bottom of this. Why are you here, Miss Puccini? Don't tell me the toilet stopped up."

"Um, but it is. I think it's about to overflow."

The nun trudged toward the bathroom. She figured they stopped it up on purpose, but she couldn't catch them doing it and she couldn't take a chance on it flooding.

"How'd you know where I was?" Theresa said.

"Just figured. Charlie came by to tell us he got accepted at Georgetown. We're going to Johnny Harris's Restaurant to celebrate. Come on."

Someone was knocking hard and persistently on the Puccini's front door. Mary Margaret, Pauline and Catherine were dancing to *Love, Love Me Do* from the Beatles with the volume all the way up.

"Charlie, get the door," shouted Mary Margaret, forgetting that Charlie and Theresa had gone out to the garage apartment to say goodbye. The girls were celebrating the end of their sophomore year with one last get-together before they all went in different directions for the summer. Pauline and Catherine were heading to Tybee, Marnie to visit her grandmother, Mary Margaret to New Orleans to visit her sister Joan, and Theresa was going to Paris for an art class at the Sorbonne.

Pauline stopped mid-twirl. Catherine turned. Ben was standing in the doorway. "No one answered, the door wasn't locked, so I let myself in," he said.

"Charlie's in the garage apartment with Theresa," Mary Margaret shouted over the music.

"I came here to see you. I want to talk to you about something. Can we go out on the porch?"

Mary Margaret's heart was racing. When he put his hand on her arm, it felt electric. How quickly this came back after all these months. He led her to the porch swing and sat next to her.

"Is everything okay?" She scanned his eyes looking for some kind of indication. They looked sad.

"I just wanted to talk to you about last summer. And that thing about the Commissioning Dance. I know I hurt you. I didn't mean to. I did care for you, I still do." Ben shifted awkwardly in the swing and looked down. "But we being together could never be."

"Why, I don't understand?" Mary Margaret asked, "Is it something about me?"

"No, it's not that. You're wonderful and beautiful. So full of life. Whenever I see you, my heart skips a beat. But I have had to ignore it."

"Then why?" Her eyes began to well. "If you cared, why have you ignored me all this time?"

"It's about me, Mary Margaret," his voice raised and he took a deep breath. "I've been so confused because of conflicting feelings I've kept inside. Finally, I talked to Father James about it."

Mary Margaret brought her hand to her mouth. "Oh my God. Are you queer?"

"Oh, no, it's not that at all. It's…" He stammered. "I want to be a priest."

Mary Margaret felt like someone punched her in the stomach. She started to cry. "What? You want to be a priest? You want to waste your life? Why Ben? You can't. How could you be a priest if you had those feelings for me? I don't understand."

"I know. I'm sorry I didn't say something before. I just didn't know how. I leave tomorrow for the summer session at St. Vincent's Arch Abbey. If I don't do this, I'll never know. Please understand." He stood but turned away so she couldn't see his tears.

Charlie and Theresa walked up the sidewalk onto the porch.

"Hey, Ben, what's going on? I didn't know you were here," said Charlie. Mary Margaret got up and pinched her face into a fake smile.

"Bye, Ben," she said sadly, giving him a little wave as she went into the house.

Upstairs, she grabbed her Maddie doll, went into the bathroom, and cried her heart out.

After Ben told them about the conversation, Theresa ran up the stairs and knocked on the bathroom door. "Pucci, it's me, I just heard. Let me in."

The lock on the door clicked open. Steam emerged from the bathroom. Mary Margaret had turned on the shower to cover the sound of her sobs.

"Mac. I thought I was over him, but I'm not. Can you believe he wants to be a priest, a damn priest?"

"Charlie and I thought something was going on with him. He's been so distant and quiet. But I didn't see this coming. I'm so sorry, Pooch."

"Mac, what do I do? I thought for a minute when we were talking, he was going to tell me he was a queer. I tell you, in a way I wish he was and not that. How can I compete with God?"

Savannah, Georgia August 1963

Summer was over and all the girls returned home from their various trips. Mary Margaret and Ted Grant were sharing a Coke float at Central Pharmacy when she jumped and turned to see who was touching her shoulder. The petite girl in ballet flats had soundlessly approached the couple. "Oh my God, Mac, I'm so glad you're back."

"I wanted to surprise you." She looked at the young man Mary Margaret was with. it was a second before she recognized him. "Is that you, Ted? You've changed so much," Theresa said, hugging Mary Margaret, then Ted. "You look like Troy Donahue."

"You're one to talk," said Mary Margaret. "You look so French in your pedal pushers and Pixie haircut. I wouldn't have recognized you across the room. She stared at her friend's wide blue eyes with their mascara-coated fringe of eyelashes."

"I'm going to leave it to you, girls," said Ted, throwing a quarter on the counter.

The girls immediately launched into details of their summer, each as excited as the other.

"I was so blown away by the architecture in New Orleans that I've decided to become an architect," Mary Margaret said.

"I see you've been drawing buildings on the napkins. I'm impressed. Maybe we can go to the same college where you can study architecture, and I can major in painting. I have some paintings I did this summer to show you."

"Did you meet any cute boys in Paris? I'll bet those European guys are really groovy."

"No, most of the boys in my art classes liked boys. Are you dating Ted?"

"No, we just ran into each other. We were getting our school supplies. He is kinda cute, isn't he? He asked me to the Commissioning Dance."

"Well, good, you should go. I'm glad you're not still pining over Ben."

"Yeah, but the thought of him being a priest still makes me sick. What a waste."

Every time Theresa stopped by the Puccini's, Ted was there. She found herself preferring to play cards with Nan than to hang out with those two making moony eyes at each other. He and Mary Margaret were going out together almost every weekend.

Theresa was lonely and missed Charlie, but found solace working in the studio her grandparents built for her behind their house.

One weekend, Mary Margaret came out to spend the night. She informed Theresa that she and Ted had gotten her a date for the Commissioning Dance.

"I don't know. Pucci, I really don't want to go," Theresa said.

"Why not? It will be a lot of fun, and it's the Commissioning Dance. It's just Tommy. He's Ted's best friend. Besides, I really want you to go," Mary Margaret said. "Where else would you wear that beautiful embroidered strapless your grandmother bought you in Paris?"

"I feel like I would be betraying Charlie."

"Charlie would never know, and Tommy, are you kidding? Everyone knows he is probably a queer, except Ted," Mary Margaret said, rolling her eyes upward, shaking her head.

Theresa went to her closet and pulled out her dress. "Are we allowed to go strapless?"

The girls and their dates arrived at the dance dressed in gowns and military whites. St. Thomas's School hosted the dance in their auditorium.

"Look at this place," said Mary Margaret. "They sure did a great job decorating. It looked pretty bleak at Charlie's graduation last year."

A thought went through Mary Margaret's head about Ben and how it was just a year ago when she hoped to go to the dance with him. Things were different now. She was with Ted.

Tommy was a terrific dancer. He introduced Theresa around and encouraged her to dance with the others who were lining up. When she sat down while the band was on break, Mary Margaret and Ted came over.

"Why don't you grab Tommy and get us some punch, Ted?" Mary Margaret said sitting down next to Theresa. "So, how has your date been? Are you having a good time?"

"Pooch, I just love Tommy. He is so much fun. You really think he's, you know, that way?"

"Ted doesn't think so. He says he's a mama's boy. But come on, Mac." The two looked over on the dance floor at Tommy flitting all around with several of the girls. "Now if that's not queer, what is?"

"I know, I just hate it for him. What do you think it is that makes somebody like that?" Theresa looked back at Tommy and grimaced when she saw him flipping his hands in the air while doing the twist. "Remember that guy we saw with John Gray a few years ago? He looked like James Dean. Nothing about him was girly acting. And then look at John Gray. He sure doesn't flit. I wonder what makes some like Tommy and some like John Gray."

"Daddy says you're born that way. A missing chromosome. Nothing you can do about it. I guess the John Gray type try to hide it."

They watched Ted maneuver through the crowd and coerce Tommy to help with the punch. Theresa noticed a change in Mary Margaret's demeanor.

"Pucci, what's going on? Why are you acting differently with Ted?" Theresa asked.

"It's nothing, we're fine."

"Pucci, I feel like you're not telling me something."

Ted and Tommy were approaching carrying punch. Mary Margaret plastered that fake smile across her face that Theresa knew so well.

After the dance, the girls were getting ready for bed at the Puccini's. Theresa asked her again what was going on. "You're so preoccupied. Ted monopolizes all your time, and you don't want to go anywhere with your friends. Tonight, there was something weird between you two. Is everything okay, Pucci?"

"Ted is always around and wants to be alone with me. He's so domineering and jealous. Tonight, when I hugged a friend I've known for years, he got mad. Do you think I'm always looking at other guys?"

"No, of course not."

"Well, he does, and I don't like it. You looked like you were having a great time, dancing with everyone."

"It was fun. I think you're right about Tommy. He was a great date, almost like being with one of the girls. I can tell Ted is crazy about you. Maybe you're not ready to be that serious."

"You're right. I care about him, but I'm certainly not ready to go steady. I like making out, but he wants to go further, he gets mad when I push his hands away. I don't know what to do."

"Please be careful. He shouldn't force you to do anything you don't want to do. Don't you dare go all the way."

"Jesus, Mac, give me some credit."

The Friday before Thanksgiving, the girls at St. Bernadette were lingering in the hall before class, chatting about their plans for the weekend and the upcoming holidays. Mary Margaret was nervous about going to the Grants for Thanksgiving dinner. Theresa was excited about Charlie coming home and had an appointment to get her hair frosted that afternoon.

"Your hair looks fine just the way it is. I don't know why you want to go through the torture of having it pulled through that cap, then sitting under the bonnet dryer for an hour. I like your dark hair," said Mary Margaret, reaching over and flipping up a few strands of Theresa's hair.

"It'll look natural, like in the summer when the sun highlights it," said Theresa, combing through her hair with her fingers. "You know I haven't seen Charlie since school started and I want it to look good."

"Well, Mac, I hope it doesn't turn green like a certain 'natural' blonde's did," she pointed behind her with her thumb toward Bunny.

Their laughter was drowned out by the sound of the bell and stomping footsteps as the girls raced to their first-period classes.

Sister Fatima felt like letting the girls in her third-period class go home. They weren't paying attention. She knew next week would be even worse on Monday and Tuesday with the upcoming holiday distracting them. There was a mechanical squeal then a crackle before Sister Hope's voice came over the loudspeaker.

"May I please have everyone's attention? I have received a bulletin that an assassination attempt has been made on the life of President Kennedy in Dallas, Texas. We will proceed to the chapel in a quiet and orderly fashion. A monitor will come to your classroom when it is your turn to go."

The classroom erupted in a cacophony of squeals and questions. Sister Fatima stood there in shock trying to speak but no words were coming out of her mouth. She reached for the bell on her desk and rang it until the girls began to quiet down and let go of whomever they were embracing. Sister dropped to her knees, the girls followed suit and they all began to recite the Hail Mary.

It suddenly felt like the world was turned upside down. For the first time ever, all network programs were suspended. Eyes were glued to the television all day. Shortly after the shocking news that three shots had been fired at Kennedy, the announcement came that the President of the United States was dead. Viewers focused on the footage of Jackie climbing onto the back of the limousine and stared as she stood by Johnson's side in her blood-stained Givenchy suit while he was sworn in as the next president.

Theresa took Mary Margaret home.

"Come in, Mac. Please don't leave me."

"No, I really need to go see about Nana and Papa. She loved Kennedy. I'm sure she's taking it very hard. I guess Anne will be happy."

"Please, she's not that hard-hearted. Well, maybe a little."

The Puccini house was quiet, the light from the TV danced in the darkened den. Every day at one-thirty Essie took the ironing board into the den to work while she watched her soap operas. The ironing board was up but Essie wasn't ironing. She was sitting on the sofa next to Anne. Mary Margaret didn't recognize her mother's clouded features.

"Mama, they let us out of school early. Are you okay?"

"What's this country coming to? I can't believe someone shot that man. He didn't deserve that. Right or wrong he was our president."

As soon as Theresa parked the car, she heard the unmistakable keening from Delia and Pearly. Her heart sank remembering that sound from her parent's funeral. Inside, she found them and her grandparents in the den huddled around the television. They didn't even notice Theresa come in. She put her arms around her grandmother and felt her jump.

"Oh, dear Lord, girl you scared me," said Sara, and locked Theresa in such a tight embrace she felt she was going to suffocate.

"Nana, I'm so sorry. How did you find out?"

"Delia and Pearly were watching *As the World Turns* and Walter Cronkite came on with the news."

Theresa went to them and gave them each a hug.

"Our story had just come on when they interrupted it with this terrible news," said Delia drawing in a breath.

"I was just back from the club," said Oliver. "Thank God, I didn't hear it there, like before." He walked across the room and gave Theresa a hug.

"Look at that poor thing in that soiled suit. They ought to get the poor chile some clean clothes," said Pearly. "I'm gonna get this here chile something to eat. I bet you're famished."

But no one moved away from the TV. They were transfixed as the horrible images played over and over.

On Saturday, Theresa met Charlie at the train station. He was wearing a camel wool overcoat and carried a dark brown briefcase in his right hand, a small leather valise in the other. She almost overlooked him among the businessmen getting off the train. They all had sad serious looks on their faces. Charlie's lit up when he saw Theresa. She grabbed him around the waist before he even had time to put down his luggage.

"I can't believe you got to come home early."

"Yeah, they let us out after class. Washington's a mess. You wouldn't believe the rumors flying around. I was lucky to get a seat on the train. People are panicking and want to leave. They're afraid there's going to be a coup."

"Oh Charlie, it's so scary. I feel so much better now that you're here. Thank God they arrested that man. I'm so sick of watching the news. Let's go to a movie tonight. I'm going to spend the night with Mary Margaret. Maybe she and Ted can come too."

"You know it'll be all over the newsreel."

After Mass on Sunday, the Puccinis and Theresa gathered in the den to watch the transfer of Lee Harvey Oswald from the Dallas jail to the state penitentiary. They watched on live television as a man stepped out of the crowd and shot the prisoner who was surrounded by a crowd of police officers.

"It's pure anarchy," shouted Anne. "Never in my life have I seen such a thing." She stood and marched out of the room. Theresa slipped her hand out of Charlie's afraid his parents would notice them holding hands. The night before the twins caught them making out on the porch and started taunting them singing, *Theresa and Charlie sitting in a tree KISSING, first comes love, then comes marriage, then comes Theresa with a baby carriage.*

Sixteen

Theresa couldn't believe her eyes when she opened the Christmas present from her grandparents. They had all been trying so hard to be cheerful. Pearly baked the traditional goodies that Elizabeth always loved to share with neighbors. They had never had a more beautiful tree, but pulling out the ornaments, each with memories of the past, sent Theresa to her room. Despite everyone's efforts to be merry the absence of her parents hung over the house like the Spanish moss on the trees outside. Now the room was filled with nostalgic pine scent and beautifully wrapped packages.

"Tickets to the Beatles concert. How did you know?" She hugged the tickets to her chest then examined them. "But it's in New York."

"Well, there's another surprise. You can take Mary Margaret on the train and Claudette will meet the two of you. She's going there on business. Her friend was able to get the tickets before they actually went on sale in January. She has a connection at Carnegie Hall," said Sara, neatly folding some used wrapping paper.

Theresa hugged her grandmother then her grandfather.

"I wish we could take credit, but it was all Claudette's idea. She was able to get the tickets and apparently knew something about this 'Beatlemania' which is sweeping the world."

"Weren't they expensive?"

"Worth every penny just to see the look on your face. I wish Claudette had been here. I'm going to get the camera and take a picture to send to her."

Theresa ran to the phone to call Mary Margaret. She couldn't wait until later when they would be together at the Puccini's for dinner.

"Holy Moly, far out," Mary Margaret said, kissing her fingers then the phone. "I'm so excited. Let me go talk to Mama. When is it again?"

She hung up and ran into the kitchen where Anne and Essie were preparing Christmas dinner.

"Those mop-haired Brits? No, ma'am, you're entirely too young to be going to a concert, especially in New York City."

"But Mama, Claudette will be with us."

"I don't know this Claudette person. Who is she? How old is she? How would I know she would be a proper chaperone?"

"She's Theresa's second cousin from France and she's at least thirty. I would have met her if I'd gotten to go to Paris."

"Get on out of here now. Essie and I have dinner to organize."

"Please, it's a once-in-a-lifetime opportunity. I promise to be good, and I'll do everyone's turn with the dishes for a whole month if I can go."

Anne handed the bowl of washed cranberries to Essie. "Now don't you look at me like that Essie?"

"Lord, I'll talk to Sara and see what it's all about, but don't get your hopes up."

Mary Margaret stood and put her hands in the prayer position. "Oh, please, please, please."

At the table, the trip to New York became the main topic of conversation.

"You know, Anne, I wouldn't be sending Theresa with Claudette if I didn't trust her. She's a delightful person, but she's also extremely responsible. She's been there for Theresa since she lost her parents."

"Mama. I can't believe you'd deny Mary Margaret this opportunity. I got to see Elvis in Savannah. Besides, it's in Carnegie Hall. You're familiar with that place. I wish I could go. How 'bout me going in Mary Margaret's place?" Charlie said.

"No way. You'd better not." She threw her napkin at him.

Theresa looked up, "That's not a bad idea." She winked at Mary Margaret. "Just kidding. Grandmother wouldn't let me go if it was with Charlie."

"Ok, but I insist Mary Margaret has to pay for her train ticket and meals out of her allowance," said Anne and raised her wine glass. "Merry Christmas."

A cheer went around the table. Mary Margaret jumped up to give Anne a hug.

"You can start your dish duty today," said Anne pointing to the stack of dishes on the table.

When Pauline found out that the girls were going to see the Beatles, her mother was able to get one ticket through a New York friend. When Marnie and Catherine tried, they were sold out.

New York, 1964

The girls acted very grown-up on the train, smoking in the dining car, and ordering pots of coffee. Mary Margaret got that look on her face and before she could utter a word Theresa said, "No, whatever you think is a good idea I'm not going along with it."

"But this is for later. Can't I just tell you what I'm thinking?"

"No, I know you'll get us into trouble, and we promised our parents. If we mess up, they'll never let us do anything again for the rest of our lives," said Pauline.

Mary Margaret sat back in her seat, folded her arms, and looked out of the window pouting.

"All right, all right, what's your idea?" Pauline said.

"We've got to figure a way to meet the Beatles."

"Yeah, and so will all the millions of other girls that will be there," said Theresa taking a sip of her coffee.

"You don't have to be sarcastic. You know if anyone can figure it out it'll be me."

Theresa and Pauline looked at each other and shook their heads. The conductor announced Grand Central Station. The girls gathered their things and descended from the train pushed along by the crowds.

"Grand Central Station, look at this place," Mary Margaret said. "It's more beautiful than I thought. Those windows are huge."

"Look at that dome ceiling with the constellations of the Zodiac, and that grand staircase," said Theresa, putting down her suitcase and looking up. "This suitcase is so heavy. I thought they'd have porters like they do at home."

"There must be a million people in here and they're all rushing around. I hope I don't get knocked down. How will we ever find Claudette?" Pauline said. "Why'd you bring such a big suitcase?"

"I couldn't decide what to bring so I brought all my best clothes. She said to meet her at the west entrance. Look for a black car. You guys are going to love Claudette. She's cool."

Mary Margaret did a double take when she saw Claudette. "Mac, she looks so much like your mother."

A tall slim lady leaning against a black car stepped forward. Her hair was pulled back into a chignon. Dark tendrils softened her pretty face. She looked like she stepped out of a recent issue of Paris Match in her tweed Chanel suit.

"Theresa, Mon Cheri," Claudette called out. She rushed over and embraced her cousin. "Girls, I'm so glad you are all here. And this is the famous Pucci I've heard so much about. Did you get these two into mischief on the train?"

Mary Margaret blushed as Claudette pulled her close and kissed her on each cheek.

"The French way. And Pauline. Enchanté. You will keep these two out of trouble. No? I heard all about your dress-up scheme at the beach."

"That wasn't my idea," Pauline said. She shrugged her shoulders and pointed to Mary Margaret. Behind her back, she shot Pauline a bird.

"Are we staying where Eloise had tea in that book?" Mary Margaret said, looking at the crowds and stores as they drove down Fifth Avenue.

"No, our hotel is the Warwick, only a few blocks away," said Claudette. "I have a surprise for you. We check in first. After, you are to have tea at Eloise's Plaza before the concert. I'll join you after my meeting."

The girls giggled as they tried out the beds in their room. Theresa fed Pauline a grape from the fruit assortment on the table. Mary Margaret bit into a huge strawberry and let the juice run down her chin. Claudette stuck her head through the door that joined her room to theirs.

"Au Revoir petites, I must go to my meeting now. You understand my instructions to get to the Plaza. No?"

She kissed Theresa on the top of her head and blew a kiss to the others before exiting.

"God, I love her, Mac. I love her accent. I almost feel like she's singing every sentence."

"Oui, oui, we must go to Paree soon. No?" Pauline said, throwing elaborate air kisses to the girls.

At the entrance to the Plaza, a bellman was unloading luggage from a very long black limousine onto a cart.

"I swear that looks like musical instrument cases. I'll bet the Beatles are staying here," said Mary Margaret drawing in a breath.

Another bellman and a man in a suit came out and said something to the one unloading the limo. He released the cart and walked over to the door with balled-up fists. He swung a mock punch at the door after the suited man went in.

"It must be for the Beatles," said Theresa.

"I'll bet they went in a secret entrance," said Pauline. "I've heard they do that."

"That doorman who was unloading the limo is mad. Let's go talk to him," said Mary Margaret. "I'll just bet he knows something."

Their protests fell on deaf ears. They followed Mary Margaret as she approached the bellman.

"Hey, we heard that was the Beatles' limo," she exaggerated her southern drawl. With a coy smile, she batted her eyelashes.

He looked down into the excited faces of the three girls. "I take it youse aren't from around here," he said in a thick Bronx brogue.

"No, we're from Savannah, Georgia. We've got tickets to the concert tonight. We know they're staying here," said Pauline, also drawling and smiling sweetly. Theresa looked incredulously at her friends.

"Any way we can meet them?" Mary Margaret said.

"For ten bucks, I might can divulge some information."

"Ten bucks? That's a lot of money," said Theresa.

"Well, if you want the info, that's what it'll cost you. Come back after the concert."

"We'll go have tea and discuss it," said Theresa, marching toward the door to the hotel.

Claudette spotted the girls across the Palm Court dining room. Their eyes peeled to the door, saw her immediately, and waved. They had the waitress seat them at a table where the view of the door was unobstructed by the palms and columns. Before Claudette arrived, they pooled their money and managed to come up with ten dollars and a plan to come back after the concert.

"Claudette, this is fabulous. Can you believe all these goodies," said Theresa stuffing a cucumber sandwich in her mouth, "it's even better than I remembered." She looked up at the domed stained-glass ceiling.

"Have you yet to see the Beatles?" Claudette said taking a place at the table. She buttered a scone and bit it daintily. "You know they are staying here. They have a whole wing. That's why we couldn't get a room."

They looked at each other with wide eyes.

"We saw their limo out front when we were coming in," said Mary Margaret.

"Now you girls put your money away," said Claudette looking at their cache on the table. "This is my treat."

In unison, they all said thank you. Mary Margaret put the money in her pocketbook. After gorging on finger sandwiches and cakes, they excused themselves to go to the ladies' room while Claudette settled the bill. Once inside, they let out all of their bundled-up excitement causing a lady to rush out of the bathroom.

"I told y'all so. Now we know for sure they're staying here. We have the money, we just need to figure out how to sneak out of our hotel," said Mary Margaret. They could see by her expression that she was hatching a plan.

"You girls ready?" Claudette said pushing the door open. "We go back to the hotel. You can dress and make yourself dolls."

"You mean we can get all dolled up?" Theresa said.

"Yes, of course. I know you will use all the makeup in your bags." They all laughed as Claudette locked arms with Theresa and led the way back to their hotel.

"A car will arrive for us here at six o'clock. We will drop you at the concert before I join my friend for dinner. We'll pick you up as soon as the concert is over. If you jeunes filles are still hungry later, you can order room service at the hotel."

Inside the room, they unpacked their suitcases spreading makeup items across the dresser. Mary Margaret caked pancake makeup across her nose trying to cover her freckles. She wet her eyeliner cake with a brush and painted a thick black line across the lid, lifting it at the corner.

"You look like a wildcat. I love it. Let me try some," said Theresa extending her hand and leaning closer to the mirror.

"Is this color Blush-on right for me?" Pauline asked coming out of the bathroom.

"You look like a clown. Rub some of it off, but that beauty mark under your lip looks great," said Mary Margaret, spreading frosted strawberry glaze over her lips and smiling into the mirror.

"Allez, allez, beauty queens," shouted Claudette outside of the girl's room.

The traffic slowed to a crawl as they approached the concert hall. A symphony of horns echoed through the streets.

"Mon Dieu, girls, please calm down. We're almost there. I promise we won't be late," said Claudette, stroking the side of Theresa's face.

"If we hadn't gone back to get our coats, maybe this wouldn't have happened," said Pauline.

"Chill, girls, we have plenty of time, it's still an hour before the show starts," said Theresa.

"We don't even need our coats," said Mary Margaret fanning her face. "It's not cold in here and probably won't be in the concert."

"Aw, girls, it is only because you are so excited. We are arriving now so it will be quite chaotic after the concert. Be sure and meet us in this exact spot," shouted Claudette elaborately throwing air kisses.

Almost before the car came to a complete stop, the girls jumped into a sea of screaming teenagers.

Theresa gave her a thumbs up and the girls joined the crowd.

Claudette turned to the driver.

"I do hope they will be okay. What is it about those young British men that drives the girls crazy? Their name is of bugs. No?"

"I think they'll be okay, there are so many police around. What could happen?" He said, slowly maneuvering the car into a stream of traffic.

"They could get trampled like those poor girls in England."

Mary Margaret elbowed her way to the front. The usher looked at their tickets and pointed to a row further back. They settled in their seats.

"I wish we were up on stage. Who the hell are those people behind the mics?" She asked.

"We're lucky to be here at all. Catherine and Marnie couldn't even get tickets," said Pauline.

"Look at all those cops. How are we going to get to the stage afterward? I want to see the Beatles up close."

"What? I can't hear you. Everyone is screaming," said Theresa.

It only got worse. After the first line, "After the first line of *She Loves You*, the audience echoed the lyrics and jumped to their feet. Everyone jumped to their feet. There was a commotion up front when a girl fainted and had to be escorted out."

After the concert, the police formed a shield and forced the sea of fans up the aisles.

"No, Mary Margaret, there's no way we can get up to the stage and certainly not backstage."

"Mac, I'm sure there is a back entrance they have to leave from."

"No, Pucci, we have to meet Claudette. Let's go."

Theresa and Pauline locked arms and allowed themselves to be pushed along by the crowd. Outside, Theresa took in a breath and looked all around for Mary Margaret. The crowd began to thin and still, she hadn't shown up. The car pulled up to the designated spot. Claudette stepped out.

"Mon Cheri, you look like you've been to a dogfight. Now where are Pauline and Poochie?"

"Oh, Claudette, it was a zoo. Pauline went to look for her and we got separated coming out. What should we do?"

"We wait here. She's a smart girl and knows where to come. You don't think she did anything foolish, do you?"

Mary Margaret came running toward the car waving her clutch purse above her head. "I dropped my purse and almost got trampled trying to pick it up. I'm so sorry," she said, trying to catch her breath. "Where's Pauline?"

"She went to look for you," said Theresa. "I'll go find her."

"No, wait," said Claudette, grabbing Theresa's arm. She knows where to come. "You girls look a fright. Let's go back to the hotel."

In the limousine, Claudette introduced the girls to her friend Monica. They thanked her profusely for helping get the tickets. They described the performance, all talking at once.

"Could you even hear the songs?" Monica said.

"Well, no, not really," said Theresa.

"It really didn't matter. We got to see the Beatles. Just wish we could have gotten closer," said Mary Margaret. "Here comes Pauline now. Let's get out of here."

At the hotel, the girls got out of the limo.

"Aren't you coming?" Theresa said looking at Claudette. The other girls were already through the hotel's revolving door.

"Non, Monica and I are going out. I know I can count on you to behave. I will be late, so don't wait up," Claudette said. She threw another one of her kisses as she rolled up the window.

"There is nothing like the enthusiasm and excitement of teens," said Monica, laughing as the limo pulled away.

"I think I know why I never had children. I would be a terrible mother. I probably should stay here and make sure they don't get into trouble."

"You didn't come all the way across the ocean to babysit."

"Yay, now we don't have to wait and sneak out. Let's hurry up and get ready, I thought we'd never get back here with all that traffic," Mary Margaret said.

"Which dress should I wear?" Theresa pulled out the beautiful designer dresses Claudette had brought her from Paris and laid them on her bed. Pauline and Mary Margaret pursed their lips together and sighed at the same time as they looked at their ordinary dresses which did not begin to compare. Theresa noticed their faces.

"Okay y'all, let's draw straws and see who gets to wear which dress. We all wear about the same size. Pauline, you go first."

Pauline took her selection into the bathroom. A minute later, she shrieked. "Oh no, wouldn't you know, I've started my period. Could one of you go into my suitcase and grab me a clean pair of panties and a tampon?"

Theresa and Mary Margaret looked at each other. "She wears tampons? Does that mean she's not a virgin? That's what Anne says."

"Don't be silly, Mary Margaret. Here, hand her these." Theresa closed Pauline's suitcase and proceeded to pull up her stockings and attach them to the garter belt. "I use them myself. Oh damn, this one has a run. Good thing I brought extra."

"Hey, look at us, we look like we stepped out of Vogue magazine," Mary Margaret said, viewing herself in the elevator mirror. "Thanks, Mac, I love this dress. These black heels look okay. No?"

"Good Lord, you're going to kill yourself in those. Besides, you're so tall you'll tower over everyone," Pauline said.

"Exactly, then I'll be able to see," Mary Margaret kicked up her heel.

"Should we have gotten our coats? It's freezing outside," Pauline said.

"And cover our dresses, no way."

After walking several blocks up Fifth Avenue, Mary Margaret stopped, "Y'all wait, my feet are killing me. I can't go this fast," she pulled off one of her shoes and rubbed her foot.

"I told you not to wear those stupid shoes," Pauline said. "Where did you even get 'em?"

"They're Joan's. I borrowed them from her closet. Where is this place? It's freezing."

"I also told you it was cold and we needed to get our coats. But oh no. You didn't want to cover your dress." Pauline wrapped her arms around herself to get warmer.

"Good Lord, quit arguing. We're on Fifty-Seventh. We've only got two more blocks. Come on, or we'll miss them," Theresa said.

At the corner of Fifty-Ninth and Fifth, they could see a commotion at the hotel. Mary Margaret put her shoes back on and they ran to the front entrance.

"Oh, my God we're going to miss them. Where did all these people come from?" Theresa said as she started in the hotel. The others followed.

There must have been a hundred teenage girls running and screaming through the lobby of the Plaza. They were taking napkins and items off of the dining tables and ransacking the place, throwing pillows off of the furniture. One girl was crying and clutching a cushion saying that she just knew Ringo had sat on it. The hotel's security people were trying to calm everyone down and get them out but to no avail. The three girls huddled by a palm tree and watched as policemen entered the hotel.

"Mary Margaret, that bellman is the one who was going to tell us how we can meet the Beatles," Pauline said, pointing in the direction of the lobby desk. "They're yelling at him."

They walked over to see what was going on, hoping there was still a chance to pay him to meet the Beatles. Mary Margaret took out the ten dollars.

A policeman walked over to the bellman and pulled out handcuffs.

"They're arresting him?" Mary Margaret said. "Sir, what's going on?" She asked one of the men watching the whole scene.

"Evidently, he took money from those girls promising them they would be able to meet the Beatles after the concert. They aren't even here."

Mary Margaret looked down at the ten dollars in her hand and quickly put it in her purse. "Well, at least we have our ten dollars."

"Come on y'all, let's get out of here. You and your bright idea, Pucci."

They trudged back to the hotel shivering and deflated. In their room, they flung themselves on the bed.

"I don't think I'll ever be warm again," said Pauline, wrapping her robe and then her overcoat around her.

"We can't dare admit to anyone that we almost got swindled," said Theresa.

"I can't believe we fell for that."

They both looked over at Mary Margaret who was sound asleep.

"Wake up your sleeping heads. It's almost ten o'clock. Time for breakfast," said Claudette bursting through the door of their adjoining rooms.

Mary Margaret mumbled something as she limped to the bathroom.

Pauline pulled the pillow from on top of Theresa's head. She sat up and went into a fit of coughing.

Claudette sat down on the edge of the bed. Pauline sneezed.

"So, you girls stayed here last night. No? I called the room several times and no one answered."

"Pucci, get back in here. You have to tell Claudette what happened last night."

"Cheri, I know that look on your face. What kind of mischief were you up to last night? The bellman told me you girls went back out."

Mary Margaret stepped back into the room blowing her nose.

"No point in lying to me."

After they confessed the whole story, Claudette burst into laughter. "You girls are safe now, even if you are being punished with colds. I can't believe you fell for that bellman's scam. Now hurry and dress so we can go downstairs and have breakfast before they quit serving."

In the restaurant, Claudette ordered hot tea for the girls and coffee for herself.

"Ah, American coffee, it tastes like something you might wash the dishes in." She took a sip of the coffee and made a face. "You girls really thought that Monsieur bellman was going to introduce you to the bug men? No?"

"Claudette, you're not going to tell Nana what we did. Are you?" Theresa cocked her head and squinted her eyes at her cousin.

"Non, Cheri, I have a secret of my own and you must promise not to tell either. What you call 'Code of the Road'. No? After all, I was myself partly to blame. I never should have left you."

"No, Claudette, we were foolish. We'll never tell. Where did you go?"

"I had promised Monica I would go to the Headliner Club with her. After she went to the trouble to get the tickets for you, I could hardly refuse. Besides, she had some insider information."

She handed a newspaper to Theresa. "We met some interesting people."

Theresa looked at the headline with a picture of the Beatles. *Beatles enjoyed the New York Headliner's Club after the Carnegie Hall Concert.*

"Oh my God, did you get to see them?"

"Look at who's in the picture, sitting next to Ringo."

"No way," said Theresa. She handed the paper to Mary Margaret. "Show it to Pauline."

"How, in the world? I am so jealous," Theresa said, sitting back in the chair.

"I do have a surprise for you girls," Claudette said. She reached into her pocketbook. "One for you, Poochie, one for you, Pauline, and one for you, Mon Cheri."

The girls looked to see their names signed by each of the Beatles on a cocktail napkin.

"Claudette, merci, merci merci," said Theresa. She jumped up and gave her a hug practically spilling her cup of coffee. "This is the best thing ever." She kissed her prize.

"Boy, I sure do wish Bunny was around so we could gloat," Mary Margaret said.

Seventeen

March 1964 St. Patrick's Day, Savannah

"Come on, y'all, it's getting late. Charlie's going to be hollering for us any minute," said Mary Margaret. She was rummaging through her dresser drawer looking for her green sweaters. "Here, Marnie, I have an extra one."

Mary Margaret's room was a mess with clothing strewn all over the place, mattresses for sleeping on the floor, and makeup lining the dresser and vanity.

"Pucci, you think we'll get into trouble at Mass wearing a green sweater under our uniform blazers?"

"Just keep your jacket buttoned up. We can't go to the parade and not wear green."

"I wish we didn't have to go to 8:30 Mass," said Pauline. "Catherine's gonna be in the parade again this year. Her family has been doing it forever. They call themselves, Riley's Raiders. I'll bet Catherine is mortified."

"Marnie, can you put the water balloons in your tote bag? We only have four, one for each of us. I'll throw mine at Tommy, Pucci you get Ted and you two, whoever you want," said Theresa. "I can't wait to see their faces."

"Y'all, I have a scathingly brilliant idea," said Mary Margaret.

The three looked at each other and on cue said, "No way."

"I don't know, Mary Margaret. You and your schemes always somehow get us into trouble."

"Geez, Marnie, now you sound like that one." Mary Margaret pointed to Theresa.

"Okay, what?" Pauline said.

The girls sat on the edge of the bed while Mary Margaret laid out her plan.

"Skip Mass? Are you nuts? There is no way to pull that off. Someone will notice we aren't there," Theresa said. "Why can't you ever do something for once in your life that will get us praise and not put in jail?"

"After Charlie drops us off, we can go into the church and then up to the loft. When Mass starts, we'll leave. No one will notice. You know it's always so crowded with people waiting outside and all. We just need to be sure someone we know sees us, just in case."

"All right y'all, let's go," Charlie yelled from the bottom of the stairs.

Charlie, Essie, and the four girls with the twins and Nan piled into the station wagon. Essie put the foldaway chairs and a cooler in the way back along with the bag of food she had packed for everyone's lunch. Anne hated the parade. She sent Essie to watch the three little ones while she stayed home and prepared snacks for the children's friends who always congregated at the Puccini house after the parade.

"Jesus Christ, look at all these people dressed in green. And that lady over there, her hair is green." Mary Margaret scanned Forsythe Park as they drove down Drayton Street toward downtown.

"Miss Mary Margaret don't be sayin' the Lord's name in vain," Essie said. She was shifting in her seat trying to get comfortable. The children were crushing her.

"It wasn't in vain, Essie. Geez."

Charlie let the girls off, then headed to park the car at Dr. Puccini's office which was just a couple of blocks off of the parade route.

"Meet at Daddy's office the minute the parade is over. We have to get home and help Mama get ready for our friends to come over later," he called out to the girls as they raced up the steps to the cathedral. "Mary Margaret, don't do anything stupid."

"We won't, Charlie," Mary Margaret crossed her fingers behind her back.

The steps to the cathedral were swamped. Most of the men were wearing green blazers, hats, and carrying shillelaghs. They were feeling good after their traditional breakfast with bloody Mary's, screwdrivers, and a big bowl of green grits laced with grain alcohol, then lit.

"I'm not so sure about this, Pucci," said Theresa. Mary Margaret was elbowing her way through the crowd and getting everyone's attention by yelling.

"Just go with the flow, for God's sake. Sister Hope, Sister Fatima, Happy Saint Patrick's Day." She stood on her toes and waved to make sure the Sisters saw her as they entered the church. Several minutes after Mass started, Mary Margaret nudged the others. They got up and left the choir loft, one by one.

They ran through the square where people were claiming space and setting up their picnics. One family even had a portable grill. When they were a safe distance from the church, they stopped to catch their breath.

"That was good but it's only 8:45," said Mary Margaret, looking at her watch. "What are we going to do until the parade starts?"

"I have an idea," said Theresa. Pauline and Marnie looked her up and down and squinted their eyes.

"Don't look at me like that. I can have an idea sometimes. Why don't we go over to the Desoto? We can wait there on the side porch. The owner knows Granddaddy. I don't think they'll mind."

The girls headed down Harris Street toward the hotel. As they passed Pinkie Masters' Lounge, Mary Margaret slowed down. "Let's look in here, y'all. I've always wondered what it's like inside."

The bar was noisy and smelled of stale cigarette smoke and soured beer. Through the smoke-filled room and sea of green-clad revelers, they spotted a familiar figure sitting on one of the bar stools. His eyes met Mary Margaret's. "Oh, my God. It's Charlie with his college roommates, he just saw us."

"Let's go over there," said Pauline.

"Those Georgetown boys are really cute," said Marnie.

"Let's get out of here. They're coming over to our house after the parade. You can flirt with them then."

They crossed Drayton Street carefully making their way through the crowd. Some were pulling little wagons, but most were carrying folding aluminum chairs with green and white webbed vinyl strips.

"Pucci, do you think he will tell on us?" Theresa was out of breath.

"He better not, I'll tell on him and Anne will kill him."

The girls made it to the hotel and sat on the rockers watching the people go by.

"Hey, y'all, look over there at the Knights of Columbus Hall," Theresa said. "It looks like those men are putting cans of beer in big metal buckets. They're getting geared up for when the parade gets here."

"I've heard they have great parties. We could watch the parade from there," said Marnie.

"Anne says that they're not our kind of people," said Mary Margaret. She sat up in her chair and looked across. She squinted to see better.

"My family goes there," said Marnie. She looked like she'd been punched in the face.

"You know, Mary Margaret, your mother is snooty. My parents always go there," said Pauline, standing up.

"I'm sorry, girls, Anne does have some high falutin ideas sometimes. Let's go over there and see for ourselves. Nobody's watching that beer right now."

"Don't even think about it, Pucci. There's no way. Besides, we don't even like beer."

"How do you know? You've never tried it. Come with me, Pauline. I'll bring my tote."

Mary Margaret and Pauline went across to the back stairs of the Hall. While Pauline watched the door, Mary Margaret grabbed some beer from the ice bucket. They ran back to the hotel porch.

"Tada!" Mary Margaret produced four cans. "Hey, I hear the bands. Let's go. We'll save these for later."

"I think we should go back to Abercorn near the bleachers."

"Maybe we can sneak up there, climb up the back, or something. It's definitely the best place," said Mary Margaret.

"You're kidding. We couldn't throw the water balloons from up there with all those priests and the bishop and other important people. The police guard it like Fort Knox. Pucci, sometimes I think you just want to get caught."

The area was swarming with people. The girls moved away from the crowd and positioned themselves further north. The Grand Marshal led the parade with his entourage, followed by Saint Thomas' band then their cadets in full uniform. A flock of girls ran into the street calling out to the boys, throwing green streamers, flowers, and chocolate kisses. They were unable to get the attention of the well-drilled cadets. They stayed in step and looked straight ahead. In the mix of people, Pauline got knocked down and broke her balloon. When the cadre came close to the girls, Marnie dropped hers, splashing water on her feet. Mary Margaret was too far away to reach Ted.

"Tommy," yelled Theresa and threw with all her might. The green balloon splattered against Tommy's back. He missed a step and like dominos the guys behind him went down, causing a pile-up.

"Let's get out of here," said Theresa. "Oh, God, Tommy is going to kill me."

They snuck into the parking lot of a lawyer's office when the security guard stepped away to get a closer look at some scantily clothed majorettes. Beside the big tent, a platform in front of a brick wall overlooked the parade route. No one appeared to notice them. They watched as the floats and cars of the Irish families continued past. Sitting on the top of the back seat of a red Cadillac convertible were Catherine and her mother all dressed up in long sparkly green gowns. Catherine's hair was pulled back in a French twist, her mother's in a beehive. They smiled and waved, arms at ninety degrees and hands oscillating from the wrist.

On a float behind, all the Riley children wore camouflage outfits. A banner across the back read Riley's Raiders. The four girls stood with their mouths hanging open.

"Would you look at that? What the hell?" Mary Margaret said. "Isn't Mrs. Riley the picture of innocence? Mrs. America next to Miss America."

"Yeah, she's so glamorous," said Marnie.

Theresa and Mary Margaret nudged each other.

"Hey, Pucci, there's Charlie. I think he's three sheets to the wind." Theresa pointed across the street. She and Mary Margaret started laughing. "We better go get him. Oh, Lord, I think he's throwing up."

"Ugh, I just remembered Marnie and I are supposed to go by the Knights of Columbus and check in with our parents," said Pauline.

"Yeah, we'll see y'all later. Wonder where Charlie's college friends are?" Marnie said, looking across the street at Charlie leaning against the fence. She waved and took Pauline's arm.

Mary Margaret and Theresa headed across the street dodging the marchers to help Charlie, who stood looking dazed, vomit on his pant legs. Theresa and Mary Margaret held him up and pushed their way through the parade again.

"Come on, Charlie, you've gotta help us. How'd you get so drunk? Let's get to Daddy's office and get you cleaned up before somebody sees you."

Through the crowds and Forsyth Park, the girls managed to get to the office dragging Charlie along the way. They struggled to pull him up the office stairs. Theresa lost her footing and fell into a puddle of his vomit. Before they reached the top, they saw Essie standing in the doorway with her hands on her hips. That startled Mary Margaret and she dropped her tote bag. The cans of beer went rolling down the steps.

"Those your beers, Miss Mary Margaret?" Essie said. She blocked the door pushing the children back inside.

In all the commotion, no one realized Tommy and Ted were watching the whole scene from the bottom of the stairs. The four cans stopped at their feet.

"Mary Margaret. What's going on? I thought we were going to your house for a party."

"Jeez, my leg is bleeding. I must have cut it when I slipped trying to catch the beer. Will this nightmare ever end? God, Ted, I'm so glad you're here. They're Charlie's, not mine," Mary Margaret said, looking up at Essie. "I was just carrying them for him."

Charlie was sitting on the top step, his head in his hands. The twins were trying to peek around Essie's enormous frame and Nan was inside wailing at the top of her lungs.

"Ted, you and Tommy take him somewhere and get him sobered up," said Mary Margaret pointing back to Charlie. "I'll drive the children and Essie home."

"I guess Charlie and I aren't going out tonight with you and Ted," said Theresa watching the guys load Charlie into the car.

Spring Break

Mary Margaret went to stay at Theresa's for spring break while her parents and the younger children were in New Orleans visiting Joan.

"Too bad we're not double-dating tonight. Charlie has this orientation thing for his summer job. We may go out later."

"Ted's picking me up here. He has something important to tell me."

As usual, Ted was late. He grumbled about having to drive all the way out to Isle of Hope to pick Mary Margaret up. He turned east on Victory Drive.

"Where are you going?" Mary Margaret asked. "We're going to be late for the movie!"

"I have a surprise for you. I got accepted into The University of Pennsylvania. We're going to celebrate."

"That's wonderful. Your dad's always wanted you to go there. You can get a business degree and run the family business," she said, rolling down the window, smelling the warm damp stink of the marsh. "Are we going to the beach?"

"You'll see. I want this night to be special," Ted said, as he reached into the back seat of his car and handed her a bag with a bottle of bourbon and some club soda.

"Jesus, Ted, where did you get this? I've only had bourbon once. Ugh! That was an awful time. Are we heading to the cottage? Remember what happened the last time we were there? Luckily, Charlie answered the phone when the neighbor called to say someone was in the beach house. He covered for me."

"Don't worry, I'll park down the street, and we can go in through the side door."

Inside, the cottage was musty. Shells the children had collected last summer lined the windowsills. It was quiet and Mary Margaret half expected one of her siblings to come through the door and beg her to play cards. She opened the windows and doors, being careful to keep the lights dim.

Ted poured them each a drink. She didn't like the taste and scrunched up her face.

"Here, try it with Coke, I found some in the ice box. You might like it better," he said, taking her glass and handing her a new one.

"Yeah, that tastes good," she said, drinking it a bit too fast. "Fix us another one, and let's go out on the porch. It's warm tonight, and the air is so fresh."

After two drinks, Mary Margaret began to feel woozy and warm inside. It was a beautiful night. The full moon cast a reflection across the water. She was content, sitting on the porch swing in Ted's arms, listening to the ebb and flow of the ocean.

"Oh, I like the way I feel," she said, with a smile. "Fix me another one." Her empty stomach growled. The drinks went straight to her head.

"Sure." Ted wobbled a little when he got up and headed to the kitchen.

He handed Mary Margaret her drink then settled down beside her on the swing, putting his arm around her shoulder.

"You're shivering. Let's go inside and sit on one of the sofas. This swing is making me dizzy," he said.

"Ahh…need to lie down." Mary Margaret's words were slurred.

The last thing she remembered was holding onto the dresser and hoping that the bedroom would quit spinning. From a deep doze, she felt Ted's hand under her blouse and wondered how she got onto the bed. She turned away only wanting to sleep. He unfastened her bra and turned her toward him. With his arms around her, he kissed her and touched her in places she had never let him. Her whole body tingled. It was like a warm pleasant dream. He pulled down her panties and got on top of her. Part of her didn't want him to stop but the dream faded. She realized where it was going.

"No, Ted, we can't. It's not right, and I don't want to do this. Stop, please stop," she said, fully awake now. She tried to wriggle free.

It was too late. There was a feeling of something tearing into her, a horrible pain, and she cried out. Ted ignored her cries and continued to move in and out of her until he was finished and rolled off.

All she could do was to lie there and wait until the pain went away. *Please, God, tell me this didn't happen.* She began to pray under her breath, "Hail Mary, full of grace." She turned on her side into the fetal position and whimpered. Ted put his arm on her shoulder. She shrugged it away.

"Hey, look, I. I didn't mean to. It was just that, God I don't know, I just couldn't stop."

"Take me to Mac's," she said, pulling on her panties. Ted went into the kitchen to gather his things. She noticed blood on the sheets as she was changing them. A lump grew in her throat, and she felt she couldn't breathe. The feeling passed, but she knew what was done could not be erased. She dialed Theresa's private number, told her something bad had happened, and asked her to please wait up. On the way there, Ted pulled over to a public trash can where he stuffed the sheets into the dumpster.

"It was that alcohol. I had too much to drink. Please don't be mad at me," Ted said, breaking the stony silence in the car.

Theresa was waiting on the porch. Mary Margaret jumped out before the car completely stopped. She slammed the car door and ran down the walkway and up the steps. Ted put the car into park, and followed, calling her name.

She turned and screamed, "Can't you see what you've done to me. I'm ruined. Leave me alone."

Theresa held Mary Margaret's head while she threw up. Afterward, she snuck downstairs and fixed her a sandwich. They talked through the night. Mary Margaret told her the whole story.

"I'll never drink again. I really didn't mean for it to happen. In a weird way, I think he felt bad, too. You know boys get to a certain point and there's no turning back."

"I know, I keep holding Charlie at bay, but it's so hard."

They both giggled a little bit at her choice of words, but neither was in a mood for humor.

"Pucci, we've had so many conversations about what it would be like, but it sounds dreadful."

"The sad part is, I'm not a virgin anymore." She looked around Theresa's room with its bulletin board of high school mementos, Beatle posters, and I love Charlie signs drawn in red magic marker with a heart for the word love. The innocence of the room confounded her feelings. "I keep hearing Sister Hope's lectures about how important it is to save yourself for your husband. How many times did she say it doesn't matter if you do it once or a hundred times, you can't replace your God-given purity."

"I'm so glad you asked me to go to New Orleans with you after school is out. Maybe it'll take your mind off of all this, Pucci."

"You're right, Mac. I need to get away from Ted. We'll explore the French Quarter and eat beignets at the Cafe du Monde. You could bring your paints."

Mary Margaret refused to take Ted's calls. She started going out with her friends again. Theresa was relieved when Mary Margaret organized an egging of the convent before school was out. Her Pucci was back!

Eighteen

Two weeks before the end of school, Mary Margaret was pinning paper flowers to the bulletin board at school. The pinks, purples, and greens swirled together. A wave of nausea overwhelmed her. Acid burned her throat. She barely made it to the garden. In the grotto, the statue of the Virgin Mary looked down on her. A branch of pink azalea blooms had been placed at the Virgin's feet. The bush next to her knee was now covered with vomit. She sat back, away from the offensive bush.

"Mary Margaret," said Sister Fatima, sitting next to her on the grass, arranging the black skirt of her habit. "Are you all right?" She took a handkerchief from her pocket and handed it to her.

"It's awful, Sister, it's just awful. I think I might be pregnant. I haven't had a period in at least six weeks and I'm sick a lot."

"Have you been with someone? I mean…"

A deep sob shuddered her body. She loved and trusted Sister Fatima and spilled the whole story about what happened that night with Ted.

Sister rocked her in her arms and moved the hair that was hanging in Mary Margaret's eye. "I promise everything will be all right. You know, you'll have to tell your mother."

"I can't. She'll kill me. Oh God, how could this be? My life is over and I've never felt so all alone." She wiped her tears on the handkerchief soiled with snot and vomit. The breeze brought the scent of jonquils and caused her to gag, but she overcame the nauseous feeling and listened to Sister Fatima's calming voice.

"No, it's not over, and she won't kill you," she said. "Your mother loves you and will be there for you. Go talk to her and tell her what you told me. You're not alone."

"I can't. She'll tell Daddy and it'll break his heart," Mary Margaret cried out. Sister took both of her hands and looked into her eyes, "You know, everything happens for a reason. We don't understand it at the time, but there will be a day that it will all make sense, and something good will come from it."

"You don't understand, Sister. How could you? My life is over."

"No, I promise it's not. You know, I do understand. Mary Margaret, the same thing happened to someone very close to me when she was your age."

She looked up at Sister. "What happened to her?"

"In Ireland, the oldest daughter was expected to become a nun and the oldest son a priest. She met a young man, Patrick Ryan, at a church picnic. They were immediately attracted to each other. They had so much in common. He was the most beautiful man she had ever seen," she said, with a smile. "He had thick blond hair and blue eyes. They would secretly meet at a secluded lake. Both being the oldest in their families, they knew what was expected of them. One night, she was awakened by a knock on her bedroom window. It was Patrick. When he told his parents that he was in love with someone and did not want to be a priest, they forbade him to ever see, or talk to her again. She snuck out and they ran to their spot at the lake, and it happened. They made love." Sister paused and wrapped her arms around her body. She looked away. "He carved their names on their favorite tree, Patrick and Grace. It wasn't long before she realized she was with child."

Mary Margaret noticed Sister looking sad and put her arm around her shoulder. "She must have been someone special to you Sister. What happened to her?"

"She was sent to a home for unwed mothers in the States. It was a workhouse. They put her in the kitchen where she stood for hours chopping onions, and then washing dishes. After that, she scrubbed the bathroom floors. When her baby girl was born, they took her away." Sister began to cry.

Humm, why are you so upset? The tears, the pain in your eyes, and your quivering voice. There must have been more to this story than that. Is it you? Is she your child?

"So, what happened to your little girl?"

"She was..." Sister stopped mid-sentence. She just looked at Mary Margaret and realized she must have figured it out. They embraced.

"Don't worry, Sister, your secret is safe with me."

Sister continued. "I was never allowed to see her. She was adopted right away. I wanted to go back to Ireland, but I didn't have any money and my parents wouldn't have anything to do with me. Afterward, I decided to become a Mercy nun and went to a convent in Baltimore, and here I am."

"How did you happen to come to Savannah?"

"My family was from Wexford County. Many of my ancestors came here in the 1850s because of the potato famine. A distant cousin Bridget Flarety, a retired nun here, told my parents about the home. She was quite elderly and died shortly before the baby was born."

"Sister, I am so sorry. What about Patrick? Did he become a priest?"

"I haven't seen him since. For a while, my sister wrote to me with news. I never told anyone who the father was. Not even him. Maybe he figured it out when I disappeared. I'm sure they all did. I feel certain he pursued his vocation." She stood and helped Mary Margaret up.

"I hope my baby has a good life and is very happy, but not a day goes by that I don't think about Colleen. That's what I called her."

"Sister, I'm so sad for you. Weren't you mad at God?"

"Heavens no, Mary Margaret. It made me closer to Him. It was my calling. Now, I'm here at St. Bernadette's to help you get through this." She leaned toward Mary Margaret with a smile. "Ever since Camp Villa Veronica, I've had this special place in my heart for you."

Grace, your name is Grace, what a beautiful name.

With a heavy heart, Sister watched Mary Margaret walking slowly toward the school. She was about the same age as her daughter. She hoped someone was there for Colleen. She remembered herself so alone on that ship. The journey was long and arduous, her future so uncertain, but that was all behind her now. Her life was here. She went into the chapel and found strength in her prayers.

Essie came in the back door with a broom and dustpan, grumbling under her breath. She found Mary Margaret in the kitchen rummaging through the pantry. "What you lookin' for, Missy?"

"Do we have any Saltines?" Mary Margaret said, turning to face Essie, suppressing a gag. She reached beyond the girl and handed her the tin of crackers. Mary Margaret stuffed two inside her mouth. The dryness masked her nausea.

"Miss Mary Margaret," said Essie. "You don't look so good. Come here girl, tell your Essie what's wrong," her eyes scanned Mary Margaret. "I see you throwing up a lot. You pregnant, ain't you? You got yourself in a family way."

"Oh Essie, how'd you know?"

"Honey, I done seen a lot of pregnant women. I know what to look for. Have you told your mama?"

"No, how can I?"

"Just tell her the truth." Essie took Mary Margaret in her arms. "It gone be all right."

Mary Margaret sobbed uncontrollably. Essie patted her back and then held her away so she could look into her face.

"You know you ain't the onliest one this ever happen to."

"It feels that way. I just don't know how I can face anyone. My parents will kill me."

"I was just fourteen years old when it happened to me. I thought my daddy gone kill me. I wouldn't tell him who the daddy was. I just couldn't. It was his boss man who took advantage of me. Daddy would have killed that man. Then where would he be? They would had hung my daddy. I was so relieved when my son came out dark. My grandmother took care of the baby so I could go to school, and my mama could keep on working. I love my son more than anything in this world. You'll see. That baby gonna be a blessing."

"Was that baby Arthur? The one who picks you up every day in that Cadillac and sometimes even brings you lunch?"

"Yep, That's him. He's a good boy. Never given me a piece of trouble. I don't know what I'd do without him. He's helped me raise my other young uns. Makes them do their homework and be serious about their schoolwork."

"Oh Essie, I'm so sorry you went through that."

"What I'm saying, Missy, is sometimes the things that seem the worst turn out good."

"Mary Margaret, are you up?" Anne asked, opening the bedroom door. Mary Margaret sat up and tried to wipe the smeared mascara from under her eyes, hoping her mother wouldn't see that she had been crying. It was

Saturday. The bright light coming in through the blinds indicated that it was late in the morning. She had been up several times, sick.

"Hey, Mama," she said. Through the open door, she could see her sister looking in. Joan was in town to take Theresa and Mary Margaret back to New Orleans later that week.

Anne sat on the edge of Mary Margaret's bed and put a hand on her forehead. "You don't feel hot, Nan said you'd been throwing up."

"There's a bug going around school. I must have gotten it."

"Look, I wasn't born yesterday. I've been pregnant seven times, and I know the signs," Anne said. She moved closer to her daughter and took her hand. Her expression hardened. "You've been sick for weeks. Something is going on with you. Is there any chance you could be pregnant?"

Mary Margaret sat up. She shielded her eyes against the light. "You mean eight?"

"Eight?"

"Eight what?"

"Times pregnant."

Anne drew in a breath. "Of course, that's what I meant. I know you haven't been seeing Ted lately. Did something happen?"

"Mama, we were just messing around. I couldn't stop him. I didn't want him to go that far. Could I be? It was only one time."

"It only takes one time. I think you might be. I'll call Dr. Houston and see if you can get in to see him right away."

"Mama, please don't tell Daddy, I don't want him to know," she cried.

"He'll find out, anyway. It's better to tell him now."

Mary Margaret felt sick. "What will I do if I am? What about my trip to New Orleans and college?"

"Well, you won't be doing either of those things. Have you told Ted?"

"No, please don't tell him," Mary Margaret begged, "I don't want him to know."

"He has to know. You two will have to get married, and soon. Now get dressed, and I'll call John Gray."

The antiseptic smell of Dr. Houston's office lingered in Mary Margaret's nose as Anne drove home. They both were silent. The positive urine test hung between them like a dead weight. Her examination confirmed that she was about eight weeks along. Mary Margaret looked out of the car window noticing the children playing in Forsyth Park. *Oh God, I'm going to be a mother. I can't be, I don't want to be.*

"What's going on?" Jeanne said as Mary Margaret walked up the front steps with Anne. "Everybody's acting weird. When I asked Daddy, he got a sad look and left. Joan won't tell me anything, either."

As she passed, Mary Margaret looked at her, tears in her eyes. "I'm pregnant."

"Jesus Christ, God Almighty. What the hell? You're not even married," Jeanne exclaimed. Anne glared at her and told her to get inside.

"You need to call Ted," Anne said, handing Mary Margaret the hall telephone.

In the kitchen, she poured a cup of coffee from the percolator, "Essie, I think I need something stronger." She walked to the sink and dumped out the coffee. "Please get me the scotch."

"Miss Anne, you don't never drink in the daytime."

"I think I will today."

"Miss Anne, it gone work out. Every child is a blessing."

She carried her drink up the stairs and went to her room. A family photo from Christmas on the bedside table drew her attention.

It will never be like that again. Why is that child always making trouble? This time, I believe she's telling the truth about what happened. The consequences are going to be life-shattering. Only seventeen, so much ahead of her. Adoption is out of the question. I was adopted, abandoned really. I don't want that for my grandchild. Abortion? Not even an option.

Mary Margaret was waiting out front when Ted pulled up.

"Ted, you're a mess and smell," she said, jumping in his car.

"Tommy and I were shooting baskets when Mrs. Olsen came out and told me you needed to see me right away. What's up? You look like someone just died."

"We need to talk."

He drove to Daffin Park. As he pulled through the street that divided the park in half, he chose to stop in front of the metal swings reserved for toddlers.

Behind them, through the oak and magnolia trees, they heard the chirping sounds of children playing ball. He had never seen Mary Margaret like this.

"So, what's going on?" Ted listened intently.

"I'm pregnant," said Mary Margaret, looking away from him out of the window. Her hands balled into fists and rested in her lap.

"Pregnant? Jesus, how did that happen?"

Mary Margaret glared at Ted. "Because we did it, that's how."

"What are you going to do?"

"Me? How about what are *we* going to do?" She snapped, fumbling in her purse, and pulling out a cigarette. "My parents want us to get married."

Ted's face turned pale. His eyes widened with panic. "You know I hate you smoking in my car," he said, snatching the unlit Kent from her hand. He rolled down the window and threw it out. He looked out at the park, and she thought for a moment he was going to open the door and run. Instead, he put his face in his hands.

"Married, I can't get married," he exclaimed. "I'm going to Philadelphia for my internship in a few weeks. I have college in the fall. I can't. I just can't."

"How do you think I feel? I have my trip and college. I want to be an architect, not a mother. We don't have any choice. My parents won't consider any other option."

There was total silence until Ted dropped Mary Margaret off at her house.

"I'll talk to my parents. I'm so sorry. I'm sorry for everything," he said. Deep down he hoped that his parents would see the insanity of their getting married and offer a solution.

Ted was surprised to see the Puccini's car in his driveway. He didn't turn in, but drove around awhile, thinking. He reached deep inside himself, trying to find the man who would do the right thing. Do I really love Mary Margaret? The song, *I Wish We Were Married* came on the radio. He pulled up in front of his house. The Puccinis were still there. He listened to the words of the song. Rain pelted the windshield as he tried to relate to the lyrics. He and Mary Margaret weren't even going steady. *I can't do this. But I have to. I have to do the right thing. But what about my life? College and the fraternity. It's over. I'd rather be dead. Oh, God please give me the strength.*

Ted was startled when his father pounded on the window, "Come in the house at once." Mr. Grant was very strict and by the look on his face, Ted knew his parents had no other option for him.

At the Willingham's, Mary Margaret was greeted by Delia. She wrapped her arms around her. "You sure is gettin' all grown-up, Miss Mary Margaret," she said. "Miss Theresa is upstairs waitin' on you. She's packing."

"Hey, Mac," Mary Margaret said, as she entered the bedroom. Theresa held up a sundress. "Should I take this?"

Theresa took one look at her. "What's wrong? You look like somebody died," she said. "Did we get caught for egging the school?"

"No, it's nothing like that," she said, putting her head down and walking toward the bed. "Will you be my Maid of Honor?"

"Pucci, you have a weird sense of humor."

Mary Margaret sat down on Theresa's bed and picked up one of her stuffed animals. She pulled the bear to her face and began to wail.

"You're not kidding, are you? God, so you are pregnant." Mary Margaret looked up and nodded. "I knew you were worried. I guess neither one of us wanted to believe it. That explains why you've been sick so much lately. Oh, Pucci, I'm so sorry. Do you have to get married? You're too young."

"There's no other way."

"When's the wedding?"

"Two weeks, two weeks from today. Looks like we won't be going to New Orleans after all. No college, no nothing. Jesus, Mac, can you believe this?"

"Pucci, Pucci, I know you didn't want this. All those schemes when you didn't get caught. Now when you didn't even mean to do it, you get caught. Life's just not fair. I'll be here for you no matter what, and of course, I'll be your Maid of Honor."

When the door closed behind Mary Margaret, Theresa felt something inside her close, too. What they had been to each other would never be the same. Deep within, she found the place she kept her sorrow.

Nineteen

The night before the wedding, Mary Margaret was sitting with her parents at the kitchen table. Anne recited all the things that everyone needed to do the next day.

"Mary Margaret, did you hear what I said?"

"Yes, Mama, I heard you. I'll do whatever you say," she said in a hollow voice. She looked pleadingly at Joe.

"Honey, do you really love him? Do you want to get married?" He shook his outstretched palm.

Before she had a chance to answer, Anne chimed in, "Of course, she loves him, otherwise she would not be in this predicament." She swirled the ice cubes around in her glass then held it out for Joe to fix her another drink. "You shouldn't have let yourself get in that situation. You can't tell me you didn't do something to encourage him. Why'd you even go to the beach?"

"Don't you think I'm being punished enough?" Mary Margaret said. She stood and glared at her mother then turned to her father.

"Daddy, are you disappointed in me?" She bit her lip, knowing she could never tell him how she really felt about Ted and getting married. At the end of the day, Anne always won.

He reached over and took his daughter's hand. He shook his head and smiled sadly. "You'll always be my Piccola Stella, no matter what."

Charlie burst through the back door. "That jackass, Ted," he said, before rushing upstairs. "I'm not going to the wedding."

Mary Margaret followed him up the steps. He slammed his bedroom door in her face.

Joe put his arm around his wife. "You know Anne, what happened between Mary Margaret and Ted can't be undone. No good comes from trying to blame. They have to face the consequences and it's not going to be easy. I'm not so sure making her marry him is the right thing." She's just a baby. "Maybe we could...."

"You better not be thinking what I think you're thinking, like sending her to that quack friend of yours. I just won't hear of it." Anne finished her drink and stood, "These children are going to be the death of me yet. And that one," she said pointing to the steps. "The apple doesn't fall very far from the tree."

Joe pushed back his chair and held out his hand to help her up.

"I guess we'd better get some sleep. Tomorrow is going to be a big day." She kissed Joe on the cheek and headed up to bed.

When Mary Margaret heard her parent's bedroom door shut, she tiptoed down the steps. Joe was still sitting at the kitchen table his head in his hands. She could tell from the way his shoulders moved that he was crying. She didn't know what to say so she moved into the living room and sank down on the sofa.

As Joe headed up the stairs he looked over and saw Mary Margaret sitting alone in the dark living room looking like a scared kitten. *What must she be thinking about? I wish I could turn back the clock for her. Too young to be going through this. Too young to be a mother. I've seen this so many times with some patients. It was never a good outcome. I'm so sorry my Piccolo Stella, I'm so sorry I'm not strong enough to fight for you.*

Charlie had hitchhiked home from Washington as soon as he heard about the pregnancy and the wedding. When he got to Highway 17, the traffic was light. No one pulled over to pick him up and he was exhausted. So close to home, he used his last dime to call Tommy from Hardeville. It had already taken him a day and a half to get that far. Tommy agreed to come get him but warned that they would have to go directly to the Grant's for Ted's bachelor party.

Tommy pulled up next to an unshaven young man he almost didn't recognize as Charlie.

"Hop in, Buddy. I've got to tear up the road in order to get to the party on time. Get out your Rosary beads and pray the Fuzz Dicks don't stop us. Ted will be furious if I'm late with the booze. He's going to be so surprised to see you."

"Gosh, man, I'll owe you one. I'm still in a state of shock. I didn't see this one coming."

"Yeah, imagine how Ted feels. His whole life ruined, interrupted. No college. A family to take care of. He'll have to go to work and to night school."

Charlie looked at Tommy, incredulous. Tommy was looking straight ahead, turning the steering wheel slightly back and forth to keep the speeding car steady on the road. Charlie opened his eyes to speak but realized the uselessness of venting his anger on Tommy. He reached over and turned the knob on the radio to try and erase the static and find a station.

"Try 95.1," Tommy said. "We may be close enough now to tune in the big APE. They play the best music. All top hits."

"Yeah, I miss that station," said Charlie, unwrapping a piece of gum and chomping down on it, trying to assuage his anger and not lash out at Tommy in defense of his sister. "You know, this the hell sucks. She's just a kid. That son-of-a-bitch bastard."

"Charlie, it's just one of those things. It's not all Ted's fault. This is going to be as hard on him as Mary Margaret."

Charlie didn't say another word. But his demeanor told Tommy, Charlie was not going to let this rest.

When they got there, Tommy jumped out and grabbed a box from the backseat.

He raced up the steps to the apartment over the Grant's garage. Charlie waited outside a few minutes debating whether to walk home or go in. As he listened to the raucous laughter from inside, bile rose up in his throat. He went home, dropped his rucksack then raced back to the party. He burst through the door, walked over to Ted, and punched him in the face. Ted had one hand outstretched to Charlie, the other wrapped around a can of Bud. He fell on one hip, spilling beer all over himself.

"Charlie, what the fuck? We're going to be brothers. That's a fine welcome to the family," said Ted, wiping the blood from the cut over his eye.

"All I can say, Brother, is that you'd better treat my sister right. Yes, it's too bad about your ruined life plans but you needed to keep your dick in your pants. Too bad you didn't think about all that sooner. What about her interrupted life? She'll be stuck home with a baby. If I hear about you once putting that thing where it doesn't belong. I won't be so kind next time."

An outburst arose from the circle of boys who had gathered around Ted. They parted as Charlie turned to leave. "The show's over, go back to your party," he shouted.

He kicked over a pyramid of empty beer cans next to the door, sending them clattering across the wooden floor.

In an off-white, tea-length dress, Mary Margaret walked down the aisle in a daze. She looked around Sacred Heart Church not believing she was the one getting married. Someone had decorated the altar with white roses. Only best friends and family were there. If she had been dreaming about a wedding, it would have been nothing like this. Ted, waiting at the altar looked handsome in his tuxedo, but his face was twitching. Pancake makeup covered the black eye Charlie gave him the night before.

Dr. Puccini seemed reluctant to let Mary Margaret go. He whispered to her, "Piccola Stella, you are my rock, be strong, and shine like the diamond you are," before handing her off to Ted.

Theresa held Mary Margaret's simple bouquet of sweetheart roses and freesia while she and Ted exchanged the rings that Tommy passed to him. She heard Father James' words but they meant nothing to her. A weak 'I do' slipped from her lips and his 'I do' echoed in her ears. She heard, "I pronounce you man and wife. You may kiss the bride."

The organ signaled the recessional.

Guests made their way to the Parish Hall where they were served punch and finger sandwiches. The newlyweds cut the cake and then retreated in a shower of rice. All the motions of a normal wedding, with none of the joy. Mary Margaret turned around and tossed the bouquet behind her. None of her friends stepped up to catch it before it hit the floor with a thud.

Outside of Savannah, Ted stopped the car at a rest stop and removed the tin cans and old shoes his friends tied to the back of the car. They drove to Saint Simons where they spent three nights in the honeymoon suite at the King and Prince Hotel, a gift from Ted's parents. When the concierge called Mary Margaret Mrs. Grant, she looked around to see if Ted's mother was behind her. When she realized he was addressing her, she felt very grown-up and began to enjoy the attention of the staff. A bottle of champagne and a fruit tray were delivered to their luxurious room where a king-sized bed was fitted with fine linens. Mary Margaret had never felt so pampered. They took a bubble bath together and laughed as they played with the foam. The sting of their situation dissolved like bubbles. The two relaxed and enjoyed each other's company.

Mary Margaret fantasized that the rest of her life would be like this until a wave of nausea returned her to reality.

While they were gone, Anne found a tiny carriage house for them in the Puccini's neighborhood. Ted struggled to carry Mary Margaret up the rickety steps, and then over the threshold. She jumped down and looked around at the motley collection of attic pieces their parents had assembled. The double bed and crowded bedroom were a far cry from the honeymoon suite.

"Mary Margaret, you look like something the cat drug in," Anne said when she saw her standing in the doorway of the Puccini's kitchen, with unkempt hair and a wrinkled shirt over cut-off blue jeans. She was carrying a basket of dirty clothes.

"I'm beat, I finally unpacked all that stuff at the apartment, and I needed a break. I've still got stuff to do. Can I have a Coke?"

Anne looked down at the basket of clothes, "If you think Essie's gonna have time to do your laundry you've got another think coming. You need to get Ted to take you to the laundromat to do your wash."

Mary Margaret grabbed the clothes and ran all the way home. In the driveway was a green 230SL Mercedes convertible.

"Mac, what are you doing in that car?"

"My grandparents gave it to me for my birthday."

"Jesus, I forgot your birthday. I've been so focused on my own situation. Mac, will you ever forgive me? Your grandparents didn't want to give you a party?"

"I didn't want one. It seemed so unimportant after all that's happened. I didn't think you'd feel like coming. I love your vine-covered cottage with this precious garden. The blooming jasmine smells so sweet."

"It makes me nauseated. I have to hold my breath when I walk by."

"Can I help with those clothes?"

"No, thanks. There are a lot of things I have to get used to."

Theresa followed her up the steps trying to think of something positive to say.

"It's kind of hot in here," Mary Margaret said, opening the screen door. She left the laundry on the porch.

"Where did all this stuff come from?" Theresa said looking around.

Mary Margaret stood in the doorway with her hands on her hips, tears streaming down her cheeks. "Pitiful, isn't it?" She said, putting her hand over a worn spot on the back of the sofa. "Everybody's rejects."

"Look, it could be cute," said Theresa, pointing. "Why don't you paint that table? I still owe you a wedding present. You could recover the sofa and that small chair."

"I'd offer you a Coke but we don't have any. How about some water?" Mary Margaret said.

"Sure." Theresa followed her into the kitchen, "It wouldn't hurt to put a coat of paint in here. How about a color to go with your harvest gold refrigerator?"

"I 'spose I could. I've just been so depressed and miserable."

"Let's go to the paint store and then go look at fabric."

"I can't wander far from the bathroom. Besides, when Ted gets home from work, he expects supper on the table before he goes to class at Armstrong."

"Are you cooking?"

"I don't know how to cook. I make him a sandwich or go beg Essie to give me some of what she's cooking. Sometimes I get those TV dinners, but they are disgusting. I think if I see one more little square carrot next to a green pea I'll puke."

"Geez, those dinners are awful. Catherine's mother fixes us those sometimes. I guess you don't see too much of Ted?"

"No, but when he's here he wants to, well you know. I don't want him to touch me. Sometimes he storms out and goes to his parents to watch TV."

"Why don't you go over to the 'chateaux' and pick out a couple of things? Pearly's there on Thursday. It's still on the market. Everything will have to go into storage, anyway. You'll be doing us a favor."

"That wouldn't feel right. I don't think I could do that."

"At least, go get that Aubusson rug that was in the little den. Just consider it a loan; I'll take them back when I get married. Mama would be pleased. She was so fond of you."

"What's with the basket of dirty clothes?"

"Anne said I needed to use the laundromat. Essie's too busy."

"I'll take you, come on. We'll put the clothes in then go get that Coke. I'll have you home before Ted gets back."

Mary Margaret burst into a fit of laughter.

"What's so funny?"

"This green Mercedes at the laundromat."

The rug made a huge difference and Mary Margaret, with help from Theresa, transformed the cottage.

"It looks so cozy," said Theresa, feeling a pang of jealousy.

"I'm really excited how it all turned out. Ted likes it too. I've even decided to take up cooking. I took your advice and got a couple of your mother's pots. Pearly made sure I didn't get her favorites. She insisted I take some of the cookbooks."

"Spaghetti," mumbled Mary Margaret to herself. "That looks easy. Ted'll love that."

She copied the ingredients on a pad and walked down to the A & P. She came home: chopped and chopped, browned the meat, ran to the bathroom, came back, added the onions and garlic, the tomatoes, and threw up again. She came back, drank a Coke, and stirred the pot. It was beginning to smell good. The red sauce was thick and bubbly.

"Boy, that smells great," said Ted, throwing his briefcase on the sofa. "Are you cooking spaghetti? I'll be right back."

"Ted," she said, but he had already slammed the screen door behind him and was clomping down the wooden steps. In a few minutes, he returned carrying a bottle of wine, the bottom was covered with straw. They sat down; plates heaped and drank a toast with the wine. The dryness puckered their mouths.

Ted took a huge forkful, spitting it out immediately.

"Ted," she said, taking a bite. She spit hers out as well, the red sauce splattered all over her white blouse. "Jesus, what did I do wrong?"

"I don't know, but I think you're trying to poison me," he said, taking another fork full and flinging it at her before storming out. He got halfway down then ran back up and grabbed the bottle of wine. "You can't do anything right."

Mary Margaret picked up the pot and ran three doors down to her parents.

"Mary Margaret, are you hurt?" Anne screamed, looking at her red-spattered top.

"No, it's spaghetti sauce. What's wrong, Mama? I worked all day and it tastes awful."

Anne took a little bite and spit it into the sink. "It is awful. Tell me what you did," said Anne, scraping the sauce into the garbage disposal.

She went over the recipe, step by step. "It took me forever to peel all that garlic. It called for the whole clove."

"You didn't put in the whole head, did you? A clove is just one little section of the pod," she said, picking up a garlic bud and peeling off a clove.

"Mama, I'm just not very good at this wife business. I was really trying." She started up the stairs.

"Mary Margaret, where are you going? You don't live here anymore. You need to go home to Ted."

"Oh, I guess you're right." She picked up her pot and left. Walking down the street, she looked back at her parent's home and realized she didn't belong there anymore. She began to run as fast as she could to get home to commiserate with her Maddie doll.

Twenty

"Ooh, Theresa, how charming," said Claudette, crossing the courtyard. "I am so excited to see your friend, Poochie again."

Mary Margaret waved from the door. At the top of the stairs, Claudette gave her a big hug, "Theresa did not tell me you had gotten so pretty," she said, holding Mary Margaret away, then kissing her on each cheek. Mary Margaret's skin glowed, and her cheeks and figure had filled out with her pregnancy.

A shadow of jealousy crossed over Mary Margaret as the two cousins laughed and smiled at each other, displaying a filial bond. They spoke rapidly in French.

"Pucci, I'm sorry, that was rude."

"Forgive us, mon Cheri, I am making Theresa speak to me only in French. She is working on it very hard."

"Thanks for coming by before you leave for Santa Fe," said Mary Margaret, turning to Claudette, "I loved being with you in New York. Mac's promised to bring me to Paris to visit you one day. Come in, I'll give you the tour. It's so tiny it'll only take a second."

It felt hotter inside the apartment than in the stifling courtyard. On the newly recovered sofa and chair, clothes hid the smart Bargello pattern which complemented the colors in the rug. The table in the corner was littered with a half-eaten sandwich, and sheets of paper, next to an old Remington typewriter.

"I'm taking a class," said Mary Margaret, holding up a practice sheet. "Ted wants me to type his term papers. Between my terrible typing and this old machine's missing r and t, he'll probably get an F. Jesus, next thing you know he'll have me working as a secretary."

In the bedroom, the windows were treated with a cerulean and gold paisley swag over sheer curtains. Theresa felt a twang when she recognized the gold sateen quilt from her mother's bed.

"Look, there is little Madeline. I remember when Theresa bought one of the Madeline books from a bookseller on the Seine. She told me that the character was just like her friend. We went to a little shop where the owner made Madeline dolls with all the finest materials."

"She's my best friend, I mean next to Mac. She understands me. I can talk to her when Mac is busy. She listens to all my troubles," said Mary Margaret. "I call her Maddie." She picked up the doll and gave her a hug.

"Remember, Pucci, when I brought her to you from my first trip to Paris? You said, 'A doll, you brought me a doll? From Paris?' But then you read the book and came to like her."

"I'm sorry, Mac, I guess you knew me better than I knew myself." The two girls hugged.

"Pucci, I'm so glad that you're feeling better."

"It's strange, but after I made that horrid spaghetti, my morning sickness disappeared. Maybe I could bottle it and sell it as a cure. I only ate one bite."

Theresa didn't notice the sadness behind Mary Margaret's smile that had been present for some time and left feeling better about her. She and Claudette sped down the highway in the wood-sided wagon singing French songs.

Mary Margaret waved goodbye and watched the station wagon disappear around the corner. She stretched out on the bed and held the doll next to her face.

"I feel so alone now, Maddie. All my friends are gone for the summer; I'm not part of my family anymore. Ted and I are always bickering. We're both so angry about our situation. What am I going to do?"

Postcards from Theresa were piled on the little mahogany chest by the front door of the tiny apartment.

"Why aren't you reading these?" asked Ted, fanning out the cards.

"Oh, I glanced at them. She's just bragging, and that Claudette writes little PS's in French, like I can read them."

Mary Margaret glared and scrunched her mouth.

"Why are you making that face? What's a PS anyway?"

"Jesus, Ted, it means postscript. You know, an add-on. Don't boys ever write letters?"

"Sounds to me like they're having a wonderful time."

"Yeah, and rubbing it in. I'm so pissed off I could scream. They stopped to see Joan in New Orleans. I wanted to be the one to show New Orleans to Mac. Now I can only imagine her excitement at all the charming sights. She would point out things I wouldn't have even noticed." She picked up a postcard and examined the picture.

"Why can't I go down to the beach with my family? You could come on the weekends like Daddy does."

"Mary Margaret, we've been over this a million times. Your place is here. You need to keep going to that typing class so you can type my term papers."

"It's so boring. It's a bunch of stupid women who just want to be secretaries."

"Why don't you go to the beach for the day and see everyone? I'll borrow Mom's car and you can take mine. I know you're lonely, but I need you here. Between working and going to school, I don't have time to take care of myself. After all, you are my wife."

Mary Margaret tried to squeeze her growing torso into one of last year's bathing suits, to no avail. She pulled a loose sundress over her head, grabbed a pair of shorts, and headed for the beach. When she crossed Lazaretto Creek, her stomach lurched, and she knew she couldn't go back to their cottage. She parked at Pauline's house and made her way to the beach. She spotted her friends. Next to the beach towels, a transistor radio blared the Beatles *I Wanna Hold Your Hand.* Pauline was rubbing baby oil and iodine on some guy's back. Mary Margaret didn't recognize him. Catherine was flipping through a magazine. Their skin was perfectly bronzed, and they were both wearing new bikinis. Mary Margaret turned around and crossed the sand dune back to her car. *Is this how it would feel to land on Mars, a total outsider?*

The rest of the summer she spent lying on the bed reading a Photoplay or Movie Star magazine, with a damp towel on her head to cool her down. The sound of the oscillating fan made her sleepy. She dozed, sometimes waking abruptly, shocked to see it was five o'clock and time for Ted to come home.

Mary Margaret picked up the mail that was on the floor by the front door. A postcard from Theresa in Santa Fe described a production of La Boheme. The picture that showed an adobe theater with breathtaking views of the surrounding mountains sent Mary Margaret into a breath-stealing sobbing fit. A fond memory of her daddy sitting on the living room sofa with a cup of coffee, waving his cigarette to the rhythm of Muzetta's Waltz, popped into her head. Another flood of tears made her unable to hear Ted's approach. She was startled when he put his arm around her.

"What is it, Mary Margaret?" He said, taking the postcard. "Looks like Theresa's having a wonderful time."

"That's just it. I'm not. Imagine seeing Anna Moffo in person."

"I know your daddy taught you to love opera, but personally, I don't understand the draw. It seems to me to be a lot of fruits running around in fancy clothes, screeching."

"Ted, you're so uncouth." Mary Margaret went into the bedroom and grabbed her Maddie doll, sat on the bed, and cried.

The next night, Ted quietly opened the door of the cottage and watched Mary Margaret spreading mayonnaise on slices of soft white bread. She peeled the plastic off a piece of cheese and then added a slice of baloney before slapping the bread together and cutting the sandwich in two. Overcome with tenderness, he cleared his throat.

"Ted, hey, what's up with the goofy smile?"

She licked the mayonnaise off of her fingers and took the record album from his extended hand.

"Jesus, Ted. It's La Boheme. How did you know what to get?"

"I took the postcard to the store. There's a new record player too," he said and pointed to a box by the door.

She grabbed him around the neck. He felt her tears on his cheek and gently wiped them off each of their faces. They embraced but were interrupted when Ted realized he had to rush to make it to class on time. She wrapped his sandwiches in wax paper and poured some freshly perked coffee into a thermos bottle, then placed them along with a Moon Pie into a Superman tin lunch box from Ted's grammar school days. "Here, Ted, you can eat this in the car or on your break."

The crisp air smelled like fall. Ted insisted that they go to St. Thomas' opening game. His brother was playing quarterback. It was cool enough for Mary Margaret to cover her belly with a trench coat. She hadn't realized how uncomfortable the backless seat would be for her, or how often she would have to trudge down the bleachers to the filthy bathroom underneath.

On one trip, she ran into Bunny who was all smiles and concern. She stared at the bulge under Mary Margaret's coat and grilled her about what it was like to be married. She asked about Charlie. Mary Margaret sensed she was really just prying, looking for ammunition for her meanness.

When she got back to her seat, Theresa and Pauline were there. They hugged and squealed like the three little pigs after the fox died.

"Did you see Catherine down there behind those pom poms? She made cheerleader this year," said Pauline.

"Can you believe those splits?" Theresa asked.

"Makes me hurt to think about it," said Mary Margaret.

They all laughed. They were trying hard not to look at her stomach, but the idea of her doing a split was funny.

The crowd went wild when St. Thomas scored a touchdown in the last two minutes. "Come on, Mary Margaret. We're going to an after-game party," said Ted.

"No, Ted, can't you see how embarrassed I would be? Why don't you go? I'll get the girls to take me home."

Mary Margaret and Theresa went to the car while Pauline found Catherine. At the Triple-X, they ordered French fries and Cokes, like in the old days. It was easy and Mary Margaret loved being with her friends. She felt like she had been let out of jail. They lost track of time when they went to Theresa's where they played records in her studio and gossiped about school. Theresa took photographs while they struck crazy poses. Mary Margaret allowed herself to forget about the past and savored every moment but eventually, the clock struck twelve and it was time to go back to reality. It was three o'clock in the morning by the time she got home.

Ted wouldn't stop screaming at her. "Where were you until three in the morning? I was worried."

She cowered, defenseless, and for the first time, she felt afraid of him. His enraged face was florid. He raised his hand but stopped just short of her face. *What kind of animal am I married to?* When he slammed the front door, she was afraid that it would come off its hinges. She spent the night curled around her Maddie doll, dozing occasionally, but mostly she was wide awake waiting for the sound of his car. He never came home. Sadly, a part of her wished he never would.

The next day, Mary Margaret expected Ted to come in the door any minute. She had that sick feeling all day trying to figure out what she should do. She knew she had to leave before he got there. In the early evening, she pulled out a suitcase from under the bed and threw in some clothes. In the bathroom, she glanced in the mirror and saw the reflection of a distraught person with swollen bloodshot eyes ringed with dark circles. She ran her fingers through her unkempt hair.

I haven't done anything wrong and don't deserve to be treated that way. He really scared me. I want to get out of this hellhole and go home to my room, my old life, and to my daddy. Everyone's going on with their life. How could anyone understand what I'm going through?

She ran as fast as she could to her parent's house, holding her stomach with one hand and her suitcase in the other.

Anne was sitting at the kitchen table, drinking a cup of coffee. "Mary Margaret, what in the world? It's so late." Anne looked around at the clock. "It's nearly six. Why aren't you at home cooking dinner?"

"I left. I left that place and Ted. I don't want to be with him."

"I don't think you have any choice in the matter."

"Please, Mama, Ted's mean. He got all mad because I stayed out late with Theresa and the girls last night," Mary Margaret cried. She looked down and touched her stomach. "I don't want to be married and I don't want a baby."

"Too late now. You've made your bed and now you'll have to lie in it," screamed Anne. She pounded her fist on the table, spilling the coffee everywhere. She got up to get a dishcloth to clean up the mess.

"But Ted was so angry. I was afraid he would hurt me. He's always yelling at me and he's mean."

"Well, you had no business being out with the girls until all hours of the night."

"But Mama, it's the only fun I've had in months."

"Well, that's just too damn bad. You need to get that bag and prance right back down the street to your apartment."

Joe turned down the stereo. "For Christ's sake, quit yelling and come in here, and let's discuss this in a civilized manner," he called from his study. "Honey, your mother's right. You're married and you need to be with your husband."

"Daddy, please, I don't want to go back. Why won't anyone listen to me? I'm miserable. I don't want to be there. I won't go back, and nobody can make me," Mary Margaret screamed. She balled up her fists and stomped her foot. Her face was crimson, and she was crying so hard she could barely catch her breath. "Don't you even care that he could hurt me?"

"Oh, Jesus. You're so goddamn dramatic. The boys are home, and I've got things to do," Anne said, unfolding her arms and pointing at Joe. "You need to talk to her."

"Mary Margaret, calm down. I know this is hard, but you've got to remember, this is not just about you. You have a baby to consider. You need to go back to Ted and make the best of the situation. Give it time. Things will get better," Joe said, taking her in his arms. "You're strong, Piccolo Stella. Stay here a few days until Ted calms down and you've had time to think."

Joe shut the door when Mary Margaret left, locked it, and lowered the blinds. He turned up the volume on the record player and let the sad aria of Madama Butterfly wash over him, shutting out the clamor of his household. He transferred his heartache to Cho-Cho-San's sorrow.

Each morning at breakfast, Anne hounded Mary Margaret about her responsibility to her marriage. They stuck her in the tiny bedroom off of the kitchen, which had a narrow bed and half-bath. She had to go upstairs to shower. She usually found Jeanne or Nan occupying the bathroom. Jeanne was making a career out of practicing her smile in the medicine cabinet mirror. The twins had turned into brats. One night, she found a frog in her bed, another she'd been short-sheeted. They recited a chorus to, 'Mary Margaret two by four can't get in the bathroom door, so she did it on the floor'.

The Friday typing class she hated gave her relief from the chaos. After one week of being with her family, she felt broken and returned to their cottage. After dragging up the stairs, she stopped at the front door, peered inside, and went in to turn on the lights.

It was a pigsty. *Oh my God. What a mess.* A half-eaten bucket of Kentucky fried chicken and Chinese food containers littered the kitchen counter. She saw ashtrays full of cigarette butts and beer cans on the living room tables. In the bedroom, she saw clothing, dirty towels, and unopened mail scattered everywhere. Next to the overflowing trashcan, balled-up pieces of paper lay. She spotted her Maddie doll and picked her up.

"I'm so sorry I left you here, Maddie."

Mary Margaret sat on the side of the bed and sighed. An unfamiliar shoe box on the side of the bed caught her eye. Pictures of her with Theresa, the girls, Tommy and Charlie spilled out. It made her reminisce. When she picked up the crumpled pieces of paper, each one began a letter to her.

"Dear, Mary Margaret, I am so sorry…Dear Mary Margaret, please forgive me, Dear Mary Margaret, I just don't know how to put into words how sorry I feel…"

"Oh, Maddie, I guess he does love me. Daddy's right. Ted and I are having a baby and I've got to get my act together and make the best of it for the baby's sake."

She cleaned up the mess, cooked dinner, and waited for Ted to come home. Like clockwork, he showed up at 6:00.

Sister Fatima was surprised to see Mary Margaret standing in the doorway of her office. She waited until school was out to go see Sister in hopes of not encountering anyone. Unfortunately, Chorale was getting out and several of the students saw Mary Margaret. They stared at her and whispered to each other. She could sense their disapproval.

"Mary Margaret, come in." Sister got up from her desk and gave her a hug. "To what do I owe the pleasure?" Sister could feel her stiffness and pulled back to look at her. She could sense something was wrong. "Are you okay?"

Mary Margaret brought her hands to her face and sobbed uncontrollably.

"Tell me what's going on?" Sister walked her over to her sofa and they sat.

Mary Margaret told about everything that happened about Ted a few weeks before. When she went back, he bent over backward to try and make things right. She felt bad for hating him and wishing he would just go away. But most of all, she felt guilty because she didn't want the baby.

"I don't know what I should do. I don't like the way I feel, but I can't help it." Mary Margaret looked at Sister searching for an answer.

"I can't tell you what to do. All I can say is what I said to you months ago. Everything happens for a reason. You don't understand it now, but one day you will." She took Mary Margaret's hands into hers. "I can certainly attest to that. It was meant for me to be right here. What happened to you and Ted is unfortunate. But it's God's plan." Sister put her hands on Mary Margaret's stomach. "And something precious is inside of you. Cherish every moment you have with this child now and in the future. Not everyone is so fortunate."

The two talked for a great deal of time. When Mary Margaret left, she felt a sense of calmness.

In the hall at school, Bunny began taunting Theresa with comments about Mary Margaret. Everyone knew she was pregnant, but her showing up at the football game and some students seeing her at school reminded the gossip mongers. Bunny followed Theresa into the locker room. She sat down on the bench while Theresa opened her locker.

"You should have given Pucci the little package I left for you last year. Then maybe she wouldn't be in the predicament she's in. Maybe you used them all yourself," she said with narrowed hate-filled eyes.

Theresa took a step to confront Bunny but thought better of it and turned away. Furious, she hurled her history book into her locker. It veered to the left and hit the locker next to hers bouncing off and hitting Bunny in the head. The sharp corner glanced off Bunny's forehead followed by a stream of blood.

"You hit me, you hit me," she screamed. "I'm bleeding."

Theresa's hand went to her mouth. "It was an accident. I didn't mean to hit you." Other girls crowded around.

"Let me through," shouted Sister Fatima.

Someone brought wet paper towels and pressed them against Bunny's wound. The crowd parted.

"Take Bunny to the infirmary. Come with me, Theresa," said Sister Fatima, leading the crying girl toward her office.

Sister Hope and Sister Fatima tried to calm Theresa. By the time her grandmother got there, several of the witnesses confirmed that it was an accident. Someone heard Bunny admit to having put the condoms in Theresa's locker last year. Theresa fully expected to be expelled but the nuns decided on a short suspension for both girls until things died down.

Theresa picked up Mary Margaret at her typing class one Friday afternoon. When she got into the car, she told her about the book incident and how Bunny was going around showing her black eye.

"It still looks pretty bad especially since she enhanced it with eye shadow," said Theresa.

"Pull over there in the Medical Arts Motel parking area," said Mary Margaret.

"Why?"

"I could have sworn I saw Bunny's Thunderbird over there the last couple of Fridays. Look, it's back there. Pull over, and let's see if she comes out."

At five o'clock, the door opened, and Bunny came out with a man.

"Jesus, who is that?" Mary Margaret asked.

"Oh my God, that's the new basketball coach, Mr. Adams. He's so handsome. I wondered why Bunny joined the basketball team. I hate that. He has a wife and a bunch of children," said Theresa.

"What a creep he must be. This is bad, even for Bunny."

"I have a scathingly brilliant idea." Theresa started the car and drove across the street to a phone booth.

"Hey, that's my line."

"Got a dime?"

Theresa found the number she wanted in the phone book.

"Hi, Mrs. Adams, I'm on the basketball team and I need to ask the coach a question about practice. May I speak to him?" Theresa winked at Mary Margaret. "No, ma'am, we don't have practice on Friday, that's why I thought he would be at home. Thanks so much. Oh, maybe that is his car I see outside the Medical Arts Motel every Friday afternoon."

Theresa hung up the phone and giggled.

"Mac, that was good. That was really good."

"Well, I learned from the pro. Let's just hope it works."

The next Friday, Mary Margaret and Theresa sat in the far corner of the motel parking lot. They watched. Bunny and Mr. Adams came out of the motel room. His wife was there with her five children in the car, waiting. The couple lingered at the door sharing one last kiss. Mrs. Adams sat on the horn and the two jumped apart. Bunny ran to her Thunderbird. Mrs. Adams bolted out of her car, grabbed her husband by the arm, and slapped him across the face.

"I figured you were up to something. Ever since you've been coaching those girls."

He stood there stunned as she retreated to her car and started backing up wildly. She barely missed Theresa's car and another one in the parking area.

"Oh God, I hope she doesn't have a wreck. Maybe Bunny will finally get her just due," said Mary Margaret.

On Monday, Theresa was shocked to see Bunny sitting demurely at her desk in homeroom. They said the morning prayers and the pledge of allegiance to the flag and sat down. Sister Hope came to the door and asked for Bunny. She was told to get her things and bring them with her. A hush fell over the room as all eyes watched Bunny retreat. As soon as she left, the room broke out into a cacophony of voices. Theresa remained quiet. Unless Bunny had told someone, she was the only one in the room who would have known what happened.

By lunchtime, the whole school knew that Coach Adams was fired, and Bunny was expelled. Many were putting two and two together. Catherine and Pauline sat down at the table with Theresa. The food on her tray was untouched.

"Well, it looks like Bunny's finally done herself in," said Catherine. "Members of the basketball team suspected there was something between Bunny and Coach."

"I just wish Mary Margaret was here to enjoy it," Pauline said, taking a bite of Theresa's banana pudding. "You're so quiet and look sort of sad. I thought you'd revel in this."

"I know, I should, but somehow it really doesn't feel so good." Theresa picked up her tray after passing the rest of the dessert to Pauline. "I guess revenge isn't so sweet, after all," she said, walking over to the conveyor belt and placing her tray of uneaten food on it. The noise in the cafeteria was deafening. Theresa went to the infirmary and said she felt sick. All she could think about was the look on Mrs. Adams' face. She went straight to Mary Margaret's and told her what happened at school.

"Bunny will probably be sent off and later no one will even remember it, but what about the Adams and their five children?" Theresa said. "I really don't feel so good about what we did."

"Me either. We were so intent on getting back at Bunny. We didn't think the whole thing through."

"Maybe it's better that someone found out. He's a creep. It's good he got fired. It could have been some other girl he would have been inappropriate with."

Twenty-One

Theresa was sitting in her grandfather's study. College applications cluttered his desk. Mrs. Willingham came in with a cup of coffee.

"I know you're having a hard time deciding," she said, placing a hand on Theresa's back and peering over her shoulder.

"Nana, it's so difficult. Of course, I want to go to Paris and study art, but it's so far from you and Granddaddy."

"I really think you should get a liberal arts education here, then go to the Sorbonne."

"What about Parson's in New York, like Mother."

"They don't offer the kind of broad education I'm talking about. You need that for life. Afterward, you can pursue your art."

"Charlie was telling me about this girl's junior college near Georgetown called Georgetown Visitation. What do you think of it?" She said, handing her grandmother the brochure.

"This looks good. Let me check it out."

"I always thought Mary Margaret and I would be deciding this together. I feel so bad for her, Nana. I hate to leave her alone. I know she has her family but all of us will be graduating and going off somewhere. I just can't imagine."

Savannah, 1965

After the Christmas holidays, the buzz at school was about who was accepted at which college. There was a noticeable lack of drama since Bunny left. Theresa joined Catherine, Pauline, and Marnie at their usual table in the cafeteria.

"I wonder what's going on with Mary Margaret," said Marnie. "I haven't talked to her in a while."

"I'm really worried about her. She still seems depressed about her situation. She hasn't bought the first thing for the baby," said Pauline.

"Her mother has a bassinet for her, but Mary Margaret won't let her bring it over until the baby comes. It will have to be in their bedroom, and the room is so small," said Catherine.

"Why don't we give her a surprise shower? We can do it at my house," said Theresa.

"The baby's due in three weeks so let's do it Saturday. I hope we can get her to come out. Now that she's so big she mostly stays home and eats."

"I never thought I would see her fat. She was always so thin. I'll make her favorite chocolate cake," said Marnie.

Mary Margaret had no idea that the so-called lunch with the Willinghams would be a party for her. She figured Sara would expect her to look respectable so she wore the only dress that fit. She looked in the mirror and shook her head. When she turned to the side, she sighed and slumped her shoulders. "Boy, what a whale. Just what I want to do. Go to lunch."

All the girls, Anne, Mary Margaret's sisters, Sally Grant, and Mrs. Willingham hid quietly in the den waiting for Mary Margaret to come in. Theresa met her at the front door.

"Good Lord, what took you so long? I was beginning to worry. Let's go in the den, Nana is waiting to see you." She took Mary Margaret by the hand.

"Mac, it was so cold and I couldn't find a coat that fit and then the traffic was awful and…"

"Surprise!"

All of the guests ran to greet Mary Margaret. She stopped mid-sentence.

"How in the world did y'all keep this a secret."

The room was filled with pink and blue balloons and streamers. Beautifully wrapped presents lined the fireplace and the dining room was set for a feast. She noticed Pearly, Essie, and Delia standing in the doorway to the kitchen. They were grinning like Chessy cats.

"Oh my God, I can't believe this," Mary Margaret leaned into Theresa and whispered in her ear, "I'm going to f.ing kill you."

Mary Margaret groaned as she hefted her heavy body up the steps to their cottage. She made a beeline for the bed where she picked up her Maddie doll. "My friends are so wonderful. Wait until Ted brings up all the gifts. You won't believe what Mrs. Willingham gave us. She's going to have Pearly come for three months to help us two days a week."

"Where do you want all this stuff?" Ted yelled, from the front door.

"Bring the changing table in here next to where the bassinet will go. Just put all the other stuff on it, and I'll find places for them later. I'm just so tired."

"Why are all the clothes either yellow or white?" He said, fingering one of the tiny garments.

"We don't know if it's a boy or a girl yet, so yellow or white will work for either one."

"Which brings up that we haven't decided on a name yet," he said, picking up the yellow legal pad from the bedside table. "You've listed so many and have only crossed out a few."

"Ted, we don't have to decide right now. We've got two more weeks," she said, lying down on the bed. "Of course, Anne says he or she needs to be named after a saint."

After Ted left for class, Mary Margaret fell asleep and didn't wake up until the middle of the night. Ted was asleep next to her. Her stomach growled. She hadn't eaten supper, still full from the shower. She felt a strong cramp. It hurt in a different way from her usual period cramps. In the bathroom, a rush of water ran down her legs. *Oh no, I didn't make it! My bladder was really full. Oh, another pain. Was that what I think it was? Did my water break? No, it's too soon. I have two more weeks.*

She changed underwear and returned to the bed. Ted was snoring gently. Should she wake him? He looked so peaceful. She tried to get comfortable on her side but another pain grabbed her.

Early dawn light crept through the sheer curtains. She shook Ted. Her hand was trembling. "Ted, wake up. I think it's time."

It took a couple of tries to roust him.

"Time for what?" When he cleared his eyes, he saw her doubled over in pain. "Jesus Christ, the baby? It's too soon." He jumped out of the bed and ran to the phone to call Dr. Puccini.

"Son, calm down. Everything will be fine. Time her contractions and when they are about twenty minutes apart head to St. Josephs. I'll meet you there."

"Your dad said to wait until the pains are twenty minutes apart."

He tied his shoes and stood to zip his pants, "Have you been timing them?" He could tell when she winced and grabbed her stomach that she was having another pain.

"I think we better go now," Mary Margaret said. She wrapped her coat around her pajamas and picked up the overnight she packed weeks before.

"Holy shit. Where's your bag?" Ted tripped all over himself looking for his keys and wallet. He ran out the door, headed down the apartment steps, and jumped into the car.

"Ted, wait, what about me?" Mary Margaret stood at the top of the landing with her bag in her hands.

Dr. Houston took Mary Margaret's hand. It calmed her immediately. Months ago on her first visit, she dreaded him examining her, but he made her feel at ease, even while she shivered naked under the inadequate cover. Now he looked down at her writhing in pain. To him, it seemed like yesterday that she and her friend Theresa had pursued him at Central Pharmacy. They thought he didn't know what they were up to. Another contraction caused her to cry out and ask for her father.

Dr. Puccini looked down at his child gripped with pain and choked back a sob. *She was just a baby having a baby.* He knew the pain would pass but wondered if she would be up to the responsibility of being a mother and wife.

"It's time," said Sister Josetta. "I need to prep her now."

"What are they going to do, Daddy?"

"You're in the best hands with Sister Jo. She'll take great care of you," said Dr. Puccini. He let go of her hand, kissed her on the cheek, and whispered in her ear. "Be strong, my Piccolo Stella."

She never felt so scared and alone in her life. She could hear Ted and her father talking to Dr. Houston in the hall.

"It's time for your enema, and I'll have to shave you," Sister said, lifting the sheet. "Shave me? Down there? I don't need an enema," she said, sitting up and grabbing Sister's arm.

"I'm sorry, dear, but it's what I have to do," she said, gently pushing Mary Margaret back down. When she was ready, Sister wheeled her past the men in the hall to the delivery room. She was waving to them when another contraction split through her almost causing her to fall from the gurney.

Bright light bounced off gleaming white walls as figures in green scrubs and masks bustled around the room. Her legs were in stirrups. Sister put a mask over her nose and the lights went out. She felt a slight sensation like something cut her. A baby hollered and someone said it was a girl. She fell into a peaceful sleep.

Theresa and Anne flipped through well-worn magazines while Ted paced the floor of the waiting room. A pattern worn into the green linoleum tile suggested he wasn't the first expectant father to do this. Theresa went to the vending machine where she managed to get three cups of coffee. Twice she watched the machine malfunction, pouring coffee out with no cup to catch it. By the time she got back to the others, the coffee was cold on top of being tasteless.

Ted stood and looked out the window. His mind was going a thousand miles an hour. *I can't believe it's that time. I'm really going to be a father. What the hell am I going to do? What kind of father could I possibly be? Like Dad? God, forbid. I don't want to be here. I should be at college with my friends. Jesus, Grant, get a grip. There's nothing you can do but make the best of it. You need to pull up your big boy pants and...*

"Ted, Ted, Doctor P is here," Theresa raised her voice to get Ted's attention.

It seemed an eternity before Joe came out of the restricted area removing his green mask. He ran his fingers through his hair exposing the gray at the temples. His eyes looked tired as he wiped his brow.

They all descended on Joe and were shouting questions at him.

He raised his hands to quiet them.

"Mary Margaret's fine and the baby is healthy and weighs six pounds. Mrs. Puccini, you are now a grandmother."

In chorus, they shouted, "What is it?"

"It's a beautiful baby girl. Anne and Ted, you can come to see her now."

Theresa smiled and gave them hugs, but inside she felt left out and alone. She looked out of the window at the cars in the parking lot. The sun was setting, adding a fiery backdrop to an otherwise dreary view. Couples walked two by two. A group of medical personnel gathered, laughing and talking. An ambulance wailed in the background. When a hand touched her shoulder, she jumped.

"Theresa?"

"Dr. Houston, you startled me," she said. Her heart skipped a little. He took her hand.

"You would be proud of your friend. She was very brave and had the most beautiful six-pound baby girl."

I want to finish that dream. Theresa and I were leaving for Paris. Mary Margaret turned over. *Jesus, that hurts. Where am I?* She put her hand on her stomach. *It was flat. Oh, my God. I've had the baby.*

She smelled coffee and looked at the familiar figure standing by the window. "Daddy?"

"Hey, Sweetheart, little mother." He walked over to the bed and helped her sit up. "Your little girl is beautiful. Looks like you, when you were born."

Memories of the day before came flooding back. She tried to get up.

"Hold on, you have to stay in bed."

"But I have to tinkle."

"I'll get the nurse. She'll bring a bedpan," he said, pressing the buzzer next to her bed.

"Oh, dear God, no. I'll be all right," she said struggling to get up. She felt a wet spot on her gown above the waist and put her palm over it.

"No, Mary Margaret, we can't take a chance on infection. You can't get up for a few more days."

A nurse came in carrying a bedpan. She gently removed the hand covering Mary Margaret's breast.

"Now, dear, that's perfectly natural. You're going to leak a little."

"But I don't plan to nurse the baby." *Oh God. Anne always said only poor people nursed their babies.*

"The doctor told us. We gave you a shot to dry up your milk, but it takes a little while."

Sister Jo came in with a tiny bundle in a pink blanket. She placed it in Mary Margaret's arms. She was nervous to hold such a little squirming thing, but she took her in her arms and felt a surge of emotion, unlike anything she had experienced before.

"I made you," she whispered. The baby girl nuzzled Mary Margaret's breast. "You're beautiful. Look at your perfect skin and pink cheeks."

Anne and Ted carefully opened the door. They were both dressed in white coats with face masks. Sister Jo motioned for them to come in. The nurse passed the baby to him. His smile was broad, he used his shoulder to try and catch the tears that were streaming down his face. He and Mary Margaret looked at each other as if for the first time.

Family and friends were in and out over the course of Mary Margaret's stay. The room was filled with flowers and gifts. There was no question in a nursery full of crying babies, which one was the Grants'. Her pale pink skin and strawberry blond hair gave her away.

They still needed to choose a name. Ted brought the pad and Mary Margaret studied it and scratched out some names. She showed Ted, one name that was circled.

He smiled, "That's one of my favorites too."

When Theresa saw it, she choked back her tears and told them how pleased her mother would have been. "Her first name is so appropriate since she was born on Tuesday," said Theresa. "Monday's child is fair of face. Tuesday's child is full of grace."

"Oh, my God, Mac, isn't that ironic, but you remember how I told you." She stopped, remembering she hadn't told anyone what Sister Fatima had revealed to her. "I've always loved that name."

"It's beautiful, Grace Elizabeth," Theresa said, rubbing her necklace,

"Will you be her godmother?"

"Of course, Pucci."

Sister Fatima visited Mary Margaret daily. When she heard the baby's name, she was overcome with emotion and had to leave the room. The next day she came back with a wicker hamper filled with hand-knitted baby clothes.

"It was a while before I gave up hope that I could find a way to keep my baby, but I never even got to see my little Colleen. Now these clothes will be for your Grace."

"They're so soft," said Mary Margaret pressing a tiny sweater to her face. "Did you knit them?"

"My sister sent me yarn from Ireland. We had a knitting circle at home. I couldn't bear to get rid of them."

"She'll love them. There's even a pink one. How did you know it would be a girl?"

"I figured if it was a lad he'd be so tiny he wouldn't even remember his mam dressed him like a girl."

Mary Margaret thought going home from the hospital must be like being released from prison. As she stood up from the wheelchair, an unworldly feeling, like she was looking through the wrong end of binoculars, came over her. She leaned on Ted's arm. She wanted to dance for joy, but after a week of confinement her legs were wobbly, and she dared not drop her precious bundle. She snuggled the warm baby closer, shielding her against the chilly January air, taking in her warm delicious smell. Passersby smiled at the beautiful baby in her pink knitted hat and a matching blanket of soft Irish wool. One even commented that she would be a perfect Gerber baby.

Pearly was at the cottage putting away the diapers the service had delivered. Baby bottles were lined up on the counter in the kitchen. Pearly, worried Mary Margaret would kill the child, showed her what she needed to do to take care of her. Ted had filled the bedroom with pink roses. The bassinet sat on the wall across from the bed next to the changing table. An old chest of Anne's held Grace's clothes in the hall.

After Ted left for work, Pearly sidled through the tiny space to put Grace into the bassinet. She pointed out to Mary Margaret the foil-wrapped dinner she had prepared for their supper and said she'd be back first thing in the morning. The door clicked closed. Outside, Pearly started the Imperial, then all was quiet. Mary Margaret checked to make sure the baby was breathing. Her own bed had never felt so luxurious. She woke up feeling all was right with the world, but somewhere, a baby was crying.

"The baby needs to be baptized," said Anne, pushing open the cottage door with her shoulder. "And you need to start going to church again, young lady." She set the long flat box she was carrying on the dining room table.

"Mama, I've been so tired, Grace is a night owl. On Sundays, Ted takes care of her so I can sleep. What's in the box?"

"The family christening dress."

"But I thought…"

"You did, but your aunt, Sister Mary Margaret was able to repair it," she said, taking the dress out of the box.

Mary Margaret's ears still burned, remembering how her mother had screamed at her that day. It was so bad her father took her with him to make a house call. "It's beautiful, you can't even tell,"

"I'll never know what possessed you to go on the top shelf of my closet and get down the dress and cut it up," Anne said in a bitter tone. "Sister made it by hand. All of my babies wore it."

"I just wanted my doll to wear it. It was so pretty. I'm sorry." She put down the dress and hugged her mother. "I promise to keep it safe for all the future Puccinis." As if on cue, Grace let out a scream.

A flowery scent from a bouquet of fresh flowers filled the tiny apartment. Grace, in the christening gown, was propped up on pillows in the middle of the bed.

"That baby-chile should be in a picture book. Good Housing or that Ladies Home Journal. She's so pretty," said Pearly.

Theresa came by with a small, wrapped box which Mary Margaret ripped into.

"Her first gold bracelet," she said, placing the little bangle on Grace's chubby wrist.

"Come on, we'll be late for the Mass," said Ted, opening the door for Pearly and the baby.

"Wish we didn't have to sit through Mass and could go straight to the Baptism," said Mary Margaret, donning her ecru mantilla.

"Tommy's meeting us at the church," said Ted. "He has Godfather duty."

"Tommy? I thought Charlie would be the Godfather. I thought that's why he's here," said Theresa, covering her mouth with her hand.

"He's here? Charlie's here? Are you sure? He hasn't really spoken to me since the wedding. He was so upset about everything that happened. I've missed him so," exclaimed Mary Margaret. "He literally said ten words to me at Christmas."

"We had a date last night. I'm afraid I've spoiled his surprise. He talked to Ben. He convinced Charlie that you just made a mistake, anyone could, and that you are a good person and have suffered enough without him adding to your trouble. He realized Ben was right and decided to come," Theresa said, guiding Mary Margaret toward the door. "The others are already in the car."

Easter Sunday at St. John the Baptist Cathedral with the bishop, was the only option Mary Margaret considered for Grace's Baptism. The Puccinis slipped in through the side door and sat in the first two rows in front of the right-side altar. Lilies on the altar filled the air with their pungent smell.

Mary Margaret loved the lofty Nave and the French Gothic style of the church. The Stations of the Cross along the side walls made her shiver as she remembered the dreaded custom she was forced to participate in every Friday during Lent. *Why did they have to replay Christ's suffering so often?*

Theresa walked up to the side altar and lit two candles for her parents, another custom Mary Margaret failed to understand. She knelt at the altar for what seemed to Mary Margaret an eternity. Pearly held the sleeping child as the worshippers filed in, clad in their Easter finery. Mary Margaret pulled the lace veil over her face. The congregation turned to watch the clergy march in, surrounded by a cloud of incense. *Oh my God, that's Ben swinging that incense thing back and forth, dressed in his priest clothes. Look at him, he's still beautiful. What's wrong with me? Why do I still have feelings for him?*

The Mass dragged on. Mary Margaret watched as Ben assisted the bishop never taking her eyes off of him. She saw in him a piety she never realized he had. When she took Communion and he was inches in front of her, he looked at her as if she was just another communicant.

During the Benediction, Charlie slipped into the pew, next to Mary Margaret. He took her hand. The look that passed between them stood for all the words they each wanted to say. She took the baby from Pearly. "Grace, meet your uncle Charlie," she whispered.

After the Christening, close friends and family gathered at the Puccini's. It was supposed to be a simple reception, but Essie got carried away, adding all her specialties to the bakery petit fours with pink flowers that Theresa brought. The usual chaos at the Puccini's was heightened by the crying baby who was still angry at being doused with water at the church. John Gray Houston, Tommy, Ted, Mr. Grant and Charlie were on the porch smoking the cigars Ted passed around.

Dr. Puccini came to the door, "Come inside for a toast but please leave those smelly butts outside."

"Well, they certainly weren't Havanas," teased Charlie.

"They were all I could afford," said Ted, slinging his arm over his father's shoulder, "on my salary."

"I declare, you deserve a raise," said Mr. Grant.

"Does that mean I'll get one, Dad?"

"We'll see," he said, patting Ted on the back.

The baby quit crying. A little pink icing on Mary Margaret's finger did the trick. Dr. Puccini poured champagne around. Mary Margaret held out her glass. He started to hold back, then laughed and filled her glass. "Of course, you're old enough now," he said.

There were toasts all around. Mary Margaret and Ted were laughing and posing for pictures. The rosy glow of the wine on their cheeks. A shared pride in the beautiful child.

Ben and Father James walked in. The pair worked the room, shaking hands with everyone. Ben gave Mary Margaret a perfunctory hug. He showered her with compliments. She felt her stomach lurch.

Mary Margaret changed the baby and put her down for her nap. She met Theresa in the hall.

"Pucci, I'm so proud of you. What a day. This is a great party. Hey, did you notice that John Houston and Tommy were off in the corner talking away? Maybe they'll like each other," Theresa winked, noticing Mary Margaret just staring off. "What's wrong, you seem a little down."

"It's just Ben; do you think I'll ever get completely over him? I never thought he would really become a priest."

"My God, Pucci, what in the hell is wrong with you? What would you do if he did decide to leave the priesthood? Leave Ted and Grace, and run off with him? Can't you get it through your thick skull, what you had that summer was just a teenage romance, nothing more? Just get over it. He made his choice."

"I know, you're right. You're always right," Mary Margaret said, giving Theresa a hug.

"Look, I know it's hard to get over your first love. But it is what it is. Things don't always work out the way we want. I know it's not what you expected but it's your path. You, Ted, and Grace looked so perfect for the photos."

"Charlie has invited me to Georgetown for the May Day dance. I can look at Georgetown Visitation then and decide for sure if I want to go there."

Twenty-Two

The air in Washington was different, charged like an electric current ran through it. At the airport, everyone was bustling about, each with an air of importance. Theresa had to ride a bus to the main terminal where Charlie was waiting for her. She ran to him, dropping her magazine and shoulder bag.

"I thought we'd never get here. The plane aborted the take-off, so we had to change planes," said a breathless Theresa.

"I was so worried when the plane was late," said Charlie.

"All I could think about was the Orly plane crash and how much fear they all must have felt," she said, sobbing, and clutching Charlie. By the time they broke apart, the roses he was holding were crushed. They both looked down at the pitiful bouquet with blossomless stems and laughed.

"Let's gather your things; I've got so much planned for us."

Theresa's neck was swiveling from side to side looking at all the charming homes in Georgetown.

"That's where the Kennedys lived before he became president. See where all those people are gaping and pointing? You won't believe what these houses sell for."

"Savannah could look like this if people would move downtown. There are a few brave people who have, but most of the fine old homes are rentals."

"I don't know, there's an awful lot of crime there."

She loved the campus. Stately gothic buildings were surrounded by quadrangles, beautifully planted and maintained. She stayed in the dorm at Georgetown Visitation, where the girls were friendly. She learned she could take classes at Georgetown University in addition to the ones that were offered at Georgetown Visitation. Theresa was on cloud nine when she boarded the plane to go home.

Mary Margaret picked up Theresa at the airport.

"You'll never believe who I ran into. Remember Katie Sullivan from camp? She's going to be my roommate next year."

"Katie, I really liked her. She'll be a lot of fun."

Mary Margaret stared blankly out of the window of the car as Theresa relayed every detail of her trip to Washington. Grace, in her lap, cooed.

"Pucci, I must be boring you."

"Jesus, no, Mac, I'm just trying to imagine what it would feel like dancing to the music of Lester Lanin. I think it sounds like Washington was fabulous and you saw everything there was to see. And you've already found a divine roommate."

Deep down inside, Mary Margaret felt a pang of jealousy. All her friends would be going off to college, joining sororities then coming back to make their debut during their sophomore year. But not her, she would be at home being a mother.

A week before graduation, the rental shop was packed with St. Bernadette's girls trying on their gowns.

"Over here, Theresa," yelled Marnie.

"I can't believe you are going to be Valedictorian, and Marnie, Salutatorian," said Pauline, tearing the wrapper from her gown.

"God, I'm a nervous wreck. What will I say?" Theresa said.

"Just say how thankful you are for all your wonderful teachers and friends and how glad you are that Bunny's gone and that you're getting the hell out of here," said Pauline, tipping her mortarboard to a rakish angle.

"That's what I was going to say," said Marnie.

They laughed and hugged each other the way teenage girls often do.

"Do you think Mary Margaret will come?" Catherine asked.

"She's thinking about it," said Theresa. "But I don't know. She's been pretty bummed."

"What a beautiful day," said Sara, pulling up the shades in Theresa's bedroom. "I've brought you breakfast in bed. Your graduation day and you're the star. Delia made you French toast and bacon, your favorites."

"Oh Nana, thanks," Theresa said, sitting up and reaching for the orange juice. She patted the side of the bed for her grandmother to sit down.

"Last night, I dreamed Mama and Daddy flew in from Paris for the graduation. It was so real. I could smell her Je Reviens perfume with a trace of cigarette smoke underneath. Daddy picked me up and swung me around. I hugged Mother and cried, telling her I hadn't written my speech yet. She told me what to write. I woke up and wrote it all down. It's so much better than what I'd written."

"Would you like to read it to me first?"

"No, Nana, I'm going to go with it. You'll hear it later."

The afternoon light slanted in through the stained-glass windows of the cathedral. Dust motes floated in the shafts of light surrounded by the scent of beeswax and Sunday's incense. Mary Margaret pulled toward a back-row seat, but Ted pushed her forward into an aisle seat near the front. She bowed her head and looked down at her program hoping no one would see her.

A tap on the shoulder made her turn around to see Catherine's and Pauline's parents sitting behind her. They showered her with compliments about how good she looked. They asked about the baby. She wanted to go through the floor. Relief flooded over her when the music began and the procession started.

All stood. Theresa and Marnie were leading the class. Mary Margaret felt she should be the one walking with Theresa. As everyone sat down, Ted grabbed Mary Margaret's arm sensing she wanted to bolt. After Father James blessed the congregation, Sister Hope gave the introduction and presented the awards. The graduates came up one by one in alphabetical order to receive their diplomas. Mary Margaret gnawed down her last fingernail as they called out the name McDermott. She detected a pause after McDermott, a pause where Puccini should have been. Ted heard a low guttural sound, almost a growl coming from her.

Marnie up next, gave a peppy talk and thanked the nuns for their selfless service. With her braces off, perfectly applied makeup, and new hairstyle, she stood with an air of confidence. Mary Margaret couldn't believe the transformation. She really liked Marnie but resented that she had become the fourth in their group, her replacement.

When Theresa stepped up to the podium, Mary Margaret was shocked at how tall she had grown. Her neck was long and regal. How had she failed to notice? Her complexion was flawless and even from where she sat, she could sense her eyes sparkling and saw how she drew the audience in.

Theresa looked past a sea of black robes and black habits. She spotted Mary Margaret in the center of the church and took courage from her. It was brave of her to come and face her graduating classmates.

"Last night, in a dream, my parents came to me. As most of you know, I lost my parents only a few months after coming to St. Bernadette's. I bring this up not to garner sympathy from you today. You have already showered me with sympathy and support. I mention it because I was able to get inspiration from that dream. As we go out into the world feeling alone in our endeavors there will always be a source of guidance, whether it is from a teacher, a friend, a family member, or the Lord. It is all within us. All the lessons we've learned in life, all the wisdom our teachers have bestowed upon us, the faith we have been shown. It is all within us. This inner intelligence will guide us. Our job is to listen and trust. We are never alone."

The audience gave Theresa a standing ovation. After Father James' benediction, the graduates threw their caps in the air, hugging and squealing.

It took everything Mary Margaret had to keep from falling completely apart. She charged out of the church, fighting the flow of friends and relatives heading for the front. Ted ran after her, only catching up with her in the car.

"What's wrong? Why did you run out like that? You need to stay and congratulate your friends and Theresa on her amazing speech," Ted yelled.

"No, and I'm not going to Johnny Harris' with the Willinghams and everyone they invited," she said, jumping in the car and slamming the door. "I've never felt so out of place. I don't belong there anymore. Take me home."

Ted jerked the car into reverse and squealed out of the parking place.

At home, Mary Margaret rushed past Tommy who was giving Grace her bottle.

"I guess that didn't go so well," he said, shifting the baby to his shoulder.

"No, she couldn't stand seeing her friends moving on," said Ted, grabbing a beer from the fridge, "Want one?"

"No, thanks," said Tommy, patting Grace on her back. "Why don't I take this one out for a stroll?"

"Thanks, Tommy, you're a real pal to babysit. I'm so angry. Why can't she accept her life now?" He reached down to the stroller and caressed Grace's cheek.

He could hear Mary Margaret on the other side of the door still crying. He slammed down his beer bottle and burst into the room.

"Please don't start yelling at me again. You never let up, the whole way home," said Mary Margaret, who was curled up on the bed with her doll. She pulled the pillow over her ear.

"Look at you with that doll. You walked past your own baby to talk to that stuffed doll. What's wrong with you? I'm tired of you acting like everything is the end of the world and telling me you missed out on your goddamned life. This is your life. You are a wife and mother. What about my life? Can't you see how hard I'm trying?"

As he yelled, she rocked back and forth, clutching the doll. Tears streamed down her face. It enraged Ted. He snatched the doll from her, ripped its head off, and threw it in the trash. Mary Margaret heard the door slam. Ted's stomps echoed on the wooden steps. She listened to the familiar sound of his car starting.

"Charlie, please don't ask me one more time to stay here this summer," said Theresa, standing up from the porch swing at the Willinghams. "Claudette has rented an apartment in Florence and she's counting on me being there."

"But Theresa, I'm stuck here working for Mr. Grant. Ben's not here and half my class is away, Mary Margaret's married, with a baby, and now my girlfriend is leaving. After Washington, D.C., this may as well be Mayberry."

"Are you crazy? You want me to stay here with you, in this boring town? They're predicting the hottest summer on record. Why don't you come to Italy with me?"

"Now you're the one who needs her head examined. Where do you think I could get that kind of money?"

"I'll buy you a plane ticket. It can be an early birthday gift."

"Now, I know you're nuts. You think I'm a gigolo? Just because you're so spoiled. You never have to worry about money. I have to make my spending money for the school year."

"I really think this time apart from each other will do us both good," she said, walking toward the door.

"Well, you certainly don't expect me to sit around and wait while you prance around Europe and flirt with those smooth-talking Italian men. Do you?"

"No, Charlie, we aren't exactly engaged or even going steady for that matter. Good night, Charlie," she went into the house and turned off the porch light.

There had been a lot of tension between Charlie and Theresa that summer. She, feeling more relaxed about her relationship with Charlie, was willing to let things develop. Dr. Houston had put her on birth control pills to regulate her periods. She didn't tell anyone, especially Charlie. Of course, the pills went against the teachings of the Church, but since she wasn't actually using them for birth control, it was probably okay.

She was curious about sex. Mary Margaret didn't paint a rosy picture about it. It had been drilled into their heads a thousand times by the nuns and priests that a girl should wait until she was married. She wondered if they told the boys that, too. Probably not. Most of the girls were complaining about how the boys were always trying to sneak a feel or pressuring them to do more. Since Pauline had been going steady, she didn't talk about it anymore which probably meant that they were doing it.

When she and Charlie made out, it left her breathless and wanting more. Mary Margaret told her about what boys do to relieve themselves but not what girls do. She was frustrated and guilty about some of the stuff she and Charlie did. She really needed someone to talk to. Mary Margaret was so busy these days that they never had time for heart-to-heart conversations anymore. It was like Grace had a radar that detected when their conversations became intimate and would let out a squeal.

Charlie, on the other hand, had been so upset about what happened to Mary Margaret he wouldn't take a chance on that happening to Theresa. He always drew back before they went too far. Claudette would be able to enlighten her. It was just a few weeks until they would be together in Florence.

Mary Margaret loved her baby but couldn't believe the number of times she had to change her diapers. Why did Grace sleep so much during the day and so little at night? When Grace outgrew the bassinet, they had to get rid of the sofa to make room for a crib and the stroller. The apartment looked more like a garage sale than a magazine spread.

The heat was stifling. When Theresa left for Italy and would not be around to help with Grace, Mary Margaret would only have one day of relief. Ted wouldn't pay Pearly after the baby shower gift ran out. She managed to pay her for one day a week out of her grocery money or the twenty dollar bills her daddy slipped her when no one was looking.

Pearly was huffing up the steps when Mary Margaret opened the door with Grace asleep on her shoulder. She started to pass the baby to her.

"Hold on a minute, Missy, I gotta catch my breath," Pearly said, collapsing into a chair and wiping her face with a wet paper towel. "You okay, you look kinda pale?" She said, holding out her arms for Grace. "That man on the radio say it gone be one hundred degrees. It sure does feel it, too."

"Yeah, it's so hot and she cries all night. My family left for the beach and Theresa's leaving for Europe soon."

"That chile right upset she done broke up with your brother."

"Me too, I want them to get married so she'll be my sister, but I'm in the middle. They each want me to take their side."

"I just bet when Miss Theresa gets back from Italy they'll get back together. Those two just been seeing too much of each other this summer. 'Besides, they're plenty of fish in the sea. They still young."

"I guess I need to get going. I have the car and need to run a hundred errands," she said, picking up the laundry by the door and kissing the baby on the head.

In the car, she rolled down the window. It was only eleven and already hot and humid. At the filling station, Mr. Dixon gassed up the car and washed the windshield. When he came over for her to sign the charge ticket, he started chatting. She glanced stealthily at her watch while listening to him talk about his wife's operation and how Dr. Puccini had come by to check on her every day at the hospital.

"Glad she's feeling better, Mr. Dixon. I'll bring the baby by next week. Thanks for asking."

Mrs. Woo, at the cleaners, gossiped on and on about who was doing what to whom. Mary Margaret didn't want to be rude and look at her watch, but an underlying anxiety made her want to scream. Most days she welcomed the old lady's gossip. She took the brown paper parcel of clean clothes.

"I'll pick up Ted's shirts tomorrow, I need to get on with my errands," she said, handing Mrs. Woo a five-dollar bill.

She drove out Highway 17 to drop off Ted's shoes at the repair shop for new soles. She headed south toward the Flying Pig to get supper. I just missed the turn-in. Damn, now what? There's not a turnaround for miles. The air coming from outside felt delicious as the car sped down the highway. Turning up the radio she sang Crying over You along with Roy Orbison. She felt freer than she had in months. Ted kept his extra cigarettes in the glove compartment. They never smoked around the baby. She punched in the lighter and reached for the pack. Her hand was trembling as she held the lighter to the cigarette. I probably should get something to eat. I feel so tired. She inhaled the smoke deeply and felt better for a moment.

The lowering sun was casting streaks across the road. The strobe effect created by the in-and-out light and shadow on the road made her feel like she had taken the pain pills Dr. Houston gave her after the birth. The car ran off the road, she swerved back toward the highway but felt she was losing control. She remembered being told to hold the steering wheel straight and not try to over-correct. She braked and came to a bumpy stop on the shoulder. The car choked down.

Oh, dear God, what's happened? A grinding sound echoed in her ears as she tried to restart the car. *I've wrecked Ted's car. He's going to kill me.*

She was sobbing when someone tapped on the window. She could see a green pickup truck in her rear-view mirror and looked over to see a bearded man beside her car. His teeth were yellow, and some were missing.

"You done run off the road and busted up your tire, Miss. You can't drive it like at. It'll bend up the rim."

She could smell the alcohol on his breath. Her heart beat wildly. Her first instinct was to roll up the window, but then he might try to kill her.

"Thank you. What should I do?"

"You got a spare?"

"A spare what?"

"Tire, young lady. You old enough to drive?"

"Yes, yes I am. Where would it be? This is my husband's car."

"Gimme them keys and I'll have a look in your trunk. There's a place just outside of Brunswick. Buddy of mine. He'll fix you up real good. 'Bout twenty miles," he said.

"Brunswick, I'm almost to Brunswick?" She said a bit too loud almost like she was screaming at him.

"You had too much to drink, Lady?"

"No, no, I'm just really tired, didn't realize I had driven so far."

"Well, come on. We'd better see about this 'fore it gets dark and my friend closes."

She followed him around to the right front tire. He clucked his tongue. Even she could tell the car wasn't drivable.

"Get your stuff and I'll drive you to the garage. He can send a tow truck," he said, nodding toward his own truck.

She looked him over, his greasy overalls, torn tee shirt underneath, a pack of cigarettes rolled into the sleeve. *Mama said never get in the car with strangers, much less, a truck. Dear God, what should I do?*

"Don't be afraid, Lady. You're much better off riding with me than waiting out here by the side of the highway for that tow truck," he said, opening the passenger side of the truck. He brushed the seat off with the back of his hand. "That hound dog gets right muddy. It's dry now, shouldn't be a bother."

She fetched her purse from the car, ran to the truck, and jumped in, ignoring her fear, and biting down hard on her molars. The truck roared off in a cloud of dust. On each side of the road, the marshes glowed in the afternoon light. Not a building in sight and only a few cars along the way. He pulled the truck over. "I'll be right back," he said.

The tinny sound of the truck door slamming. Her fear turned to panic. She gagged from the strong scent of dirty dogs. Where was he going? Why did he stop here? She looked behind her at the two rifles strung across the rear window. For the first time in a long time, she started to pray. *Hail Mary, full of grace.*

Twenty-Three

Mary Margaret did not come to pick Ted up at work. A friend dropped him off at home. He was surprised to find Pearly, still at the cottage.

"Where's Mary Margaret?" He asked.

"She left here 'bout eleven-thirty taking the laundry, say she had a million errands to run. I expected her back an hour or so ago."

"I bet I know where she is," he said. "Would you mind driving me and Grace down to the beach?"

"I'm awfully tired and that car ain't got much gas."

Ted pulled out a ten-dollar bill. Pearly looked at it, looked away. She expected more.

"That's in addition to what I owe you for today," he said, pulling out eight more dollars. "You know Essie's down there."

"Well, I reckon if we stop at the filling station."

He picked up a sleeping Grace and they headed for the car. "Better grab a bottle and the diaper bag."

They pulled up to the cottage, Ted stepped out of the car and the twins ran down from the porch calling, "Gracie, Gracie."

Anne followed. "What in the world? Where's Mary Margaret?"

"She hasn't come home from running errands," said Ted.

"What kind of stunt has that child pulled now? I was hoping her foolishness would stop now that the baby is here."

The whole family was in the driveway. The children were poking and pulling at Grace. Ted turned her over to Joel. She let out a howl. Joel passed her back to Ted.

Inside they got out the phone book and started calling anyone who might know the whereabouts of Mary Margaret. When Theresa got the call, she panicked. She had been concerned about Mary Margaret's state of mind after graduation. She said she would call a few people. They all wondered if they should call the police. Anne said no, they needed to wait until tomorrow if she hadn't shown up by then. If they called now, and it was nothing, the whole town would know.

"Can you keep Grace tonight?" He said, handing the baby to Anne. "I need to get home in case she calls. If she doesn't come home tonight, I'll get Mom's car tomorrow. I don't want to tell them until we know something."

Mary Margaret pulled on the handle. The door wouldn't open. The man was in the bed of the truck bending over. He's probably getting a knife or some shells for the rifles that are hanging across the rear window. Then her fears grew worse. What if he rapes me? She was trembling all over. She felt the truck bounce as he jumped down from the bed. She tried the door again. Nothing. Just as she reached outside through the window, her hand on the handle, he appeared.

"Sorry, that door handle's jammed. Been meaning to get it fixed. I hope you weren't sceered, I just went to get us a cold one." He handed her a bottle of icy Coke and a pack of orange cheese Nabs.

They bounced back onto the road. Mary Margaret sipped her drink, guilt descended on her like a warm wool coat. When she finally stopped trembling, she turned toward him. "What's your name? Mine's Mary Margaret."

"I'm Bubba Lee and this here truck's 'Old Faithful'," he said, patting the steering wheel. "There's Whelan's garage. I'll explain to Mr. Whelan where your car is."

They pulled up running over the annunciator. Mr. Whelan hobbled out rubbing his eyes. "What's up, Bubba Lee?"

"Lady's car done run off the road."

Mary Margaret got out of the truck.

"Afraid my mechanic's gone for the day. I'll take the tow truck and pick up the car. I'll need twenty dollars and your signature," Mr. Whelan said, pushing a clipboard toward Mary Margaret.

She handed him a twenty and asked if she could use the phone.

"I done locked the office already. Why don't you go over there to that motel?" He said, pointing across the street. "You may as well check in. Ain't nothing gonna happen tonight."

"Bye now." Bubba Lee said, "Mr. Whelan'll take care of you now." He gave a little wave before screeching off.

"I didn't even get to thank him," Mary Margaret exclaimed, as she saw his truck drive away. "I should have given him some money," she said, thinking of the dwindling bills in her wallet.

"He wouldn't take it. Ain't many souls good as him. Ev' since his wife and daughter were killed on the side of that road; he rides up and down that highway helping people."

"Oh my God, that's awful. How sad for him," she said, putting her hands up to her mouth.

"Yeah, they had a flat and were trying to get someone to stop and help when that reckless teenager hit 'em."

She walked across the street with the package of clean laundry and checked into the motel. Ted didn't answer the office or the home phone. She showered, tried Ted again, turned the air-conditioning down, shut the blackout curtains, and crawled into bed.

Her sleep was long and dreamless. She looked at her watch. *Nine-thirty? It must need winding. Surely, I slept longer than two hours.* Her stomach growled. She wondered if they were still serving supper in the restaurant downstairs. She tried Ted again, but still no answer. *Where could he be at this hour? Why can't I remember the number at the beach? It's too late to call anyone else. Theresa maybe? Damn, her line is busy. I'll try again after supper.*

When she opened the door, it was full daylight. Oh my God, I slept through the night. She ordered a sausage biscuit and a cup of coffee to go, then walked across the street to the garage. As she approached, Mr. Whelan was shaking his head. He looked at her and said, "Sorry to tell you young lady, but my mechanic said he couldn't fix your car unless he orders a part. Could take a week."

"Can you tow it to Savannah?"

"It'll cost you."

"Of course. I need to call my husband."

"That'll be long-distance."

"Okay, I'll pay for that too."

Theresa answered the phone on the first ring. She had been at the Grant's cottage since eight o'clock waiting in case Mary Margaret called. "Where are you? We've all been in a panic. Ted's gone to retrace your steps from yesterday."

"Mac, can you come and get me and bring some money?"

Nearing Brunswick, Theresa recognized Ted's car being pulled by a wrecker in the opposite direction. *Oh, Dear God, Mary Margaret didn't explain on the phone. I hope she isn't hurt. She just urged me to get there as soon as possible.*

As she pulled up to the motel, she noticed a forlorn figure in front of the cafe clutching a brown parcel. It was Mary Margaret. She looked so thin and her eyes were puffy, her cheeks sunken.

"Get in, Pucci. What in the hell got into you this time? Everyone was frantic."

Mary Margaret explained what happened. "I was so tired and needed some time to think. I didn't realize how far I'd driven."

"Think about what, Pucci?" Theresa wheeled the car onto the highway.

"I just keep thinking about my life. What if I had not gone to the beach that night? What if I had not been drinking? Would any of this have happened? What if I wasn't so stupid?"

Theresa pulled the car over onto the shoulder and looked Mary Margaret in the eye. "For Christ's sake, if, if, if. You know what they say about 'your aunt and if'?"

"I know, I know," said Mary Margaret, "'if your aunt had balls, she would be your uncle'."

"You have got to quit thinking about it. It's the past, and you can't change things. You have so much going for you. A beautiful baby, a wonderful husband who really loves you, and Grace has two wonderful sets of grandparents. Oh, and then you have me," Theresa said. She smiled and took Mary Margaret's hand. "I wonder who that is pulling up behind us in a green truck."

Mary Margaret opened the door, waved, and got out of the car.

"Hey, Bubba Lee. We're fine, we were just talking. I didn't get a chance to thank you for helping me yesterday."

Theresa watched in the rear-view mirror as Mary Margaret hugged the man. They chatted a bit and he patted her shoulder before getting back in his truck. He gave a little toot and waved as he reentered the highway. When she got back in the car, she told Theresa about Bubba Lee and the story about what happened that day. She sobbed all the way to Savannah.

"By the way, I called Sister Fatima," Theresa said.

"Mac, why did you do that?" She said, wiping her eyes.

"We called everyone. I thought she may have known something. Pucci, Sister said she had an idea that might help you. I'm not sure what it is. Here we are, so I'll just drop you off and come over to say goodbye before I leave next week."

"Will you do me one favor?"

"Of course."

"Will you call Anne and explain? She'll only yell at me. Tell her you really think I've turned around and am going to make the best of what I have."

When Mary Margaret started up the stairs, Ted ran out with Grace to greet her. "Mary Margaret, oh my God, I was so worried," he said. "Where did you go? Why didn't you call?"

She tried to explain what happened. She herself didn't really understand, but she realized that it was a turning point. She grabbed Ted and hugged him like she had never done before. Poor Grace was almost crushed between them. When she squealed and wiggled, they pulled away and laughed.

"I'm so sorry. I never meant to hurt you. I love you both so much," Mary Margaret said. When she went into the bedroom, her Maddie doll was sitting on the bed with her head, crudely sewn back on.

"Ted, it's Maddie. Who fixed her?"

"I did."

"You know how to sew?"

"I had to learn to sew on my name tags when I went to camp."

Twenty-Four

Sister Fatima tried to keep her eyes on her missal, but she heard a slight commotion near the side altar. She looked over and saw Mary Margaret, Ted, and Grace enter a pew. She made the sign of the cross and thanked God. She thought she detected a slight smile at the corners of Mary Margaret's mouth when she walked down the aisle after Holy Communion. When Mass was over, she caught up with them. They were putting Grace into the stroller.

"Mary Margaret, I've been wanting to talk to you. Can you come by the convent tomorrow?"

"Theresa, if my eyes were closed, I would know I had walked into St. Bernadette's," said Mary Margaret. "The smell of school even outside of the door." She held the door open for Theresa to get the baby stroller through. "Thank you for coming with me to look after Grace."

"I know Sister Fatima would want to see her. I'll take her out for a walk so you two can talk."

"What a sight for sore eyes, the Dynamo Duo. Plus, this precious one," said Sister Fatima.

"You knew they called us that?" Theresa said, giving the nun a hug.

"There wasn't much that went on that I didn't know about. You girls all thought you had me fooled," she said, hugging Mary Margaret before leaning into the stroller and scooping up Grace.

"Oh, you darling, darling girl," said Sister Fatima. "You know some babies and children shy away from us. The habit scares them."

"Clearly, she likes you. She held out her arms to you right away," said Mary Margaret, looking around. "It feels so strange being back. It's hard to believe it's been over a year."

"It's just not the same without the two of you. That leads me to what I want to talk to you about, Mary Margaret."

"Grace and I will go for a walk," said Theresa. She took Grace and put her back into the stroller. "We'll be back in a little while."

"Come into my office," Sister said, opening the door for Mary Margaret.

"This is Sister Hope's office," she said, reliving that gut-wrenching feeling she used to get coming into this room. It was more cheerful now. The blinds were pulled up, the walls were painted warm beige and African violets bloomed on the window sill.

"I guess you haven't heard, Sister Hope is ill and has returned to the Motherhouse. I'm interim principal now."

"I'm sorry she's sick. It's wonderful that you got the job. If only you had been principal in my day." Mary Margaret took a seat on the familiar sofa.

"I knew you wanted to finish school so I checked into your records." Sister Fatima picked up some papers on her desk. "You only need a few more hours to graduate. If you could start in September, you could complete everything by midterm and start college winter semester."

"Really, could I? Do you think I'll fit in? All the students are so much younger. I thought married girls couldn't come here."

"Mary Margaret, you'll have nothing to worry about. I've talked to the head of the Postulant Council and the bishop. You know how they feel about your father. You have been cleared."

"I'll go find Theresa and tell her the good news," said Mary Margaret. *Thank you, Daddy, for being their doctor.*

She felt as if a huge weight had been lifted from her shoulders. She knew it would be different. She looked around the room at the formerly menacing furniture and thought how ironic that the former occupant had been named Hope when she delivered none of it.

Sister Fatima watched as the three disappeared around the corner. A wave of nostalgia came over her as she thought back over the years. None of the students coming up now were as special to her as Theresa and Mary Margaret had been. They were just about the age her own daughter would be now. When she came back to Savannah in 1959 and was posted to Camp Villa Veronica, she couldn't help but wonder if any of the campers were her Colleen. She prayed daily to God to take away the longing she had to find her own child. An inner voice told her that the child was well and safe but it didn't assuage Fatima's yearning while here in Savannah. She planned to return to Baltimore in the fall but got orders to go to Saint Bernadette's. Again and again, she asked God to give her strength.

Twenty-Five

Mary Margaret put Grace down for a nap in the crib her mother kept in the small bedroom off of the kitchen. Anne was nursing a cup of coffee at the table.

"Mary Margaret, slow down. I can't understand a word you're saying."

"But, I'm so excited. I'm going to get to finish high school."

She told her mother about her visit with Sister Fatima.

"That's wonderful news. Essie and I will work it out with Grace. I'm glad you're here. Why don't you sit? There's something I wanted to talk to you about. Let me grab another cup of coffee."

"I'll take a Coke, please."

Mary Margaret wondered if she was going to get a lecture. She couldn't think of anything she had done wrong this time.

Anne returned and put the drink in front of Mary Margaret. "You and these Cokes. I never let the boys have them. They can't be good for you," said Anne, lighting a cigarette.

"You remember Aunt Ruth? She used to visit us at Easter." She put the coffee on the table and took a drag of her cigarette.

Mary Margaret started to say something about her smoking. Anne was trying to quit, but she noticed the distressed look on her face and decided to stay quiet.

"Mama, did something happen to her? I do remember her coming a long time ago."

"She passed away. I knew she had been sick."

"I never did know how she was related. You haven't talked much about her."

Anne scrunched up her face and wiped her eyes. Mary Margaret had rarely seen her mother cry. She stood and put her arm around her shoulder.

"There's something I've never told you. I preferred not to talk about it. Aunt Ruth is not my aunt, she's my birth mother. I was adopted."

Mary Margaret felt a stab in her stomach. She looked aside, her eyebrows knitted together, her voice stammered. "I…I don't understand. You were adopted? Are Granny and Grandpa not my grandparents?"

"Granny and Grandpa will always be your grandparents. Don't ever forget that." Anne stubbed out her cigarette, put her head on her arms, and cried softly. Mary Margaret fell back into her chair with a thud. She wasn't quite sure what to do. *Adopted, how awful. How would someone feel? I would just die if I found out I was. Thank God I'm not.*

"How long have you known?" She asked. She handed Anne a paper napkin from the holder on the table. "How did you find out the truth about Aunt Ruth?"

Anne wiped her eyes and began her story. "I was left as an infant in the waiting area at the train depot in Macon, wrapped in a quilt. Ruth was only sixteen and couldn't take care of me. She watched from behind one of the pillars in the station until a porter noticed the bundle and picked it up. He took me to the Salvation Army. There was a note pinned to the blanket."

Anne reached behind her and pulled a cigar box from the side table. She passed a note and some newspaper articles to Mary Margaret.

Mary Margaret's mouth dropped open as she read the note: *Please take care of my baby. Let her know her mother will always love her.* The headlines: *Beautiful Blue-eyed Baby Found at the Train Depot, Beautiful Blue-Eyed Depot Baby Adopted.* Mary Margaret read the articles.

"I can't believe they put Granny and Grandpa's names in the paper. Adoptions were so private then."

"Because of the first article, there was so much interest. I was adopted the day after it appeared. It always made Ruth feel better that I didn't have to be without a family for very long."

"When I was five years old, Ruth appeared at the door of our home. She had seen the names in the paper and had been watching our house to make sure that I was okay. One day, she got up the nerve to ring the doorbell. She asked Mother if she could just see me for only a few minutes. She promised not to cause any trouble. Mother invited her in and she became Aunt Ruth."

"How wonderful of Granny, Mama."

"Yes, it was. She let Ruth come see me when she could and even invited her to Sunday lunch on occasion. At thirteen, my mother told me Aunt Ruth was my real mother. Every birthday and holiday Ruth sent me money. She encouraged me to go to nursing school and helped me financially. Over the years, she was always there if I needed her and came here when each of you was born."

Anne reached into the box and pulled out a nurse's pin and passed it to Mary Margaret.

"When I graduated, she gave me this."

"Mama, who was your father? Did you know him?"

"No, she never told me, only that Charlie looked just like him"

"Once you knew, how did you feel about Granny and Grandpa? Did you love Ruth more?"

"Not for one minute. Mother and Daddy were my parents and I loved them deeply. Ruth was like an aunt. I cared for her but she was not my mother. I was very lucky to have her in my life and was grateful to Mother for letting her in."

Grace belted out a scream from the other room. Anne and Mary Margaret looked at each other for a minute and smiled. They stood and hugged.

"Oh, Mama, what if I'd given her up? I'm so glad I listened to you."

"Even though being adopted was good for me and with you…um, um…" Anne stammered.

"What were you about to say?"

"That you did keep your child. I personally know of other adoptions that have worked. Sometimes they don't. I remember the anguish Ruth went through giving me up. That's why I'd never let a grandchild of mine be adopted."

"You always knew what was best. I'm sorry for all the times I rebelled. But I always felt you were being harder on me."

"It was because I saw your potential. I wanted you to meet it and now I think you will be able to do that. I'm glad we had this talk. I wish I had told you sooner. Maybe we would have understood each other better."

Mary Margaret put Grace in her car seat and drove out to Theresa's. On the way, she was trying to process the story her mother told her. How had her mother lived that lie all these years and been so self-assured all-knowing with all her elitist ideas and judgments of other people? She was always saying so-and-so wasn't to the manor born and here she was a foundling.

Her whole life she never felt she measured up to her mother's expectations. All the while Anne was suffering. Of course, she wouldn't admit it. She had built a shell around herself with her family and her volunteer work.

Mary Margaret handed Grace off to Delia and bounded up the steps to Theresa's room. Clothes were in piles all over the place. Some were folded and in a suitcase.

When she was telling Theresa her mother's story she suddenly began to sob, surprising herself.

"You know I guess I really didn't realize how I felt about all this until I told you. I don't even know what I think unless I have you to bounce it off of. And now you're leaving."

"Pucci, I'll be back in six weeks. We can write and talk on the phone. Here, blow your nose." Theresa handed her a box of Kleenex.

"I know, but it won't be the same."

"Nothing will ever be the same. I'm a wreck too. I'm especially nervous about flying and distraught about Charlie."

"So, what really is the deal with you and Charlie? You say you two mess around but that Charlie is worried about going all the way because of what happened to me. It's got to be hard, no pun intended." The two looked at each other and laughed. "No really, my relationship with Ted doesn't count. I have no idea what wild passionate sex would be like. I'll probably be with Ted the rest of my life, so I'll never know." Mary Margaret walked over to Theresa's dresser. She picked up a picture. "You and Charlie were a cute couple. I hate to say it but he is probably going to be one of those ho-hum sex people. You need to spread your wings. If I was going to Italy, I would find Omar Sharif and drop my drawers."

"Jesus, Pooch, I'm not going to Egypt. He doesn't even live in Italy."

"Mac, don't be so damn literal. You know what I mean. You need to live a little."

"Well, I don't know. I can't see myself in that position"

"Neither can I, but it's like this." Mary Margaret laid down on the bed, grabbed a pillow, and wrapped her legs around it.

Theresa took the other pillow and swatted Mary Margaret with it. "You are so nasty. Hey, I have a scathingly brilliant idea. Why don't we walk down to Barbee's and get a peach ice cream cone?"

"I have an even better one. Why don't we let Delia take Grace for ice cream and we sneak a bottle of wine and go out to your studio?"

Twenty-Six

Mary Margaret dumped out a huge jigsaw puzzle onto a table. She began to put the pieces together and wondered if it was a Georges Seurat painting. As she completed more of it, she realized the figures were people in her life. Ted was pushing a baby carriage by the water. Sister Fatima was holding out a diploma. Her parents were sitting on the grass, Jeanne was dancing. She saw Charlie standing with Bunny. She made out that the twins were in a bateau in the water and most of her girlfriends were nearby. She finished the puzzle and scanned the painting to find Theresa. She wasn't there. She ran her hand across the puzzle and noticed she was wearing the friendship ring Theresa had given her years before.

Next to the puzzle was a box. Inside was another puzzle. As she began to complete this one, crisp washes formed an image of a table laden with Italian dishes and bottles of wine in the foreground in the style of Maurice Prendergast. At the end of the table was Theresa, toasting with a glass of wine. Around it, her parents, her grandparents, and Claudette had raised glasses. In the background, a villa stood on a hill above an olive orchard. Next to the villa was a replica of Michelangelo's David. Mary Margaret put in the last few pieces and was studying the man at the opposite end of the table from Theresa. His head was turned away. There was something familiar about his back but she couldn't quite figure out who it was.

"Mary Margaret, wake up. You promised Theresa, you'd take her to the airport."

"Ted, I was having the most vivid dream. It seemed so real. Where's Grace?"

"I fed her breakfast and changed her. She's excited about going to the airport. I made an appointment for this afternoon with the realtor to see that house your father told us about."

"Oh, Ted, that's great. This place is just too damn small for us. Grace will need a yard and maybe you can get that boat you've always wanted."

"Hey, I really appreciate you driving me to the airport," said Theresa, turning to wave at her grandparents. "I always thought I'd be the one taking you places."

"I'm happy to do it and Grace is excited. After talking to you last night, I think I understand Anne. I feel much better about our relationship. I tell you what, if I ever found out I was adopted and Daddy was not my real daddy I would be devastated."

"Well, you don't have to worry about that." The two glanced at each other.

"You know, think about your aunt Ruth," Theresa said. "Think how she felt about leaving her baby in a basket and just waiting for someone to find her. Then to see her at a distance for years and not able to be a part of her life. Now that would be devastating."

"I know, I think about Fatima and…" Mary Margaret stopped short realizing she was about to reveal Sister's secret. She flushed and hoped with Grace's babbling Theresa did not pick up on her comment.

"What about Fatima?" Theresa looked at Mary Margaret and could see an uncomfortable look on her face. "This is not the first time you said something about her and changed the subject. Do you know something I don't know?"

Mary Margaret squirmed in her seat. She figured Theresa would not let up and she might as well tell her.

"Mac, there's something about Fatima that's a secret. I'm probably one of the few people that know. You have to swear to never say anything or it would be damaging to her."

"You know I would never."

Theresa listened intently, tearing up several times as Mary Margaret relayed the story. It made her sad to know Sister went through this and that her friend had kept it to herself all this time.

"So, that's where the name Grace came from." Theresa turned and smiled at her precious Godchild in the back seat. "Don't worry, Pooch, this secret is safe with me."

The girls sat silent for some time.

"Oh, by the way, when I got home last night, Ted told me he had gotten a raise and we're going to look at a house this afternoon. It's on the water. Ted's dream. Things are really good between us now."

"I'm so pleased for you, Pooch. I wish I could go with y'all to see the property," Theresa said, rooting in her pocketbook. She checked her ticket and passport; her hand was shaking.

"Nervous about the flight?"

"Always, but I know there's a pot of gold at the end and I have my lucky necklace," Theresa said. She fingered the cross around her neck. "Claudette has so much planned for our adventure. She's going to meet me in Rome and we'll drive to Florence. I'll have to do the driving. I've always heard those Italians drive like there's no tomorrow."

Grace was cooing in her seat in the back.

Mary Margaret told Theresa about her dream and the puzzles. "It was so real. But it was weird. In one puzzle, you weren't in it and there was Bunny standing next to Charlie. In the other, I think you were in Italy, at a table. There was a man there at the end of it."

"Who was it?"

"I don't know but he had dark hair."

"I had a weird dream last night too. I took one of Nana's tranquilizers. Otherwise, I knew I wouldn't sleep at all."

"What was it about?"

"It was so awful, a nightmare. I almost don't want to say it. It might make it come true."

"Oh, don't be silly, Mac. It was just a dream."

"But you and I were fighting. There was water all around us and you wouldn't believe me about something. I kept trying to reason with you. You were so mad at me that you even said for me to stay away from you and your family."

"You know that would never happen. We are family, you and me. Somewhere, somehow, in another life or something. Even if you never marry Charlie, you and Grace and I will always be family."

They chatted on, each about their own future. When Mary Margaret turned into the airport, they both grew silent.

Mary Margaret and Grace watched from the gate window as Theresa walked across the tarmac to board the plane for Rome. She stopped before she went up the stairs and turned around. She lifted her hand and pointed to the ring on her pinkie finger, her friendship ring from Mary Margaret.

"Bye, Pucci. Bye, Grace, I love you," Theresa yelled, as she waved.

Mary Margaret read her lips and mouthed the same words even though she knew Theresa couldn't hear. Grace waved and giggled as they watched the plane take off. She pressed her tiny fingers into her mother's eyes to feel the tears.

THE END